SECTOR 73

SECTOR 73

A Gypsy King Sci-fi Thriller

GREGORY C. RANDALL

WH
WINDSOR HILL PUBLSIHING

Created in the United States of America

Published by
Windsor Hill Publishing
Walnut Creek, California 94596

ISBN: 978-0-9987083-8-6

Cover Design: Gregory C. Randall

Twinkle, twinkle, little star,
How I wonder what you are!
Up above the world so high,
Like a diamond in the sky!

—*Jane Taylor*

PROLOGUE

You call yourself Tassos. Really? The Resurrection? From what universe did you extract that macho moniker? It sure as hell wasn't the tag your parents gave you. Maybe it was in that go-go bar in Luna 3—you know, the one with that strange high priestess, with a deep voice and sharpened teeth, asking for coin. Money, which, right now, means nothing, stuck as you are inside this rock. You push ahead and crash through the shielded door and stumble into the tunnel; finally, you've escaped. Escaped from who? Your crew—where are they? No freaking clue. You owe them. Bullshit, they owe you.

Your helmet's light bounces schizophrenically off the rough, glistening, metallic walls. They look moist, even wet—that's impossible. Here in the infinite vacuum of space, there's nothing. Your breathing, heavy and raspy, fights with the air escaping from the tears in your P-suit—they both demand a fix. Is it better to die? End it here, pull the plug, cast off this mortal coil. Fear? Tassos wouldn't be afraid; you were never scared of anything—until now. Your suit's hissing. Add that to the booming and pounding of your heart, and it makes you sound like a snake with a bad head cold. That's it, the symphony of your last hours: the fitful suck-suck of your busted lungs, the snake-like hiss of irreplaceable air, the thumping beat in your chest. Moisture fogs your faceplate; it rolls down the glass to your chin; will it turn to frost? If that happens, that's more than enough—you think frosted faceplate, high priestesses, go-go Luna 3, snake in your pants, and the lights. Yes, the goddamn lights. You run your gloves over the slap-patches; a dozen stuck on the tears on your spacesuit. All try to retain your air, Tassos's air. Air you won't or can't share. Five minutes, that's it, five minutes before you'll be sucking space. Stumble on, push out against the impossibly wet walls, walls that are squeezing you. That's it, air out—walls in. Don't forget the damned illuminations, the lights—the incessant flickerings of those impossible beings that buzz inside your helmet like a thousand gnats on fire. They will haunt you forever—if you live. They were there with the crew, your crew—the missing crew. You swat at them; they go through your gloves like . . . like your gloves aren't there. They swarm in the vacuum around you; you can't wave them away. They land, first on your helmet, next on your arms, then over your whole suit. You are like a man on fire, lit up like a Christmas tree; you are the tree of life. You will be dead in minutes.

For a dragger, you, Tassos Orion, are a man of the endless universe. The tunnel crushes you with a suffocating vise. You are smaller. Your own blood's coppery-iron stink fills your nose. Are you, Tassos, macho-dragger, starman, bleeding to death before your lungs stop sucking? You don't care. Your lamp swings upward to the ceiling, then down to the slick floor. Confused, you stumble forward. You are blind because of the thousands of lights filling your fogged visor. Gravity decreases; your boot toes just touch the glistening floor. You are drifting, floating. There, a dozen meters ahead, the wash of stars from the Milky Way fills the opening. Beyond those stars—extends eternity. You again push away the lights; they are your own universe of impossible things, your own Milky Way. You swing your arms wildly; the damn lights instantly move away like ghostly specs of bright dust. They flow through you. More confusion—fogginess and shock are setting in, no air, it's gone. You are becoming your own vacuum. Your suit is doing its best to both save your life and kill you. To your suit, it's all the same. You are sucking nothing.

It was money that brought you here, money that you, Tassos, ace dragger, crave. Money, the stuff that makes you go to the belt, hard money, rock money. This rock, this asteroid, this piece-of-shit man-killer, showed promise. The assay numbers were off the sensors, and the probes went ga-ga. Its density was unheard of, unnatural. It was the holy grail of draggers, more metal than any had ever seen or remembered. Your crew, the now missing crew, pushed hard to initiate the three-hundred-million-kilometer drag to Mars. They wanted that paycheck for the prize. Greed was your first mistake. Your ego, Tassos, was your second.

This chunk of the eternal universe was still an asteroid then, a promise of wealth and fortune. Not the trap it is now. It's your executioner. You push off the floor, your toes drag the surface. The annoying specs follow in a swirling cloud, like dust kicked up on an earth-side road. You reach for the handholds on the walls, just uneven enough for your glove tips to barely grab and pull. The mouth of the tunnel, enlarging with each painful tug, is ahead. Starlight floods and reflects across the impossible wet surface. The cold light of your sun, tiny and almost lost a half of a billion kilometers away, leaves a ghostly shadow across the entry. You and your million specs of dust confuse the shadows and ghosts of the universe.

Thirty meters beyond, hanging in the void, is the yellow hull of the donkey. Grab, pull, grab again, pull harder. Save the air. You must live.

Your suit is talking now; it answers your labored breathing. It's a ghost. Words are not helpful. "One hundred and seventy seconds until complete system failure," *it affirms with a soothing voice, the kind that greets you in an elevator. What it really is saying is:* "Going down—three minutes until you are fucked and dead—have a nice day."

Shit, you don't need your P-suit to tell you what you already know: total system failure—a technical euphemism for death due to nothing, the void, the vacuum, the big empty, the eternal suck. Your last hand pull takes you to the lip of the tunnel. The service donkey slowly drifts toward you, now just ten meters away. So close, yet an infinite distance. No strength left in your body; the gap impossible to jump. Something hard slams into your back, and you scream. Metal pincers grab your arms and squeeze. You, Tassos, starman, dragger, girly-girl, scream, and scream again and again. Directly in front of you, the thousand lights collapse in on themselves again and again and become a blinding incandescent ball, and . . . disappear.

"No, stop. You will tear the suit. No."

"I've got you, Captain, you're safe now," *a metallic voice says, filling your helmet. Real, not a ghost.*

"Where the hell have you been?"

"*The others? The crew—where are they? Your crew?*"

"*Gone.*" *You suck the last atom of air and life.* "*All gone. They are all with the Creators.*"

i

Time is a thief. Every living moment is filled with expectations, and every past moment is filled with regrets. Time anticipates, you anticipate, I anticipate, then nothing happens according to plan. The future is stolen, i.e., time is a thief. That's the cynic in me. Call me Buster Strabo: Dragger, Captain, Mr. Cynical Bastard, asshole, that's Mr. Asshole to you. I got this way after twenty-plus years of driving iron through the vacuum of space. Space, the big nothing. Where you can go a million years and not run into one goddamn thing, and then, blam, you do. Yeah, the final frontier, it's all around you.

"Damn it, for the love of God, what are you thinking?" I yelled. "The sensors are all fouled up, I'm getting nothing. What the hell are you doing?" Down and directly below, a plasta-steel, humanoid-shaped brainbox sat on the steel deck of the lower control level. Three of its extension arms, with their gruesome mix of tools and probes, were deployed deep inside the panel of the nav-sys. The noid hummed a tune as it worked.

"This is exactly the proper way to replace the circuit board, sir," a metallic voice replied. It sounded like it was wheezed through a wire screen while whistling. "It is correct and according to the specifications."

"I wrote those specs, not you. I know what the correct procedure is. And quit using that damn nasal-cyborg-bot voice. And for God's sake, stop that infernal humming. Sweet Jesus, you sound like a tin can on the end of a string with a bad head cold."

"Sorry, sir. I thought you liked Mozart. Is this an improvement?" The voice changed to the soothing sound of Bach.

"Improvement? I'll tell you what improvement is: it's a new noid when I get back to the Prasinus. This time I'll get a red one. Yes, a nice red one, with a cute female voice, someone I can talk to late at night. Someone who understands me."

"No need to get so annoyed, sir. Besides, you already have one of those: Sheila."

"You leave her out of this, okay? And besides, I've had her a lot longer than you."

"Yes, sir. I understand the use of the action verb word 'had.'"

"Shut up. Just put in the correct circuit board. Got it?"

"Yes, sir."

"Asshole." Leaving the noid to do its job, I hand-over-handed my way up the stairs to the command level. We were not under thrust; I was as weightless as an eighty-two-kilo feather. I adjusted my shorts—they tend to ride up uncomfortably in nul-g.

"Why do you keep that sack of short-circuited wires and servo-motors around?" Garrett Borg offered from the right control seat. "You and Hank do nothing but fight and bicker; you're worse than a married couple. And that circuit board he suggested; you *know* it will work."

"See, sir?" Hank said from below, as its middle left arm pushed in the replacement board.

"Garrett, you stay out of my domestic affairs. Hank, you do as your told."

"Yes, sir." Subordinate attitude echoed throughout the bridge.

"Mutinous assholes," I mumbled again as I drifted into the left chair. The magties found their grips in the seat. Ahead, a gazillion stars filled the front screen, the slash of the Milky Way cut from upper right to lower left. Finding your bearing in the three-dimensional environment of deep space was relatively easy. Just imagine yourself in the center of an infinite sphere with the panoply of stars staying fixed around you. Directions are never left or right, or up or down. They are more like here, or there, or way-the-bejesus over there. As a dragger, "way-the-bejesus that way," is almost always the primary direction. And "way the fucking bejesus" is just too far away to even think about.

Good morning, class, I'm Captain Buster Strabo, a dragger. I am the twenty-fifth-century equivalent of Ahab in *Moby Dick*; I am always looking for my white whale. First Officer Garrett Borg, in the right-hand chair, is a dragger, and Tech-Officer Clive Jones, sleeping one deck below, is a dragger. Hank, the humanoid asshole robot, or noid as we colloquially call him, is a dragger. My four-hundred-and-thirty-meters-long-by-twenty-three-meters-thick slab of steel, titanium, gold, aluminum, silicon, and diamond glass, with its hydrogen-fueled fusion nuclear propulsion, is the *Gypsy King,* an interplanetary mining ship. It's also called a dragger, or as some call it, a BATT—big-ass tow truck. No, not really, I made that up. However, I've gotten into fights over being called a dump-truck driver. And here, in this asteroid belt between Mars and Jupiter orbiting the sun, are our oysters and pearls. You could easily say we are chasing pearls before swine and not be too far off the mark.

My *Gypsy King* is elegant and beautiful to look at, especially if you wanted to buy a one-hundred-and-fifty-year-old interplanetary package of ancient tech and dented steel. Remarkably, she looks like a twentieth-century Earth-side battleship after being pressed through the solar system's most gigantic pasta maker. And then, after being squeezed, had welded to its nose a multi-level bulbous transparent carbuncle of titanium and diamond glass. This carbuncle, with its multiple decks, holds yours truly, command and control, crew, and support. Operations on the upper level, living quarters on two, crew quarters are on three, and on its lowest deck, the ship's maintenance paraphernalia and extra-vehicular equipment. As interplanetary vessels go, it is as lovely as the last whore, in the last bordello, in the last corridor of Prasinus.

I lucked into this bucket of space junk at an interplanetary yard sale about twenty Earth years back—they threw the noid in for fun—lucky me. It had been declared salvage by the courts; I was in on that operation. I tell people that it's someone's idea of a bad joke. Some days it's like getting a free puppy that you just can't housebreak. Some call me "Star-Buc," but not usually to my face. I hate the term—it makes me contemplate wearing a tight physi-skin suit and a cape. Decorative spots would be sweet. There are those who admire me (my sister, allegedly, for one), but most think I'm just crazy. To the point, in this infinitesimal part of the universe, all us draggers are either nuts, drifters, or hiding from the law. Me, I love this bucket of twenty-third-century tech, especially when the toilets work.

Dragger is the colloquial term for a drag-miner. A drag-miner is the twenty-fifth-century version of a fourteenth-century alchemist; we turn rocks into gold. Or, more importantly, and financially, we convert an asteroid into money. Money, as defined these days by the Interplanetary Monetary Reserve Collective, as bitunits, bits, or coin. In the twenty-fifth century, draggers do it for two reasons: to make a lot of money or hide from the IPTs, the Inter-Planetary Troopers. We drift and drag so far from the home planets of Earth or Mars that even serial killers aren't worth the hydrogen to find us. In many ways, it's like the Old West, where outlaws would hide out in the canyons and mountains. They'd not come into town except to drink, fornicate, or take a bath—a real bath with water, soap, and gravity.

It's a simple job. Most Earthers and Martians imagine the asteroid belt as like the rings of Saturn, all packed stone to stone, creating a shimmering band of debris and junk. Not so. The most important stuff, stuff worth mining, orbits as far apart as the moon and Earth, most a lot farther—millions of kilometers farther. This rocky crap is found between Mars and Jupiter. Some say it all was once a planet and got blown up or run into billions of years ago. Still speculative. Space gets real big, real fast out here. So, after we find a particular rock drifting in space, we laser-drill its surface to better assay it, attach high-strength cables, and tow the bastard to one of the off-planet smelters and foundries orbiting around Mars and Earth. They process our rock into construction products for off-Earth structures: bio-domes, daises, colonies, and even spacecraft. Some is converted into metal powders used to print out everything from spacecraft parts to replacement teeth. Soup to nuts as they say. Rock to money. Shit to shinola.

Draggers find, scan, probe, and assay the rocks—asteroid sounds too techy—and establish the type, composition, mass, and mineral wealth. If necessary, we get out and walk the rock, take samples, and evaluate and verify earlier probes. If a keeper, the bastard gets massive drag rings laser-embedded and welded deep into her surface. Then we hook on ten-kilometer-long tow cables, and through a serious amount of geometry and half-ass physics, we pull the rock out of its billions-of-years-old orbit and tow it hundreds of millions of kilometers to the smelters. Centuries earlier, a few idiots tried to mount fusion engines directly on the rock. But, sweet Jesus, after a couple of incredibly impressive and deadly failures, it was found that towing was the safest and most profitable—relatively speaking. Some of those rocks are still flying out of the galaxy—damn things may never stop. I occasionally offer a prayer for the poor bastards that were stuck on its surface when it squirted off. A few attempts were made to mount a chase, but its power source was a year's worth of hydrogen, and its speed kept multiplying. By the time its tanks went dry, it may be doing more than a couple million kilometers an hour. So fast you wouldn't see it go by. In fact, so fast you wouldn't know if it hit you—instant karma.

It takes us months to find, secure, and set-up a tow. And often another year to cross half the solar system and dock at the smelters. There's only a few of these foundries, five around the earth, and two orbit Mars. In the belt, it is estimated that there are more than fifty million mineable rocks to pick from. Some are towed for their metals and others for their essential elements. Some for building, and others for H_2O—we need a lot of hydrogen, breathable air, and water out here.

"Hank, you finished yet?"

"Two minutes. I'll go through the logs to see what else needs repair."

"Recharge yourself first."

"Yes, sir."

"He knows when to recharge," Garrett said.

"I know it, he knows it. But I need to have some sense of control over that noid. Lord knows he's enough of a pain in the ass."

"I heard that!"

"That's why I said it. Recharge."

"Yes, sir."

I swung around to the ship's tow controls. Five monitors above the panel showed camera views to all areas of the ship's bays, winches, and miscellaneous tool racks hung on the exterior. Mounted on the *Gypsy King*'s stern are five enormous cable spools. Each spool is thirty meters in diameter and carries over twenty kilometers of high-strength, ti-steel flex-cable. Outriggers extend out from the stern, allowing for better control of the played-out cables. These outriggers also reduce the chance of the lines twisting together. The center spool is held in reserve. The cables are an alloy mix that is ten times stronger than steel and remain flexible even in the near absolute zero temperature of space, which is somewhere around minus 273 degrees Celsius. The cables cost a king's fortune; to lose just one cable would ruin the financials of the trip. That's why, during much of the return trip, the *Gypsy King* acts as a solar screen. We'd make sure the ship's shadow is cast along the length of the cables, keeping them at a constant temperature. Is this too techie for you?

Smaller hydrogen fusion thrusters are also secured to strategic points on the rock to permit better control. When the tow is underway, these thrusters manage the yaw and pitch of the rock. They also assist in slowing the asteroid as we approach the smelter. If not, we'd go roaring by the smelters or worse. It would be like throwing a billion-ton curveball. Nonetheless, when moving an asteroid—half the size of the *Gypsy King* and a thousand times its weight—at a quarter of a million kilometers an hour, another universal law applies: An object in motion tends to stay in motion; an object at rest wants to remain at rest. Corollary: Inertia is a bitch.

Right now, our bastard is an eighty-meter, oblong-shaped, iron and manganese potato that, by Clive's estimates, weighs about 2.2 million metric tons. It assayed out at very fine iron and nickel, low carbon, with nodules and veins of platinum, gold, and rare earth minerals. I'm positive that when the smelter starts cutting this rock apart, they will find even more rare earths, and, praise the Maker, only He knows what else. The tonnage price is based on an average mineral mix set almost two hundred years old. There is little new to be found in the asteroid belt.

It took three months of probing through this sector to find this one rock. We'd analyzed a dozen others made up of silicates and other chondrites, amino acids, and as we call it, WS—worthless shit. One rock looked promising, but when we hit it with a MEC (massive explosive charge), it fractured in a dozen places. Under drag, that would not be good. Remember what I said about cables, inertia, and enemas.

We gave this bastard the official name Castor, after one of the twins Castor and Pollux. It was found in Sector Sixty-eight, under the constellation Gemini. Hank reminded me that Castor's place in the stars was owed to Zeus kicking the twins out of Greek heaven. I thanked him profusely for that bit of historical and astronomical bullshit.

"Hank, update on the readings on Castor's rear port and starboard thrusters, please," Garrett asked.

"All systems are nominal, Mr. Borg," Hank answered.

"Forward thrusters?"

"All nominal and standing by."

"Thanks, Hank. Fully charged?"

"Aces, standing by."

I studied the screens. The main screen is from the camera mounted high over the central cable drum. Four cables, two left and two right, extended out 6.35 kilometers behind the *Gypsy King*. This left a reserve of more than thirteen kilometers on the spools. At some point, we would allow the rock to hang farther back. If something went wrong, I didn't want a two-million-ton rock slammed up my ass. The camera mounted on the stern displayed the enlarged view of Castor. It showed a spec of grey, with the four cables—like parallel railroad tracks—pointing directly outward to a sharp point in space. Other cameras are mounted on Castor. There are also two satellite cameras, one to port and one to starboard; they present views of the whole choo-choo train: locomotive, cables, and caboose.

Guidance technology, sensors, and radar provide the backup needed to keep the rock under control. The cameras and twenty years of experience dragging rocks give us a high success record. Eight profitable rocks, in nineteen years, wasn't too bad. My team is sure that two more rocks like this one, will be enough to retire. Yeah, that and a sharp stick in the eye, as Clive would say. "You have to save to retire, mate. Me? If I can't drink it, eat it, fly it, or screw it—it's not worth doing."

I love these guys.

2

Hank said a week later, his voice flat and mechanical, "Captain, there's an anomaly on Castor's stern port thruster,"

Damn, I hate the word anomaly.

"Its signal is cutting in and out," Hank said. "We lost control of the port thruster fifteen seconds ago. I cannot regain its signal, trying to reacquire."

"Pull up the camera. Show me stern port thruster, center screen," I ordered.

On the screen, a dark grey pocked and blasted landscape appeared. Centered in the view, in the shape of a thick perfecto cigar, was a massive steel structure. This thruster, like the five others mounted on Castor, is twenty-five meters long and ten meters thick at its waist. A pocket fusion reactor provides the muscle. The thrusters are mounted on pedestals that allow it to be rotated up to three-hundred-and-sixty-degrees. These pedestals, like the anchors for the cable tow rings, are deeply embedded in the matrix of the rock. It was apparent that we had a problem. This thruster is not designed to point its ass-end at the asteroid's surface at a downward angle of thirty-degrees plus. The forward anchors, at the base of the pedestal, had been ripped out of the rock. The thruster's purpose is to move the rock, not burn a hole in its four-billion-year-old hide.

Clive drifted up from the second-level living quarters.

"Goddamn thing tipped up," I said. "Prepare the bots to

stabilize and right it. The pedestal looks bent. We may then need to remove and replace the entire unit. We can repair it on the way home. Damn, this will take a week to fix."

"Roger that, Captain," Clive said.

"I have a signal, and a new problem, sir. The unit has activated itself," Hank matter-of-factly announced.

"What?" Clive and I yelled.

"The port thruster has activated itself. It is beginning to apply force to Castor; please note on the screen—"

"I can see what's happening—you shit-box of bolts and wires. Damnit!"

"What's the thrust curve on that son of a bitch, Garrett?"

"Five hours to maximum thrust—if we can't shut it off. It's at five-point-two percent and will climb at a steady rate over the next five hours. The force against the rock will initiate a slow rotation at forty percent; it will continue to rise as the power increases. In time, the rotating rock will twist up the cables until it's a deranged puppet master's nightmare."

"Nice analogy, thanks a lot. Time to initial rotation?"

"Based on the calcs, it will, with this one thruster, begin rotation in about twenty-four hours. The first full rotation will take about forty-eight hours. The rotation speed will increase as inertia is changed. Eventually, it could be spinning at a rate of once a minute or more."

I looked at the four cables, imagining them all twisted up. The winding would increase until it became one ungodly wad that would eventually tear off the back end of the *Gypsy King*. Or, worst case, the cables would snap and fling themselves back at the ship, snapping like an interstellar whip. The six kilometers of high-strength steel would strip and slice away equipment, telemetric antennas, and potentially the main engine.

"Garrett, activate and warm up the other thrusters. Hold them available to spin up just in case we need to counter the thrust of this fucking unit. Additionally, we need to prepare the *Gypsy* to rotate in concert with Castor. It looks like it wants to go counterclockwise."

"Already on it."

"Clive, you manage the bots. Garrett, you watch the *Gypsy*. If this goes sideways, I want everyone ready to bail and cut the cables. Hank, you are with me, I'm taking *Horus* out. I'll see what I can do with the bots on the thruster. Worst case, I'll blow the damn thing off the rock. I will not lose this payday."

Horus is a donkey; the *Gypsy King* has two. They are four decks below. The donkeys on the *Gypsy* are twenty-meter by eight-meter thick chunks of steel and manipulating arms. The generic term is a donk. Call sign D-1 and D-2; we never call them by their call signs. We use them with the robots to secure the cable and thrusters, take assay samples, and do exterior repairs and maintenance to the *Gypsy King*. They are identical, though *Horus* is bright yellow, and *Osiris* is orange. I've been known to hide in one when the crew gets under my nerves.

An hour later, I applied thrust to *Horus*. We exited the bay door, slid along the length of the *Gypsy King*'s belly, past the fusion engine, until we reached the cable spools. Currently, they were tight, and they would be until the *Gypsy King* and Castor were underway. They would remain so until we reached speed. Then the cables would develop a slight droop but still provide the needed tug to the rock. The thrusters on Castor would maintain its proper orientation to the ship during the six-month tow to the Earth-side smelter.

"Proceeding to Castor." I slipped the donk into the twenty-meter gap between the four cables. "All looks nominal here. However, I'm looking at the screen; the thruster has increased its power. What's up with that?"

"Numbers say it's at eight percent, that's expected. No change to Castor. Data says that we should not start initial tilt and rotation for at least five hours. That's our window."

"At least there's that. Hank, what about the other thrusters?"

"They are spooling up, all at three percent," Hank said. He was secured to his mount on the outside of *Horus*, three meters behind the command chair. "I would suggest that you plateau them at thirty percent; we can ramp them up more quickly if needed."

"I agree. At thirty percent I will put them in idle," Clive said.

"Roger that."

Horus moved steadily toward the rock. Each minute we gained another three hundred and fifty meters, sixteen-minute travel time. To tell the truth, it was agonizing. This had happened two drags earlier. That time it was one of the cables. The far port ring had ripped out of the iron it was welded to. The line snapped out and began a slow-motion worm dance, as Clive called it. The damn wire twisted and waved about. The stabilization took three bots working their way out to the end of the cable, slowly gaining control every thousand meters. During the process, the loose cable caught one of the bots, cut it in two, and slammed the eviscerated thing into the surface of the rock. It took three days to save the rock and resecure the cable. I had nightmares about what might have happened if the cable had rebounded and slashed at one of the donkeys or the *Gypsy King*.

Horus and I continued toward Castor. Four exterior bots joined us, two to each side of my seat in the control dome. Clive was driving these bots.

"Alpha, Beta, Charlie, and Duke have joined me," I said. "Nice to have company."

"I have you on the screen," Clive said.

Out the port window, I saw Charlie. The bot raised one of its two arms, did a roll, then saluted.

"Cute, Jones. Save it for the thruster."

"Roger that, boss."

I slowed almost a stop when we neared Castor. I carefully maneuvered the donk up and over the mounting rings and fittings that secured the cables. All looked nominal. Nothing the rogue stern thruster was doing was having an effect—yet. Above Castor, I took another look at the rock. It looked benign and generally harmless. A chunk of grey-brown debris, billions of years old, born at the creation of this solar system. I looked back at the *Gypsy King*, the sun hanging just above the massive shell of the ship. Sol was about the size of the tip of my little finger—its life-giving warmth nonexistent here in space.

"Proceeding to the thruster."

"Roger that," Garrett answered.

Castor is about the size of a soccer pitch, one-hundred meters by about sixty meters. Clive called it a potato and the description fit, but this singular spud was worth maybe a billion units to our account. Subtracting salaries, fuel costs, provisions, loan payments, and probably the loss of the thruster, we still might make a profit. What a way to make a living.

"The thruster is visible. It should be on *Horus*'s cameras. You getting this?"

"Five by five, Captain. All good, but it's a mess," Garrett said.

I slowed *Horus* and held back about twenty meters above the broken thruster. "The front two anchors have ripped out, that's confirmed. When the unit activated, the initial jolt must have snapped their mounts. The back of the pedestal is also bent. This is not supposed to happen. That pedestal should easily take the load. When we get back, I'm going to dump this thing in the manufacturer's lap and demand a refund. Clive, any idea why the thruster activated?"

"None that I can see or determine from here," Clive answered. "I'll do a full autopsy and diagnostic after we retrieve it. It's at fifteen percent. Captain, I suggest that you find a way to shut the son of a bitch off—soon."

"Working on it."

The left end of the thruster glowed. It was as if the lit end of a cigar was pointed at the rock. The nuclear propulsion system was old school, using hydrogen as the fuel source. Hydrogen was cheap; the unit, with its duel hydrogen storage tanks, wasn't. Almost one hundred percent of the volume of *Gypsy King*'s own tanks was for hydrogen storage, the same for the tanks on each of the other thrusters.

"It's shaking the remaining anchor bolts. I can see cavitation, and the welds are being stressed. There's no way I can get to the panels to shut them off. If the other bolts snap, the thruster will be a thousand meters away in a second."

"How about securing bots Alpha and Beta to the transport clips on the thruster," Clive said. "Maybe they can counter the acceleration if the pedestal snaps. At least they can be there to retrieve . . . holy shit."

"I see it. Thrust is seriously ramping up. Cavitation is increasing. " The whole unit began to rotate and twist, like a tiger fighting to escape with a chain around its neck. It jerked and bucked. Finally, only one of the pins held the beast to the rock.

"Captain, get the hell out of there. It can spiral anywhere."

"Backing away as fast as my . . . shit! It's busted loose. It slammed into Alpha and knocked the bot into the forward quarter of *Horus*. Compensating."

The thruster's breakaway completely distorted the pedestal and spun the unit into a tumbling and gyrating movement. Slamming the controls into reverse as fast as I could, I braced myself. The rogue thruster, now untethered, spun directly at me. Defensively, I threw up the two port arms—like a fighter pushing away an opponent. The titanium arms took the brunt of the impact; I was jammed back into my seat. The thruster glanced off the arms and continued its rapid rollout, missing the glass canopy above my head by a meter. The last I saw of the son of a bitch, it was spinning out into space, like a whirling dervish, with its ass on fire. The impact of the thruster knocked us toward the surface of Castor.

"Hank, evasive maneuvers."

"Roger that, sir. Maneuvering."

Hank worked a thousand times quicker than I could. The donkey has twelve thrusters mounted on its top side, underside, and flanks. With the style and finesse of the lead pole dancer of the Starlite dive bar, Hank fired the donk's hydrogen thrusters and managed to slow the tumble of *Horus*. We just avoided smashing into Castor. Out the window, I saw a long slash on the surface of the asteroid from one of the manipulating arms. Fuck me.

"Good job, Hank."

"You are welcome, sir. But it was my tin ass as well."

"Garrett, the thruster is spinning toward Jupiter right now—it's gone. Make a note to see if that piece of shit is covered by our insurance. And secure video copies to file with the insurance company."

"Roger that, Captain."

I'm not only a cynic, but I'm also a pessimist too. My analyst has a field day during my not so often consultations. All the optimists died hundreds of years ago during the African War. That was the proxy war between Europe and China fought over local mineral rights and African labor. The Chinese used Muslims as their proxy force. They convinced the North African countries, then under strict Islamic rule, that the European nations wanted to exterminate them in retaliation for a century of terrorist activities by the various fanatic Islamic religious leaders. The war, which began in Saudi Arabia, spread south through the length of Africa.

Tens of millions died, and it bankrupted both regions—Europe and China. And to make matters even worse, for three months, they exchanged nuclear weapons tit-for-tat. After the peace was negotiated by Brasilia, postwar revolutions swept these regions and countries; millions more died from famine and disease. Eventually, the Eurounion was established under the moral and financial control of the Catholic Church and the Vatican. For fifty years, it was as if the Middle Ages had returned. Even electricity was hard to find.

Greater America (the result of a problematic but necessary treaty agreed to by Canada, Mexico, and the United States) was established in 2235, ten years before the start of the African War. It was an economic and political powerhouse. China used this development in the Western Hemisphere as its excuse to push into Africa and agitate the Islamic states. The ensuing chaos resulted in significant steps backward socially and politically in the northern half of the African continent. Waves of refugees pushed into Europe destabilizing countries along the Mediterranean Sea. Islamic fundamentalists attacked weak points and local caregivers, and it was eventually learned that China was both the banker and armorer. This was intentional on the part of China. They believed they could weaken all of Europe.

The most radical Islamic group, centered in Wahhabi Saudi Arabia, was given ancient twenty-first-century nuclear weapons. It was never proven, but they were probably Chinese nukes. Four were detonated: the port city of Barcelona, the docklands in the Thames River below London, and in the harbors of Hamburg and Genoa. Europe retaliated across the northern half of Africa with six nuclear strikes. Kinshasa, with its massive Chinese steel factories, was vaporized. Europe, at the same time, dropped intercontinental ballistic missiles on seven Chinese cities. Its response was a hundred times greater than the four attacks in Europe. China tried to retaliate with its own intercontinental missiles—most were instantly destroyed by satellite-based lasers unknown to the Chinese. However, three missiles did get through. One hit north of Rome, the second hit thirty miles outside Paris, and the last exploded high in the Alps, causing severe flooding and damage throughout Bavaria and Austria and all along the Rhine and Danube Rivers. After that, additional weapons rained down on China, destroying ten more cities, including Beijing. China capitulated, and for the next ten years, was forcibly isolated by the world. Starvation and political chaos reigned throughout China. No one gave a fuck.

For fifty years, after the end of the African War, China regressed. In many ways, the whole nation had been placed in a prison camp of its own making. The vengeful Europeans would not forgive China for what they did. It wasn't until the beginning of the twenty-fourth century that China was permitted some economic room to reassert itself and regroup politically. In the new post–African War world, with the help of IndoUnion, Greater America, and Australia, Central Africa emerged as an expanding raw material resource provider.

After *Horus* was secured in the equipment bay, I walked around the donk inspecting the two damaged forward manipulating arms. The equipment head on the starboard arm—where claws, drills, and grips could be mounted—was gone, snapped away by the impact. When no one was looking, I kissed its cold titanium butt.

After the stabilization and remounting of a new thruster, we began our fall back toward Earth. Earth is closer than Greater America's smelter orbiting off Mars. The red planet was on the far side of the sun. It would be more than a year before it would catch us. I didn't plan on sitting around waiting.

The drop to Earth took almost six months. The climb, as we called the trip out to the belt, took four months. Hauling a few million tons of high-grade material Sol-ward was a little more delicate than humping the reverse star-ward. During the fall, Garret daily sent out the bots to patrol the cables looking for nicks and cracks. As we decelerated toward Earth, every action was made to ensure that Castor was kept under control. The *Gypsy King* took a swing around Earth, dumping speed. When we were within twenty thousand klicks of the smelter, the rock was snatched by four smelter tugs. I then released the cables and moved to the storage yard near the smelter.

We watched from the upper dome of the *Gypsy*'s command level as the smelter's tugs released the cables secured to the anchors on Castor.

"Start cable retrieval," I ordered.

"Roger that, Captain," Clive responded. Beyond the aft end of the *Gypsy*, the massive spools began to slowly rotate as they retrieved the remaining three kilometers of cable. A bot was tethered to the end of each line to reduce and control drift and potential whip of the cable's end. Over the past three weeks, as we swung around Earth, we'd recovered the six thrusters on Castor. These were now secured in their bays on the port and starboard flanks of our ship. I'm still pissed about the six-month hassle with the insurance company over the loss of the rogue thruster. The company blamed negligence on the part of the crew. I'm sure it was the fault of the manufacturer. Hell, after six months of stewing about it, and crossing the three hundred million miles from the asteroid belt, I'm positive that somebody should be sued.

With the help of two maneuvering tugs, we eased into our dock. It was a clean lock.

For the first time in almost two years, I slept like a baby. The *Gypsy King* is now secured to the port flank of Greater America's multi-gigawatt smelter called *Washington*. It is owned and operated by Greater American Metals.

After arrival, the smelter did their own analysis and assay of Castor. It proved even better than our original estimates. There is an eight percent weight windfall over earlier estimates. By the time the *Gypsy King* is refitted, the failed thruster replaced, stores and equipment replenished, and the banks paid, there would be a 21.3 percent profit.

"When are we going to Prasinus, Cap?" Garrett asked.

"When they clear Castor, and the check clears the bank. I'm not leaving that rock until I know the units are deposited. I trust these guys as much as I trust the Pope. I want to be able to grab that stone if I need to. Maybe I can get a better deal elsewhere."

"They've never stiffed us, why now?" Clive chimed in.

"Just saying—after almost two years, I want to make sure the trip was worth it. We'll know midmorning."

Clock time is elusive in space, Einstein notwithstanding. The *Gypsy King* uses Earth time, Greenwich Mean, as the basis for all our internal functions and clocks. Hours, days, weeks, even years are based on the solar-earth and historical human time management. Some of the Martian draggers used Mars as the time base, others create their own. However, humans evolved from the diurnal cycle of the earth, so when it came down to it, the human body needed its sleep, its food, and its activity. Hence, the twenty-four-hour clock seemed to be almost everyone's norm, ours included.

"What's one more day?" Clive said and took another sip of his celebratory highlands single malt from his pressure cup.

"After confirmation, we'll slide the *Gypsy* over to the off-moon dock at Marina 3," I said. "It's always been good for us. They have refitting supplies. Besides, the thruster will take another week to get here. It's in a freighter full of equipment from Mars. Glad we ordered it when we did. The six-month wait would have killed us."

"All I want is to feel solid ground under my feet," Garrett added. "This pseudo-gravity is okay, but real, stick-to-your-heels lunar gravity—nothing like it."

"I'm leaving Hank onboard—he can cover security."

"Finally, some peace and quiet," a voice echoed up from the deck below.

"That's a two-way street, Hank."

"Yes, sir. There's maintenance to be completed, stores registered, and restocking. The bots will help. We'll be ready in a week."

"Take your time," I said. "My suite in the Hilton is for one month. I don't even want to think about space or anything else for that matter—and it will be good to see my sister and my nephew."

"Does Sister Annie still live in Rome?" Garret asked

"Yes, but she's coming to the moon and she's bringing Marcus. I haven't seen the boy in four years. He's now eighteen."

"Eighteen? Time flies."

"Yes, the flics show a damn good-looking kid. Obviously takes after me."

"Poor boy," Garret injected.

"Poor boy?" Hank asked.

"Not your business, Hank," I said. "Good kid, smart. Annie says that he may go to Notre Dame in Greater America. Wants to study languages and literature, stay earthbound."

"Lots of jobs up here," Garrett said with a snort.

"She thinks he can work his way into the Vatican's ancient books and history laboratory."

"The Vatican has the money for it, that's for sure," Clive said as he injected more scotch into his pressurized crystal tumbler. "He's young. There's time to make decisions."

The Catholic Church barely survived the African Wars. A significant portion of Rome was destroyed, and the Church spent billions of units rebuilding the Vatican. There had been a resurgence in faith, and now, halfway through the third Christian millennia, it politically and economically controlled vast regions of Earth—and had grown even wealthier. The Church supported hundreds of schools, colleges, and universities. For two centuries, it had been calling in its chits. It operated smelters above Earth and Mars and owned two daisies, one on Sicily and another near Rio de Janeiro. Billions of bitunits flowed up and down the stems. Historians had written for more than a century that if it weren't for Pope Conrad I, the world would still be in anarchy—humans' seemingly natural state and course.

"Be nice, the Vatican is a big customer," I reminded Clive.

"I just drag rocks, Captain. I leave politics and religion to others," Clive said. He picked up his bottle, left the control level, and went down to the main deck.

You have been busy these past twenty-two years; they thought you were a murderer, insane, and even worse, a coward. You, Tassos, are, of course, all of those and more. If they only knew. It is impressive the way you convinced the church of your serious nature. The stars, your stars, were a perfect match to their expectations—or need. They always need prophets. If they can't find one, they will create one. You, with a million lights in your head, are the perfect religious aesthete.

The trial on the moon, they were sure they didn't want you back on Earth. You convinced them of your change, your enlightenment—if they only knew. A trial, more like a witch hunt, only they didn't believe in witches. Sure, they believe in the afterlife, the infinity beyond the universe, the miracles, but not in witches. And you have seen that universe, you have touched it—and it is in you. And if there is an infinity, an afterlife, it is something that you have touched. You would do nicely as their witch. They wanted to burn you.

You stood calmly as the charges were read: six counts of abandonment of your crew, six counts of murder in the second degree, and dereliction of duty. If the Attorney General for the Moon could have, she would have charged you with cowardice. But you know she's never walked a rock, seen the stars from beyond Mars, never looked fear in the face. Twelve of your peers heard the prosecution, good people, believers, two were even draggers, they let you walk. They absolved you—like priests of old—of your sins. The sins you made—it was all true. And they condemned you to hell— Earth, to find forgiveness. There, on your progenitor's homeworld, you endured this penance. The pain to your body as it rebelled against the crush of gravity. It felt as if your brain had settled into a well, every neuron pulled toward the center of the earth. Then gradually you healed, grew stronger, stood upright like your remotest ancestors, and were drawn to the center of the earthly universe, the Church. It was here that you found a home, solace, comfort, even the beginning of self-forgiveness. And the lights in your head forgave you.

And you drew others to you, those who believed in the lights, believed in the truth, sought you out for enlightenment and forgiveness. Sinners are easy to find. They came to you, arms and souls open. You preached to them about the lights, the infinite lights, the time before time, the beginning, the middle, and the end-all of being one.

And forgiveness.

* * *

Luna 3, or as Moon folk called it, Prasinus, sits in the shadow cast by the rim of the Bessel crater in the southern plan of Mare Serenitatis. It has the distinction of being the oldest continually inhabited Moon colony, even though it was the third to be built. This peculiarity is due to the abandonment of Luna 1 and Luna 2—Croceus and Caeruleus—in the mid-22nd century. Everyone blamed the African War. It was hard to get supply ships to the bases when there was the real threat that they would be shot out of the atmosphere. Prasinus survived due to the efforts of the Catholic Church and the Vatican's off-world investments. It was also the need for a safe place for the African and European cardinals, archbishops, and influential bishops who escaped one hour before Kinshasa and Rome were nuked and vaporized. Since then, the extensive complex of over two thousand hectares of silicon domes, underground tunnels, and biolands has become the permanent home to almost ninety thousand people. Tradition and folklore say that it acquired its original name, Prasinus, when, during a meeting of international politicians and scientists in the twenty-first

27

century, it was determined that all the Lunar outposts would be named after colors. It was a way of avoiding the usual bullshit of nationalism and aggrandizement. Outposts named after earth cities, or politicians, or men with muscle or money, that was the usual way of things during two thousand years of imperialism and colonialism. It was agreed to name the settlements after colors, and to be even fairer, the color's name would be in Latin. Sure, some wanted it to be in Mandarin or even Hindi, two of the most spoken languages. But there were enough traditionalists that pointed out that many features on the moon were already in Latin. So Luna 3 became Prasinus, the color green, leek-green, or light-green; most accepted the term emerald. There are more than a few bars named The Emerald City spread throughout its domes and backwater corridors. Hard-core Americans wanted them to be named after western towns, the new frontier. There was also talk about astronauts, Greek and Roman mythology, and even politicians and people in space exploration. Even bankers lobbied for the honor. They eventually accepted colors. Later, during the chaos of the 22nd century, there was an attempt at renaming Prasinus after influential and prominent leaders of the Catholic Church. Many of these had escaped Rome along with the then-current Pope. Here in Prasinus and for the rest of his natural life, Pope Thomas governed the Church from the small cathedral Santa Luna Perfetto, nestled among the city's glass and aluminum domes. After fifty years, when it quieted down Earth-side, and the warring nations finally agreed to peace, his successor, Pope Juan d'Luna the First, returned to Earth and rebuilt the Vatican. Since then, Prasinus has had an unofficial and quasi-religious attitude about it. It has also become a destination for off-world pilgrims and Catholic zealots.

The African War and the dozen or so subsequent sub-regional conflicts are now more than two hundred years ago. During the succeeding centuries, and after a few new and nasty neighborhood Earth-side wars, the Luna colonies were reestablished and expanded. By the early twenty-third century—to the aggravation of a few Earth nations that were its initial investors—the four Luna bases, Prasinus, Rubrum, Croceus, and Caeruleus, had become self-sustaining. When finally brought before the newly reestablished world court, the four Luna colonies effectively told the investors to go pound lunar dust; they have been independent since. This was also the time of the *Pax Domini Roma*, the Peace of Rome. China had taken one hundred and fifty years to recover. The same amount of time it took to rebuild London, Paris, Hamburg, Lagos, and Kinshasa. The collective idiocy of that era still amazes me. We humans can be seriously deranged when we want to be.

I know all this because I'm a student of history, a religious scholar, and an occasional drunkard. These traits are all mutually acceptable these days—I literally wear my dragger creds on my sleeve. During the latter part of the twenty-third century, it was advocated by the Catholic Church that the construction materials for the moon and Mars habitations be sourced from off-Earth resources, not just mined from Mars and the moon. Far-fetched and declared impossible by some, the science wasn't too tricky. All you needed to build these cities was an unlimited supply of iron, titanium, aluminum, and power. While Earth did not have an endless supply of these materials, it was too expensive to move them from Earth to the planets. The universe did—or at least our region of space on the Sol-side of Jupiter. The three initial space foundries and smelters used to supply the materials were sponsored by three nations: Eurounion, the Vatican, and Greater America. During the last century, two additional smelters have been built by the Union of Southern America and the Southeast IndoUnion. Two foundries also sit in geosynchronous orbit over Mars—the Catholic Church and Greater America own these. The Earth-side smelters sit twenty to forty thousand miles above the planet. Everything that could be dragged from the asteroid belt between Mars and Jupiter is melted down, refined, rolled, stamped, powdered, distilled, and eventually used for almost everything off-Earth.

By the last decade of the twenty-third century, these companies wanted a higher return from their investments. An unusual proposal was made by Greater America: Build a three-hundred-and-eighty-kilometers-high (or long depending on your point of view) elevator shaft that would be anchored on Earth and used to transport materials and people back and forth to space. What made the whole system even remotely possible was the profitability of moving space-made material to Earth without the problems of high-cost rockets and expensive fuels. The original tower, built near Des Moines, Iowa, acquired the cute name *American Daisy*. Called this because, from a distance (a far distance to be sure), this vertical transport tower looks like a flower with a long stem and a broad, multi-complex head of transport facilities, space docks, hotels, storage, and manufacturing facilities. Power is provided by extensive off-planet gigawatt nuclear generators and solar arrays; their energy is beamed to receiving dishes near the daisy. So, not only were these daisies used to move physical materials to Earth, they transmitted power Earth-side to most of the planet's nations. By the start of the twenty-fourth century, Earth had shut down their own filthy power generators and relied on these off-Earth power sources. Within a half-century, there were twenty-four daisies spread across all the continents except Antarctica.

Four days after docking at Marina 3, I watched my shipmates shuttle down to the lunar surface in a taxi. They knew when to return. I wasn't concerned. What I was anxious about was in what condition they would be in. "Hank, add antibiotics to the manifest."

"Roger that. Should I put them in Clive's room?"

"No, leave them in mine. I'll deal with the boys if I need to."

"Yes, sir. Are you leaving soon?"

Sector 73

"Tomorrow."

* * *

It has been almost four years since I've seen my sister and nephew. She is two years younger than yours truly. Moon born and raised; our parents taught at the Luna University of Rome branch. Our folks died when seals on a transport failed. Thirty other passengers were on the same ship; I was ten, Annie was eight. We were raised in the convent of Santa Maria de Luna. Good people, they gladly took the insurance settlement and used it for our education. And honestly, to this day, I don't believe they ripped us off. Annie took the customary novitiate vows when she was eighteen and became Sister Annie when she was twenty-two. At twenty-five, she was permitted an eight-year sabbatical to have a child—again a common thing for young Catholic women who've taken the vow. She returned to the moon where she birthed and raised Marcus, my nephew. Before he became too accustomed to the moon's gravity, she sent him to a boarding school on Earth, and Annie returned to her duties in Rome. The Church understands the need for personal flexibility. It was one of those things they had to do to maintain religious and financial control over thirty percent of the people living between Mars and the sun. Sister Annie stayed on Earth, and now, after more than twenty years, is fully conditioned to Earth gravity.

I kicked around various interplanetary jobs during this time, even a year on Mars. The toughest was the year at the Vatican-owned smelter above the red planet. As I said, I opted for the wide-open spaces of the solar system. I am somewhat of a self-serving and selfish shit; I'll admit to that. For me to walk on Earth would be painful, and I would probably end up with broken legs and a fat butt. Space is the only life for me.

Charley's is an old steakhouse that commands one of the better upper-level corners in the west wing of downtown

Prasinus. My Hilton is one corridor over. The joint is comfortable and is one of the few restaurants that provide, for a seriously hefty stack of bitunits, real beef transported up from Argentina on the Vatican's *St. Michael* daisy and the bi-weekly freighter. Besides, the bartender, Sally, is good looking, and even after being gone for more than two years, she remembered my name. Then again, ten years earlier, I'd been hitched to Sally for a stint, maybe two years. I was in the belt for half that; she got lonely. Last night, I closed the bar. Sally then took me home for a real lunar welcome. Good God in heaven, my head still hurts.

Being Sunday, the corridor near the cathedral and the Hilton was exceptionally crowded. Loaded grav-lev sleds pushed through the crowds, forcing people out of the way. Some carried pilgrims to the cathedral. The sleds, using repellors, drifted inches off the metal floor of the corridor. They were the ubiquitous tools of transport on the moon. Wheeled vehicles are rare, but they do exist. There are traditionalists, even on the moon.

I saw Annie before she saw me. Maybe it was my beard or the crowd, but as she scanned the piazza, she looked right past me. It was Marcus that spotted me. She wore the religious habit of the Sisters of the Revealment, a white robe, red scapular, and black veil. A hand-sized, simple wood cross hung on a gold chain around her neck. People would stare at the cross; wood of any kind was rare on the moon. It's a place where anything flammable was considered dangerous. Marcus was dressed in tight grey slacks, a red shirt, and a back tunic. The two of them made quite a statement. Knowing my sister, it was intentional.

She grabbed me tight and hugged hard and dropped a kiss on my cheek. "I've missed you," she said.

I turned to the young man. "Marcus, damn, you are more handsome than I remember, and at least a foot taller," I said, looking up.

He grinned. "Thank you, Uncle."

"Do you have a girlfriend yet? You are not getting any younger."

"Buster, that is not an appropriate question—and quit teasing him," Sister Annie said. "He still has his studies, and there are intentions to get him into Notre Dame. We will hear in a month or so."

"So, a member of the Fighting Irish. It's hard to believe, a good Italian kid like you in a place like that."

"What's wrong with Notre Dame?" Marcus protested.

"Nothing at all, except you're stuck in the middle of Greater America. Never heard, or seen, a more arrogant bunch of Americans. Always a pain when I have to deal with them at—"

"Buster, just stop," Annie said. "No need to drag politics into this. There's more than enough time for all that. Besides, I'm hungry, and the thought of a rib-eye steak has my mouth watering. It has been a week since we left Rome."

"I thought you came in yesterday."

"No, schedules changed at the last minute. Marcus joined me on the shuttle to Argentina. The *Siciliano* daisy was under refitting for a month. We were delayed three days in Rio— what an awful city. After vertical, we caught the first transport to Prasinus. We arrived this morning. Our bags are being sent to the convent at Santa Maria."

"So, Marcus, are you the only man in the convent?"

"No, I'm in the rectory." Marcus blushed.

"I know it well. Give Bishop Dominicus my regards."

"He told me to tell you not to forget the Church. He heard about your successful drag."

"That bishop always gets the news before anyone. He'll get his piece; he knows that. First things first—dinner."

The auto-door slid open, and both the air and the atmosphere changed as we strolled into the restaurant. The owner, the grandson of the original owner, Charley McGonagall, greeted us like old lost friends and led us to a booth halfway back in the restaurant. As we passed through the restaurant, a dozen people offered or signaled their greetings to me. A few asked for a few minutes of my time for lunch or a drink. I smiled vaguely and shook hands with a few—most were parasites or pirates. The restaurant's walls shimmered with images of Ireland and smelled of green grassy hillsides and damp perfumed air. I heard a sneeze from somewhere in the back.

"Thank you for all your notes and videos," Sister Annie said as we snuggled into the booth. "I'm happy the trip went well."

"It did go well. There was a hiccup when we started the drag, but we worked around it."

"What happened?" Marcus asked.

For the next three hours, I regaled them with stories of the drag. Probing the belt and searching for the right asteroid, finding the winner, setting the anchors, and the loss of the thruster.

"Weren't you afraid that the thruster might explode and blow you out into space?" Marcus asked.

"It was under control. My crew did a great job. I've dealt with worse."

"It seems too dangerous to me," Sister Annie said.

"Truth be told, it wasn't routine—then, in the belt, what is?"

"Sounds exciting," Marcus said.

"Never a dull moment, kid," I answered.

"Garrett and Clive? They are well?" Sister Annie asked.

"Yes, they are wandering around in the corridors up north. I'll meet with them in a few days; remind them to remain sober enough to find their way back to the ship."

"And Hank?" Marcus asked.

"Yes, for a noid, he's doing well," I said. "You always ask about him."

"He's fun, Uncle Buster. He is not like Earth-side bots. There, they are all serious about their programming. I spent a lot of time with him when I was a kid. Someday I want one like him."

"I suggest that you think twice about it—they can be a pain. I was lucky, he came with the *Gypsy King*. Not sure I could haul without him."

The steaks cost a week's wage for one of the lunar workers, but I was rolling in it. It's good to have a few bad habits.

5

Look at you, all self-important and all. For the three years you never left the island, you prayed and studied, took on the grey cloth of the Prophet, yet never once called yourself by that ancient name. They came to you, those first three. They stood in the cold rain and prayed, devout, and all believing. Why did you let them go through that? They were hooked before they arrived. Penitent and pious, they had and still have the faith of the true believer. From the three came six. From six came sixty, then six hundred. Your apostles left and brought more to the clerisy. With enough believers, mountains can be moved.

Is it mountains that you want? Those years you traveled, after the three on the island. They were troublesome for many, weren't they? All the questions, all the accusations, the righteous anger, the fear. It was all there. Some died, don't you remember? The boy in Crete, the three women stoned on the beach in Tunis—the cries of heretic, blasphemy, infidel. Why did you send them? They were each a loss of the light, and each an eternal sacrifice.

* * *

The three of us strolled through the narrow corridors back to the convent. It was late, and the crowds had thinned in the Catholic quarter. The cathedral, built with white glazed brick, rose thirty meters into the air. Its campanile stopped four meters below the translucent apex of the dome that covered this quadrant of the Emerald City. The rectory is a small grey structure to one side of the cathedral. The opulent convent for the Sisters of the Revealment sat directly across the piazza that fronted the cathedral's main entrance. The convent's glazed brick façade mimicked the cathedral. The surrounding piazza reminded me of Italian courtyards I'd seen in holo-vids. A small fountain threw geysers of water into the air; the lower gravity allowed for a more dramatic display than what might be found in one of the real Tuscan fountains a quarter of a million miles below. The piazza, church, and fountain added a touch of home to devout tourists visiting the shrine to Pope Conrad I.

Sister Annie pointed to a stone bench under real trees that offered a strange mix of earthen home and moon artifice.

"Marcus, would you mind finishing your unpacking? I need to talk to your uncle," she said.

Marcus, not wanting to be left out of anything, started to say something. I put my hand up.

"I'll take you to the bio-dome tomorrow. It has almost doubled in size since you were last here. How about that?"

"An hour, that enough time?" Marcus answered.

"Tomorrow. It's late and you need your sleep." She looked at me. "Is that okay?"

"Of course, ten tomorrow morning. We'll get a bite to eat, then tour the dome." Marcus again wanted to say something. I cut him off. "Ten tomorrow. Sleep."

We watched Marcus head toward the rectory; he disappeared into the shadow of the cathedral.

"Strong boy, and is becoming a good man. I see it. Annie, why are you here?" I asked. "You didn't need to come all this way to see me. I'm fine, in fact doing great, even have a few units put away for Marcus. So, why the trip?"

Sister Annie clenched the long shaft of her cross and fingered its polished surface. "Official and unofficial business, Brother. The official is complicated. I am here at the request of the Pope to begin laying the groundwork for a new colony on Mars. His Holiness believes that we need to ensure that the Earth-side faithful have options. Earth is doing better now than it has for two hundred years; the daisies have made a significant impact on both the environment and the economics of the planet. The importation of raw materials from space has lessened the effects of Earth-side manufacturing. Pollution is almost nonexistent, the weather is managed, food is not a problem, and even the various continental governments are at peace, relatively speaking. However, peace and safety bring population growth. The Church is seeing a population spike within the next fifty years. His Holiness believes that a second wave of emigration might be in order. They believe that more than a million will need to be transported."

"So, the Church has two options: Move people to Mars or cull the population."

"You are such an ass. Of course not; the Holy Father is not saying that. The earth's population stands at fifteen billion souls, food is plentiful, few go wanting. One million people is a statistical error, but if properly chosen, it will have an impact on the long-term growth."

"Wow, population planning. There was a time that it was anathema."

She ignored my remark, though I could see it stung.

"The international police and political tribunals keep despots from controlling more than a few million people in isolated districts. So, moving a few million to Mars would do little to change the dynamic. What His Holiness wants is to increase the Church's economic and social power. A new religious community on Mars would help that effort."

"Send the more faithful into space—develop a community that will project the Church as the leader to the stars. How sacred."

"Always a cynic. But yes, something like that. The wars of the past three hundred years have shown the Church that there must be some form of protection and safeguard for the

Church's and the Vatican's future."

"And this new colony, has it been given a name?" I asked.

"Domus Dei die Martis."

"Really? God's House on Mars?"

"Vatican III was mentioned, but the bishops thought it was presumptuous."

"Isn't most of this endeavor presumptuous? If it were here on the moon, it would be called *Civitas Aurum.*"

She ignored my remark, even though I liked the idea of the City of Gold. "I'm meeting with lunar habitat designers, manufacturers, and members of the Luna church for their input. Bishop Dominicus is managing the meetings. He was asked to lead the effort and be the bishop of this new colony. He declined. He said he was too old and was too set in his ways here at the cathedral. Another is being considered for the Martian position."

"Do I know him?" I asked.

"No, you do not. He's a bishop from a diocese in Australia, far from the politics of the Vatican."

"That's a smart move."

"He is joining me in three days. I want you to meet him. His name is Bishop Tiberius; he is forty-three and quite handsome."

"Married?"

"No, single."

"And I take it from all this preamble that you are going to Mars to help build this colony for the glory of God."

"Again, the cynicism. Yes, I'll be helping build the colony. There's much to do."

"Why not just take over one of the abandoned colonies? There're three that come to mind."

"All built with old tech. Most leak like a sieve, and the ownership of two of the domes is in question. I don't want to spend years in court trying to sort them out. We've acquired a thousand hectares in the Utopia Planitia from the Martian government. They are happy to have us join them."

"I'm sure they are, especially with all the money you can throw their way."

"Stop that—this is good for everyone. There's much we can do to help develop the colonies on Mars. It will give our Martian foundry the opportunity for more markets."

"Ah, there it is. Markets, money, and the Church. The fickle finger of capitalism, something the Church now wholeheartedly embraces. It's just a few hundred years late to the party."

"You are impossible, and you being mister big-time capitalist. That asteroid certainly helped your personal situation."

"At great risk to both body and bank."

"And the same for what I'm doing. Great things always require great risk."

"And?" I asked, waiting for the other shoe to drop. "What's the unofficial business?"

"I want you to take Marcus onboard the *Gypsy King* and get him away from all this Earth-side crap. I want you to make a man of him."

I slowly stood and looked across the piazza and then up at the cathedral. Talk about a knuckleball. "No, I can't. Marcus has no skills and would just get in the way. There's a serious risk. If something were to happen to him . . ."

"There's room. The *Gypsy* was designed to carry three times the number of crewmembers. He could be a help—he'd provide backup to Garrett and Clive."

"No. We are a tight crew. We think each other's thoughts. He would—"

"He would not get in the way. He's eighteen. You left Emerald City and went into space on the *Antares* when you were nineteen. He needs to be around men, to learn things, to grow up. The men he meets on Earth do not prepare him for the future. He needs to be a part of something bigger than himself. Most in Rome are sycophants, eunuchs, and asses."

"Ouch, and who is now the cynic? I thought he was going

to Notre Dame. There he can grow up; the brothers will knock some sense into him."

"No, he needs more than that. I don't want him to become a smart man with no off-world skills. This would give him a serious chance to be something bigger and . . . better."

"Is he going to Mars with you?"

"That is my hope, but he needs more—and you can give it to him. It will take me at least three years of preparation before we can begin. Pope Julius has approved this; he sees the need for Marcus to gain these skills . . ."

"Now the Pope is involved? The man doesn't have better things to do?"

"Pope Julius believes in the serious nature of this venture and what it means to the Church. And he believes that Marcus will play an important part in this venture and its future."

"And what it also means to you?"

She paused, a pained expression on her face. She held the cross even tighter. "Yes, to me. Yes, to me, especially. In my heart, I know that this is a task asked especially of me."

"Does the boy know?"

"He's not a boy—anymore. He's important to more people than me. He's essential to the Church. He is devout, smart, and ambitious. He reminds me of you at that age, smart, curious, and headstrong."

"You're grooming him, is that it? If Pope Julius is concerned about this one boy, what has he in mind? The priesthood, the Church . . . ?"

"The future, Buster! And the seven billion souls that look to the Church for leadership, comfort, and hope."

"Good God, Annie. He's not going to get that by tumbling through four hundred million kilometers of space with fifty millimeters of plasti-steel and diamond glass keeping him from God's own vacuum."

"Nonetheless, he must become more than that. You can help him become a strong leader who understands the future.

You can teach him that."

Chagrined, I leaned in and kissed Annie on the cheek. She held up her cross for me to kiss. I touched it with my fingertips, turned, and walked away.

"Buster, please consider it, please," she said.

I hesitated. I studied the fountain, then looked upward to the translucent glass overhead. Turning back, and against everything I held sacred, I said, "I leave in four weeks. I'll consider it."

For the next two weeks, refitting the *Gypsy King* consumed most of my time. I lived on the shuttle as I went back and forth from Prasinus to the *Gypsy King* four times. Each transit was stressful—the Gs, the security, the lousy food—and consumed about six hours. Marina 3 is positioned a few thousand kilometers above the moon. It's owned by an outfitter who controls three other marinas; the real owner is most likely buried inside some shell company whose mailing address is a small office in an alley in Rome. The *Gypsy*, due to its size, is moored at one of the stationary outboard docks on the structure. The marina and attendant facilities are enormous, even by space standards. From the surface of the moon, the marina is easily seen by flashes of the sun off the structure's exterior.

Sitting on the control deck of the *Gypsy*, Earth hangs just out of reach; it's a sight I never get bored of. When you're four hundred million miles from home chasing rocks, it's nice to know that ball is still there. Out in the belt, it's just one more very bright spot in the infinite black. The fact that I've only walked on its surface once, in my forty-five years, isn't the issue. The point is that I did, and I was younger. It hurt, but a lot less than it would now.

I took *Horus* out twice with Hank for a detailed inspection of the exterior hull. Other than repairs to a dozen micro-asteroid strikes and the fuel replenishment of the dozen bots that were secured to the exterior, everything was nominal. Hank had all the bots serviced by the Marina, and they were good to go. I replaced the lost bot; I can tell you they are not cheap. Luckily, they had a refurbished unit available. As a backup, I ordered another bot. It would be ready when we returned. The fusion reactor uses hydrogen for fuel. During my last shuttle trip, the H was being pumped into the two massive tanks secured to the port and starboard sides of the ship. They ran almost the full length of the *Gypsy*. The single fusion reactor is mounted amidships under the central mass of the vessel. The reactor is mounted so that it can be rotated without having to turn the entire ship around. While dragging a rock, turning the whole ship is difficult, if not stupid and bloody dangerous. The reactor rotates one hundred and eighty degrees and sends its thrust in the opposite direction, slowing the vessel. That and the assists from the thrusters on Castor allows for a more civilized speed as we approach the gravity well of the moon and Earth.

Some draggers haul galactic ice. At the foundries, these chunks of rock and ice are distilled into hydrogen and oxygen. Our fuel, hydrogen, is delivered to the ship by lunar-side tankers. The oxygen is piped to the various lunar bases to be used for things like breathing. The hydrogen is mainly used for fusion reactors that supply more than half of the power for the cities. The remaining H is sold to draggers, private tourist yachts, and interplanetary colonist operations. In space, nothing is wasted.

On the hull of the fuel barge is stenciled in yellow, "If you need gas, I've got it. Contact Russ at Lunar Hydrogen." Also in yellow, on the bow, is painted, *LORELEI*.

I tapped the control panel com-link of the *Horus*. "You driving today, Russ?"

"Is that the best dragger in the universe, Buster Strabo? Sure as hell is, ol' buddy. I just finished your port tank—it's full. Starboard will be full in six hours. You were drawing fumes when you arrived; that is not good. You watch yourself, Captain. I don't want to send out my tow for you. That would eat all your profits."

"Thanks, we were watching. We had enough. That wasn't the first time I've made that run."

"Did you load H at the smelter?" Russ asked as he waved at me through the forward window of the tanker.

"No, saved myself for you."

"Good, they are pirates. Thanks for waiting."

"My pleasure," I said.

"I told him ten times we were getting low, but oh no, Captain Strabo knew better," Hank butted in.

"Hank, stay out of this. This is a private conversation."

"Yes, sir."

"Bots. Can't live with 'em, can't live without 'em," Russ said.

"Ain't that the truth."

"I heard that," Hank responded.

"It was intentional," I said. "Russ, I'm going to the port side if you need anything."

"Roger that, Buster," Russ answered.

As the donkey drifted over the *Gypsy King*, I looked for additional hits or dings. I also rechecked the mounts on the asteroid thrusters. That failed unit still bugged the shit out of me; it should not have happened. The replacement was due in a week. It was a few million miles out on the freight run from the manufacturer on Mars. The void in the thruster bays on the *Gypsy*'s upper starboard flank was apparent. In two weeks, I would get Garrett and Clive up here. We'd then pull each of the cables out to their full length, and have every meter checked. That would take at least three days and required that both be onboard. Which jail or brothel I'd have to drag them out of was still to be determined. Both had been married at one time or another, but their long schedules were not conducive to lasting and intimate relationships—eventually, their wives dumped them. Back in the pre-space, pre-industrialized era of Earth, I'd read about sailing ships that would take almost two years to make round trips from England to Australia. We have a lot in common with those celibate and lonely seafaring men.

"Hey, Ranger, you still on the horn?" Russ piped in over the speaker.

"Yes, sir, starboard side," I answered.

"I found the manufacturer's plate here; it's under the starboard tank. You want a picture?"

"Jesus, I haven't thought about that thing for years. Sure, send it."

"I can't believe this box of bolts and fusion was built in 2303. That was more than a century and a half ago. And it still gets you around the universe?"

"It works just fine; the reactor is its fourth. I've modified the racks for the thrusters and added the new bots and two spools. She only had three when I bought it. The hydrogen tanks were new two trips back. Hell, Russ, you helped me pick these—came from that foundry over Australia."

"Damn, time flies, and outside of a few dings and patches, the *Gypsy* looks good, damn good."

"She does what she does; thanks for the fuel."

"See, it's good to follow the advice of your friends. I understand that last rock was solid, a good grab."

Dragging was hardly a competitive sport. Years passed between deliveries, and a foundry or smelter might survive a year or more on the content of one good rock. Payment for Castor, after the initial sale, was also long term. The price paid for the material was based on the assay at delivery. As the rock is busted up, if precious metals are found, if diamonds or other high-value crystals are discovered, hell, if a prehistoric green-skinned Catholic-eating alien is found living in the rock's heart, the price is adjusted upward. The agreed base price seldom goes down.

After inspecting the starboard side, I drifted over to the

port and watched the *Lorelei* decouple from the tank. Its fifty-meter-long hose and the maneuvering bot secured to its nozzle slowly snaked its way back to the flank of the tanker. Gas jetted from multiple thrusters on the tanker's flanks. The fuel barge was really nothing more than a control dome, cramped crew quarters, propulsion units, and four massive hydrogen tanks. Drifting over the *Gypsy King*, I watched the *Lorelei* power up and slowly head back to the moon. Russ owned another ship that was used to run emergency supplies to the belt and could be rigged to tow. It was automated and was incredibly fast. However, the cost would bankrupt any dragger who needed his help. In fact, Russ owned two draggers that were working the Mars foundries. They were ships that he acquired after saving the idiots who thought they could push the envelope just a little too much. There are bold draggers, there are old draggers, but no bold and old draggers.

My com-link pinged, but no face appeared on the screen.

"Buster Strabo here." There was a crackling hiss. I waited for the signal to clear. "Strabo here, the *Gypsy King*."

More hissing followed, then a series of clicks, then faintly: "Buster, if you get this or it's picked up by your archive, this is Titus Olivier with the ship *Chicago Glory*." More clicks and interference. Then, "I'm dragging in from Sector Seventy-two. There's something out there that you might want to look at on your rebound to the belt. It's in the adjacent sector, Seventy-three."

I knew Olivier. He is a good dragger, almost as many years in the belt as me. We once partnered on a large rock, maybe eight or nine years earlier. The radio delay said eight minutes, a minimum of almost twenty minutes round trip. I'd listen to his message, then reply.

"Ovoid, blunt ends, the highest density reading I've ever registered. Obviously, a lot of metal. We could not stop since we were underway with our drag. Couldn't assay, either. But good God in Christ, the thing metered off the chart, high-density, big. It resisted probing; most signals bounced off. It was only on the meter and the screen for less than a minute as we approached and coasted by. Spooky if you ask me, but damn, there's a lot of something in that rock. I'll send you the data and the images. Talk to you soon. This is Olivier, out . . ." More clicks and hissing followed until I shut down the com-link.

A dragger always appreciates a heads-up. Over the decades, I've mentioned a few rocks to other draggers. It was the neighborly thing to do when you're a million kilometers from home.

* * *

You are alone, more alone than any man has been in the history of mankind. You vaguely remember adjusting the thrusters and allowing the automatics to slide the donk into the supply bay. Hank pulled you from the control seat and carried you to the medi-bot. There you slept for days, or that's what the post-flight assessor said when you checked it the following week. Days, maybe a week, you remember nothing. The controls read, when you recovered enough to get out of the bot, that you were a hundred thousand kilometers from the rock. The lights were still there—they came and went. So many, then none.

Your savior, Hank, sat in his usual location watching you. Two days after you climbed out of the medi-bot, you put him to sleep. Do you remember that?

7

An hour later, the images and data arrived from the *Chicago Glory* on my com-link. After reviewing them, I was astonished. If true, the numbers were off the scale for metal density, mass-to-volume ratio, and impenetrability. The *Glory*'s sensors barely scratched the rock's surface. It was ovoid and symmetrical, very unusual for a chunk of space junk. It was blunt, it looked cut off at the ends, and swelled through its middle. The surface was pocked and scarred by eons of asteroid and meteoroid strikes; all were shallow, and they barely disfigured the rock. A few looked like glancing blows; long scars grazed the side. The radiation scans showed it was dark. No emissions of any kind.

I sent a note back to *Chicago Glory*. "Titus, thanks for the heads-up. Interesting piece. I concur, looks like metal, maybe solid. The shape is a puzzle, but you and I have seen hundreds of strange things floating around in this solar system. We are shipping out in a few weeks and heading toward Sector Eighty-One. I saw something there two trips back. However, not nearly as interesting as this one. I'll discuss it with the crew. I will let you know. Be safe. Buster Strabo, out."

I rotated the image on the screen, zoomed in, and looked again at the data.

"Hank, analyze the data and the imagery I've put into your folder. I want your opinion of what you see and what was sent."

"Will do, sir. When do you want this done?" Hank said as he stopped next to my command chair.

"On your own time. Ship status update, please."

"Hydrogen tanks are filled. All bots have been serviced, rebooted with new software, and are fully fueled. All onboard thrusters have also been serviced. The replacement is due the day after tomorrow; the freighter from Mars is decelerating. All food stores are replenished—I made a point to include more Italian; they were the biggest hits. There are also extra rations of coffee and tea. I need an update on liquor requirements. You have enough victuals to last three-point-four years under normal consumption."

"Victuals?"

"A new word I discovered in my data banks. Archaic— means food."

"Provisions works better for me."

"Yes, sir. All donkeys have been serviced. You may have noticed that when you and I took *Horus* out."

"Yes. Where are Clive and Garrett?"

"Mr. Jones is asleep in his room at the Sheraton North. Mr. Borg is also asleep, but I sense that he is not alone."

"Don't pry, Hank."

"Yes, sir."

"Send them a com to be at the Seawitch Bar this afternoon at four. There is much to discuss."

"Yes, sir."

I was scheduled to take the shuttle back to Prasinus. It was a two-hour drop to the surface, plus the boarding and deplaning. As I said, makes for a long day. I stowed my overnight bag in the upper rack; once on the surface, I'd drop it at the Hilton then meet with my crew. Hopefully, they would be sober enough to pay attention to the news about Marcus. I wanted their feedback.

Clive and Garrett, a little ragged around the eyes, sat in a back booth at the Seawitch. It was like a hundred others in the Emerald City. Vids on the walls, liquor bottles stacked on glass shelves, and a few women with love in their eyes. Many carried cred apps on their coms. A bottle of Black Label sat in the center of the steel table; it was a third empty—I'm a pessimist. A tumbler with ice sat at the empty seat across from the men. When Clive saw me, he poured.

"Thanks for coming. I know it's a day early, but there's much to talk about." I raised the tumbler and clicked their glasses.

"There's a rumor going around about a fat slug of a rock, no confirmed sector location, just a rumor. The *Chicago Glory* spotted it," Garrett said. "Could this have anything to do with that?"

"The moon is a small world, isn't it?" I said. "I only heard from Oliveira yesterday, and the word's made it to the brothels?"

"Excuse me! I'm at the Tokyo Geisha House, classy and conservative," Garrett said. "Clive, I'm not sure about him."

"So, if the word is out," I said, "I'm not going to want to waste the hydrogen to chase that rock—could be a bunch of guys wanting to take a look."

"Buster, I've never heard you turn down a chance to at least look. Even the ugliest broad has something under her skirt," Clive said.

"Well put, you're such a gentleman. By the time we reach it, it will be an additional quarter-circ around the sun, a trajectory that would be in our favor—maybe. Distance isn't the issue; it's on one of our possible flight plans. What I don't know is what it's worth. Oliveira sent me the specs."

"You got the numbers?" Garrett said.

"Yes, and images too." I placed my data-pad on the table and flicked through the images. "There's something odd about this thing, and it's not just the density and how opaque it is. There's a visceral attraction. I don't get it, but it's there."

Clive slid the PD over to Garrett, and they both studied the rock.

"It is a size that's doable, only a little bigger than Castor," Clive said. "No rotation, that's good." He looked at the numbers, then scrolled across the bottom of the images. "I've never seen such densities—maybe that's why the impacts are so shallow. Whatever the metal is, it is hard. The cut-off ends are intriguing. Both are almost the same except where an asteroid may have clipped off an edge or two. The biggest issue is inertia. This tater weighs a lot more than Castor and most of the others we've dragged. More power to pull it out of its orbit, more power to slow it down once we reach the smelter. And as hard as it is, how are they going to break it down? Oliveira never put a cutter to it. So, that's a whole other issue to deal with. But still, it is fascinating."

"Strange thing is, when I asked Hank to take a look at the numbers, he came back later and said he was too busy."

"Hank? Said he was too busy?" Clive said. "That is strange. That noid could do a billion calcs a sec. Did you press him why?"

"Yes, and he still blew me off. Never had that happen. I let it pass, for now. But I'm going to find out what anomaly is twisting his circuits."

"You said it was in Sector Seventy-three?" Garret said. "We were going to look in Sector Eighty-one this next trip; it's on the same trajectory. If this thing is a bust, we lose a week, at most. We can power up to catch Sector Eighty-one."

"I looked at the orbital data, and if this thing is a go," I said, opening a new screen on the pad, "we can tow it to Mars's smelter *Paulus*. There's a rumor that they will need a great deal of metal for some on-planet development, and this would help a lot. Plus, the money would be good."

"Is this a vote?" Clive asked. "We never voted before."

"As I said, there's something about this that's giving me a strange vibe, and with Hank jamming me, I don't know why. That's why I want your opinion, so if this a vote, sure, I'll ask for one."

"You said there was another reason you wanted to see us?" Clive said.

"Yes, my sister has asked me to take my nephew, Marcus, on the run. She thinks he needs some bonding time with his uncle Buster."

"Good God, we're not a nursery school, Buster," Clive said. "It's dangerous out there. You know that and that sister of yours knows that too. What is the kid, fifteen?"

"He's almost eighteen, strong, smart."

"And has grown up in the Church and has hung around with a bunch of acolytes that couldn't carry their weight on the moon. Buster, it's your call, but we're tight, we've been a trio for six runs. Most draggers carry five or six in their crews. Hell, the *Gypsy* once carried six plus the captain. We do just fine with bots and each other. Besides, the split is also an issue."

"I'll cover his piece. No impact on yours or Garrett's; full shares as always. Annie says that there's a colony development being planned for Mars. She wants Marcus to be involved, but he needs space-time. So? What do you think?"

"Yeah, I guess it could work. I get tired of dealing with just the two of you for years at a time. Another face would make it less boring," Garrett added. "I'm bringing a lunar slider on this trip. It needs a lot of work and refurbishing, he could help. It's like the Martian sliders, but a different transfer power source for the steamers. Faster reaction time. It would be good to have him learn some of the tech. Besides, I haven't seen the kid for eight years. He was a handful then. I can only imagine him now."

"He's a good kid—seems like he has his feet under him," I said. "But he's Earthborn. It will be tough the first few weeks," I said.

"I get it. But knowing your sister, she hasn't told him yet," Clive added.

"Yeah, she hasn't. I'm having dinner with them tonight. I will let you know tomorrow. Are we good with Oliveira's rock?"

"What the hell," Clive said.

"Go for it," Garrett added.

"In for a penny, in for a pound," I said.

"What the hell does that mean? I never understood that stupid colloquialism," Clive said.

"Me neither."

* * *

I was early and relaxed in the lobby of the Hilton, my feet up on an overstuffed footstool covered in some type of leatherette the color of lunar dust, waiting for Annie and Marcus. The thick overhead glass enlarged the stars that filled the lunar sky. There was a secondary wash of light over the furniture from the tall lamps placed around the lobby. Real trees and shrubbery filled the planters that divided the hall into the bars, restaurants, and main lounge. They grew in fantastic shapes due to the low gravity. I ordered a Kentucky bourbon from the patrolling bar-bot. He questioned my choice and asked twice to confirm. My guess, he was really checking my bank account. Many of the people in the lounge wore ecclesiastical clothing, black cassocks for priests, a few red-trimmed cassocks for visiting bishops, and red-decked cardinals. There were even a few business suits. The women, those not in religious garb, were dressed for the evening. Tourists filled the barstools, and a trio of surprisingly well-behaved children dipped their hands in the fountain. For me, it was natural and commonplace. I've lived most of my weird, off-Earth life on the moon, and most of that in Emerald City. However, now, when not dragging asteroids through space, I live in a cheap room in the Hilton. By all standards, Earth-side or lunar, I am wealthy. There are a few million bitunits in the bank; I have my own crew and my own mortgage-free ship. I am the master and commander of my life. But deep down inside, as the trite song goes, I need someone to love. All laughs on the outside, tears on the inside, boo-hoo. Then again, if you swallow that, I'll trade you the *Gypsy King* for a bottle of Highland. Being me is fucking fun.

The double bourbon cost a week's wage for one of the Hilton staff. And me? Life? Command of? Really? The money could blow up tomorrow. Financial speculators and asshole money managers fooling around in the markets haven't changed for hundreds of years. A bit unit one day could be worth a tenth the amount, or double the amount, the next. What drives everything in the universe is need; I need steel, I need gold, I need aluminum, I need diamond windows, I need a hooker, I need a wife or some other song lyric. Need and markets; that's why I spin up for the belt. There are two things that old Buster Strabo needs, a good crew and a good market when I get back. Without those, I might as well buy a bungalow in Emerald City's west wing, retire, and paint holo-slogans on moon rocks. I've been asked twice by the local trade school to teach courses in planetary science, mineralogy, rare earths, and dragging. I've got that to fall back on. My one passion is reading the old Roman classics—that's why the Latin names. Maybe that's why taking a real job would be like falling on my own sword, *Recidisset in gladio meo!*

"A penny for your thoughts?" a soft voice said from behind my left ear. The intoxicating fragrance of Martian orchids filled my nose, and then a beautiful face leaned in and kissed me on my cheek. "I've been looking for you."

I reached around and took the woman's waist and pulled her to me. God, she smelled wonderful. I stood, wrapped her in my arms, and returned the tease. As always, she tasted like the sweetest peach. Her response offered that she definitely didn't mind my attention and added her two lips' worth. We tasted like a Bourbon and peach smash. I considered ordering a double.

When we broke for air, I whispered in her orchid-scented ear, "Prasinus, for the last three weeks, then going out again. I thought you were on Earth."

"I'd have come up, you know that. You should have called."

"Maybe I should have." Her lingering taste brought back turbulent whitecaps within memory storms.

"Yes, you should have. You are a bad boy."

I stepped back and looked her over; she had undeniably improved over the past two years. "Why are you here?"

"Business, as always. We have an order for a hundred thousand tons of steel and a matching order for aluminum powders. I came up to finalize the deal. My team and I are going back to the *Washington* smelter the day after tomorrow. I understand it's your asteroid they are cutting up. When I found out, I took the opportunity."

"Business before pleasure," I said.

"Not necessarily."

"Good."

"Well, if it's not Sarah Thomason," Sister Annie said as she strolled over to us—talk about bad timing. Marcus followed in her wake. "Buster didn't tell me you were in Prasinus."

"Sister Annie, he didn't know. I just arrived today," Sarah answered, her tone far softer than my sister's.

"How convenient," Annie said.

I know I heard a cat scratch a panel of slate.

Sister Annie drew the young man to her. "This is my son, Marcus Aurelius Strabo. Marcus, this is Sarah Thomason. She is, I still believe, the CEO of Greater American Metals."

"Still am, Sister. Marcus, a pleasure." She shook my godson's hand.

"Sarah, we are having dinner," I said. "Care to join us?"

An annoyed expression washed over my sister's face, then quickly faded.

"Please, Sarah, join us. There's much to catch up on," Annie said.

"Only if I buy," Sarah said.

"Even more of a reason," I joked, then led the four of us to the restaurant that filled the open upper-level deck above the lounge and bar.

The whole time I climbed the gilded stairway, I wondered who might throw who over the balcony's railing first.

Dinner was surprisingly pleasant; the two most interesting and important women in my life behaved themselves as professionals. Marcus wanted to know everything about the *Washington* smelter. Even after two bottles of a delightful and expensive Chianti from Tuscany, I still waited for this little world created between us to explode. The two of them have a long history, the kind that makes thrillers and murder-romance novels. The three of us grew up together in an upper-class corridor in the west wing of Emerald City, just kids but close, and our folks hung out together—until our parents died. After that, we seldom saw each other. Sarah went to the public high school, Annie and me to the parochial version. After high school, Sarah immigrated to Earth to study business at Oxford; Annie soon followed and went to Rome, took vows, and joined the Revealment convent to study God; and I, as previously bragged, left for interplanetary space to escape everything. Annie took on the role of hovering angel and not the kind that floats about like in a Botticelli painting—more like one of those in a Hieronymus Bosch painting. Sarah and I have a fondness for each other, and after my busted marriage, this affection escalated a couple of times to way, way beyond friends. We were good at keeping it simple—one of us was always leaving. Annie intended to make sure it never grew beyond simple. Sarah ended up in a lousy marriage contract;

luckily, there were no children. That contract was now voided; her life, like mine, was all business.

"Marcus, your uncle, has something to ask you," Annie said.

"Really? You're making me ask now?" I said, looking at her, then Sarah. "You could have at least warned me."

She said matter-of-factly, "You *are* the man in the family."

I shook my head and took another gulp of wine. Returning to space was looking better and better. "Marcus, I would like you to join me on my next drag to the belt."

Marcus turned to his mother. "Did you know about this?"

"Your uncle and I have talked about it. We believe it would be good for you."

I wasn't sure about the correct use of the pronoun *we*, or for that matter the phrase *good for you*, either.

"The *Gypsy King* is shipping out in a few weeks," I began to plead our case. "There are some interesting asteroids to assay; some could be worth a fortune. You get a cut. A few thousand units in the bank would make your time at the university more comfortable."

"But I've already been accepted," Marcus protested.

"Notre Dame has been there for five hundred years," I continued, not sure why. "Two years more won't make that much of a difference. And besides, I've been told that an experienced dragger gets all the girls."

"Yeah, right. Is that why you're still single, Uncle Buster?"

"Marcus, watch that tone," Annie said.

"Mother, we had this all planned: college, then the Vatican; we even talked about the priesthood. There are scholarships. Now, you want to send me out into space? Why?"

"These days, the Church needs men experienced in a broad range of things, especially those that can offer more than just prayers," Annie said.

"Sister Annie, if you don't mind, may I add something?" Sarah said.

I was shocked when Annie nodded, yes.

"Marcus, I think this is a fantastic opportunity. I envy you. The future is out there; it has been since the wars. Look what we've accomplished, a quarter of a million living here on the moon, and millions more on Mars. And the other planets and moons are also available. There's talk about a permanent settlement on Ceres, even a smelter there to reduce costs. You have so much ahead of you, and this would add and expand to your abilities and your knowledge. No one in college would have your experience, and besides, as your uncle says, I think the Church needs more than priests and bishops. I understand they are building a new colony on Mars—who will advise them? Who has the skills to assist that effort? A lot happens in the solar system; it's not just in these bubbles. Your uncle Buster is out there, he knows. You will learn; your world will expand."

I was stunned. This was the first time I can remember these two women being on the same side—of anything.

"Marcus, you know my crew, Mr. Borg and Mr. Jones. They think that you would be a great addition. There are no better men to teach you about deep space and dragging. And there's a lot more to it than just towing rocks. You'll find that out—and besides, you can continue your studies as well. There is a lot of transit time. And you will be able to spend time with Hank; he is an encyclopedia."

Marcus paused, but before he could say anything, yelling penetrated the restaurant from near the entry.

I didn't believe who I saw pushing aside the maître d'. "What the hell is *he* doing here? He's banned from the moon." I looked at my sister. "Is this your doing? You are the only official with enough authority to force the Prasinus city council to permit that man to return, or even pass through the airlock."

The intruder was tall, lean, and gaunt. His face was dark, eyes deeply set, with a beard as white as Saturn ice. His cassock was brown, with a full hood that covered his head and shaded his eyes. I had nightmares about that face. A cross hung over his chest; a white cord wrapped his thin waist. Even from twenty meters, his blue eyes cut through the room. He saw Sister Annie and pushed his way past the maître d' and one of the bus-bots that tried to stop him.

He abruptly stopped at the table and glared at the nun. "We were supposed to meet this evening—have you forgotten?"

"No, I hadn't. However, *you* have forgotten your manners," Annie coldly answered, as if she were scolding a child. "Sarah Thomason, this is Prophet Tassos. Prophet, Ms. Thomason is CEO of Greater American Metals. You, of course, know my brother, Buster Strabo, and my son, Marcus Strabo."

He bowed to all of us. He then took a long moment to stare at me—he blinked first. "A pleasure again, Captain; it has been a few years. Now, Sister Annie, why didn't—"

"We will talk about this later, Prophet," Annie said, not looking at the man. "This is not the place. I will meet you in the Cathedral later this evening."

"When?"

"Just go there and wait. I will be there soon."

He glared at the nun and continued to rub his fingers over the polished surface of his crucifix. "The peace of the Universal God be with you." He waved his fingers in the air, then spun around and hurriedly left the restaurant.

"What a strange man," Sarah said.

"You don't know the half of it," I offered. "That man has stirred up more trouble during the last five years than any other drunk, zealot, tech-phobic Luddite or politician. He has called the Pope an imposter and charlatan; the leading religious orders are nothing more than corporate shills. His latest rant is that only he, Prophet Tassos, can make humans worthy of the stars."

"Scary and eccentric," Sarah said. "Yes, I've heard of him. I thought he was exiled to a monastery in the Mediterranean. Someplace away from communications and . . ."

". . . people—he has a way of mesmerizing people," Annie said. "And he has a following."

"Yes, we call ourselves Nostre Familia," Marcus said.

"Marcus, you're not following that nut?" I asked.

"He's not a nut, and he's not crazy either. We believe the future of humans is out there in the universe. We must spread ourselves into the far reaches of space, beyond our solar system, for our salvation. The word will be carried as far as humans can carry it."

"And whose word is that?" I said. "God's, the ancient bible's, the Church, or the sanctimonious ramblings of that space-dead fool? All I've heard him broadcast is babel and noise."

"Then you aren't listening, Uncle," Marcus said. "He speaks of the future and of the path that leads to it."

"Is that why you want Marcus to go with me?" I said to Annie. "To get him away from that crackpot?"

She avoided my glare.

"That's it! For a couple of years, I'm supposed to be his babysitter until he gets that man out of his system. You are as crazy as that so-called prophet."

"You know him better than most," Sister Annie said.

"You leave all that out of this. That was a long time ago."

"You know him?" Sarah asked.

"Tassos was once, more than twenty years ago, a dragger like me. I was a punk kid; two drags under my belt. He had a reputation as a bold and fearless risk-taker, hauling rocks that no one would touch—made a lot of money doing it, too. His name is Tassos Orion. He came down from Ceres, from a spec mining family. He was crazy, yet his crew would follow him to the gates of Hades. And that's where he left them."

"At the gates of hell?"

"Yes, they all disappeared."

"And the *Gypsy King* . . ." Annie said. She knew a lot about the story.

". . . was his ship. Everyone said it was cursed. I didn't and still don't believe them—the world's forgotten what happened. None of the old-timers working the runs then are still dragging. They're either retired, drifting in space, or dead."

"What happened?" Sarah asked.

"It was all over the news here on the moon back then. But I can see why you don't know; you were in England. What happens out here seldom finds its way back to Earth. Twenty-two years ago, Orion was found alone, crazed out his mind, in the *Gypsy King*. His cables still out, dragging nothing. He was the only crewmember left aboard; the others, six of them, were missing. Orion, when he regained his senses, told the investigating grand jury that they all died trying to secure an asteroid. He told the jury that they were all blown out into space, lost. The data-recording monitors confirm nothing. The data banks were wiped clean; all the authorities had was his far-fetched story. They took his license; all the smelters were ordered not to deal with Orion. He didn't care; he fled the moon and disappeared. Some thought he'd spaced himself. Others said he went to Mars. Then, maybe ten years ago, he began to have run-ins with the Church and Earth-side governments, demonstrations, even a riot in Rome. The biggest demonstration, with more than a thousand of his followers, was in St. Peter's Square outside the Vatican. Then they disappeared. The rumor was that they moved to an island in the Mediterranean. It was later confirmed. No one cared; the authorities and the Church were glad to be rid of him. The Eurounion decided to leave them alone; they didn't want to stir up the ashes. You know the rest, Annie."

"He shows up again at the steps of the Vatican; he calls himself Prophet Tassos. His followers demand to see the Pope. The Pope refuses, the guards begin to push the crowd back down the steps, something explodes, dozens are killed and hurt. Tassos is gone, again. A few years later, he is discovered hiding on the island of Lipari. I had left the convent by then and was working in Rome. Marcus was with him."

"What?" I said. "You never told me this part."

"We did not set off the bomb," Marcus said. "It was the conservatives in the Church that wanted to blame the Prophet."

"I do remember that incident. It was all over the news then; the word was it was terrorists," Sarah said.

"Religious terrorism has never gone away," I said. "Remember the low-yield explosion in Mecca, eighty years ago? Just one more chapter in humanity's love affair with a deity, any deity. Someone wanted to start the African Wars all over again."

"What happened in the asteroid belt?" Sarah asked.

"No one knows. Whatever happened profoundly changed the man," I said. "His politics—for a man who believed in nothing other than a good drink, a soft curve of a woman's waist, and a thick bundle of bits—became a religious radical. His demands of the Church were to turn away from earthly things and look to the universe. He's been preaching this migration dogma to his followers. He wants to lead them to the stars."

"Good God, not another one," Sarah said. "Which part of the asteroid belt was he working when this so-called accident happened?"

"Sector Seventy-three."

took the bottle of scotch with me when I returned to my room. Sarah did pick up the check. However, I paid for the bottle. The view from my room extended across the Sea of Serenity toward the Haemus Mountains that enclosed the southern edge of the broad basin. The greys of the moon soothed my haunted memories of those months, twenty-two years earlier, dealing with the asshole Captain Tassos Orion. I intentionally neglected to mention to Sarah (and I'm not sure even Annie remembered) that I was on the rescue ship that retrieved the *Gypsy King*. All that alerted the authorities about the troubled ship was a distress signal. Orion had powered down the ship; only life support remained on. It was found twenty-five million kilometers from the moon. I had just returned to the moon on another dragger called the *Love It or Leave It* (I was the senior chief), and had downtime after a drag. Space Command Luna (SCL) asked for a rescue crew. Being the upright guy that I am, I volunteered (and the promise of salvage, if any). We found the *Gypsy King* cold, barely a light on, one more piece of space junk—she was a ghost ship, a ghost ship with one ghost. Entering, we found a single man, wretched, and barely alive. He blathered something about the ancients, the founders, the Creators. All we knew was that six men were missing, or dead, or at least presumed dead, and that this idiot Orion knew something.

The authorities locked up Orion and took Orion back to Prasinus. He was detained, questioned, and eventually arrested. I was with the crew of five that remained behind with the *Gypsy King*. We powered her up and got her to the moon. The SCL investigated Orion. They wanted to charge him with abandoning his crew, but the evidence was circumstantial. There were no files to recover on the computers, wiped as clean as a baby's bright bottom; I thought the whole episode smelled like one too. He was released, then he disappeared. My eye never left the *Gypsy King*. The old dragger remained moored at Marina 3, for more than two years. When I returned to the moon from my next drag, I found out that the *Gypsy King* was for sale, all to cover its unpaid moorage charges and power use liabilities. I dumped everything I had saved from my past three drags into an offer, borrowed a not so small fortune of bitunits, and took command and ownership. That was ten successful drags ago. Now I own the *Gypsy King* outright, I fund my drags, and make serious coin on every drag I run. For the first ten years after taking on the *Gypsy*, I heard nothing about what happened to Tassos Orion. If I'd given him a thought, I'd have wished him wedged in a crack on the dark side of the moon. Those six lost men of his still bothered me. Space is a lonely place. Floating around out there, alive or dead, gives me chills. Then Prophet Tassos began appearing in the news feeds.

My room's doorbell buzzed. Standing in the door was Sarah, another bottle of the Chianti in her hand. She held it and a smile out to me. There is never a time to argue with a woman bearing gifts.

"Are we moving the bar up to my room, a bottle at a time?" I asked, taking her hand and drawing her into my room.

"No, just me, this is a bribe. I want to know more about Prophet Tantalus."

"And I want to know more about you." I closed the door behind her and pulled her into my arms.

Later—the unopened bottle of Chianti still on the hallway

table—she was curled up in the crook of my body. Considerably smaller than me, she fit nicely, as nicely as I'd fit earlier that evening.

"A pleasant and most unexpected surprise," I whispered. "Were corporate meetings the only thing you had on your mind coming to the moon?"

"Yes and no, so I took a chance. While it's good to have strategies in long-term business relationships—in personal ones, I've always gone for the big surprise."

"Everyone likes surprises; me, not so much. On the other hand, you are more than welcome."

She rolled over into the warm space next to me and kissed me hard.

For breakfast, we ordered room service.

"You asked about surprises," I said. "That fool Orion was one of those unexpected and unwanted surprises. My sister had to have orchestrated all this; it's what she does. I know something is going on. She knew about Marcus and his involvement with the man. Tantalus seemed overly friendly and compliant, something that he is not known for. And he acted as though I wasn't there."

"You know him?"

"All too well."

I told her the story of the *Gypsy King*, the rescue, and the subsequent investigation.

"And then he just disappeared?" Sarah asked. "How can anyone just disappear? It's impossible. If he were chipped when he was born, he would have been easily found with a warrant under Global Laws. There was no way he could have been through the legal system and not have been spotted. There may be some Earth-side dead zones, but he'd have stood out. Most of those places don't like his kind."

"And now, my sister wants Marcus to go to the belt with me, to help him become a man. She's good at manipulating."

"I've known that since we were children," Sarah said. "Had

I known she was in Emerald City, I would have found another way to meet you. She always complicates things."

"And her new role as Mars colony facilitator will only increase that Byzantine way she has of dealing with people."

"Are you taking Marcus?" Sarah asked.

"Haven't decided. I asked. He's not sure—or at least that's what seems to be his attitude. I know they are in this together and are up to something."

"I have to leave this afternoon," she said, taking my hand. "I'm on the shuttle to Croceus—meetings with their business and development council. They are looking to expand the bio-pod and the housing corridors. Lots of metal—all kinds. Our contracts with the other Earth-side smelters and foundries need renewing. After Croceus, I'll be back on Earth in ten days. I'm taking Maine's *Hamilton* daisy down. Then back to New York. When do you leave?"

"If you were staying on the moon, I'd delay my departure."

"I can't."

"I know. I'm scheduled to ship out in two weeks. A lot to do before then. I'll miss you."

"Not as much as I'll miss you." She stood, dropped her robe, and placed her body tight to mine.

"Wanna bet?"

We do fit well together.

* * *

I sent a note to Clive and Garrett to join me for dinner that night. I also asked that Marcus and my sister join us.

After reintroductions, the crew pointed out how much Marcus had grown, asked about his schooling, and did he have a girlfriend? I said nothing about the real reason for the dinner. We took our seats.

"And in Rome and the Vatican, things are well?" Clive asked Sister Annie.

"The usual palace intrigues and backstabbing, nothing out of the norm," she offered with a smile. She nervously thumbed her Crucifix.

Clive's question surprised me. I knew the man did not like the Church, its religious aristocracy, even the Pope. I gave him points for at least being sociable.

"So, m'boy, you want to ship out with us?" Clive asked. "There's plenty of room—Hank says there are enough provisions. All Garrett and I want to know, are you willing to put up with a couple of old draggers for two years?"

"I was surprised by my uncle's offer," Marcus said. "I had a lot planned for the next few years, starting with college in the fall. However, I have discussed this with my mother, and she believes it would be good for me. So, I've decided to accept Uncle Buster's offer."

I was a little shocked by the answer. I was sure there would be more negotiation and more questions.

"Excellent choice. I first shipped out when I was about your age," Garrett said. "Every drag is an adventure; this one should be a pip."

"Mr. Borg, I appreciate what you are saying and the support. Yes, I'm ready for an . . . adventure."

"Call us Garrett and Clive. Only your uncle calls us Mister, and that's when he's pissed at us."

"Which is often, Mister Borg," I reminded him.

"See, there you are. It's settled."

"What will I be doing?" Marcus asked.

"We have plenty of time to sort that out," Clive said. "We'll be in transit for about six months trying to catch up with the sector we've been watching."

"Sector?"

"The asteroid belt that lies between Mars and Jupiter is a ring," Clive began. "And like the planets, this ring lies in the same general plane as their orbits. So, spread within this ring are millions of asteroids, planetoids, and a lot of stuff that is ice and junk."

"A few hundred years ago," Garret said, "the asteroid belt was divided into sectors, three hundred and sixty to be exact, making it easier to keep track of what's what and what's where. Each sector is one degree of a circle of the arc of the asteroid belt as it rotates around the sun. It begins and ends at the largest asteroid in the band, the small planetoid called Ceres. It's the one with the oldest mining colonies in the solar system. The last sector is the last degree before reaching Ceres, three hundred and sixty total segments; it is the solar system's biggest pie. I've been to ten sectors during my career—that only leaves me three hundred and fifty to go. Laddie, there are two million asteroids larger than a kilometer across in the belt, and those are too big to drag. Best guess is that there are another twenty million rocks, somewhat equally distributed through the rest of the sectors. It would take a hundred draggers fifteen thousand years to check them all out."

"Some of the rocks are ice and frozen CO_2, and others are junky amalgamations of rock and crap," Clive added. "We look for iron and nickel asteroids and almost every other element in the periodic table. Our ticket is metals. Other draggers look for water, and there's even a few that look for rich ores like gold and platinum. It's a veritable smorgasbord out there."

"I didn't know," Marcus answered.

"The colonies on Mars, the moon, and Earth need all the stuff found in the asteroids," Clive continued. "Back before humans escaped Earth, these metals were mined out of the crust of Earth. Now, it's easier to drag them to satellite smelters, refine them, and down-ship via the daisies to Earth. When you went off Earth, the same elevators that took you to space were delivering metals and resources to Earth. Not surprisingly, the most important resources are iron and titanium powders for 3D printing almost everything."

"What do I need to bring?" Marcus asked, intrigued by Garrett's information.

"Clothing, mostly," Clive said. "Garrett will take you to our outfitter here in EC; they will fit you with a custom EVA spacesuit, and other gear. You'll be scanned and measured; it will only take a day or two to build. Our gear is being refurbished there; they will ship it all to the *Gypsy King* at Marina 3. Hank will inventory it in."

"I would like to bring my bot; he's been with me for five years. All he needs is reprogramming."

"What design?"

"He's a Hugo 3. He is still in his shipping crate."

Garrett looked at Clive, then me. "A Hugo? Good design, sure. Have it interface with Hank. It will be under Hank's total control the whole time it's onboard. It will need software updates."

"I understand."

"Good," Garrett said. "Sister Annie, Clive and I have things to do. It was a pleasure to see you again. Marcus, your uncle will give you the schedule. I suggest that you get all your gear together and check it twice. There's no store where we're going. What you have is what you bring."

After the two men left the restaurant, Annie said, "Thank you, Brother—for Marcus and me. We talked about this since your offer; he's prepared. And It will be good for him."

"Marcus, are you ready?" I asked.

Marcus paused and looked at me. "Yes, I'm ready."

"Good, because once we are underway, there is no going back."

How will your people survive without you? You are their shepherd; you are their heart, their leader. Have you considered what would happen to them if you don't return?

"Done," I heard Garrett say as he reviewed the checklist on his pad. "I can't think of anything that we need that we don't have, sometimes twice as much as we need. Good job, Hank."

"Thank you, Mr. Borg. From you, that is high praise."

"Be careful, you know I will find something we need about three weeks out, and it will be your fault."

"Of course, isn't it always," Hank answered. "Master Marcus is in transit; he will be here in thirty minutes. He has his gear. The robot of Master Marcus is also on the manifest. Should I deploy the unit when they arrive?"

"No, let's get underway," I said. "You can unpack it after we leave orbit. One less bot under my feet, the better."

Two hours later, the crew of the *Gypsy King* was belted in in their respective chairs, and Marcus was secured in the backup communications seat one level down. Clive would handle the undocking.

"Undock," Clive said into his com-link. Outside, the massive docking cables released, and puffs of white gas squirted from their control jets. Like thick fishing lines, the Marina's cables slowly reeled back to spools mounted on the legs of the month-long anchorage. Clive adjusted attitude jets on the *Gypsy*, and slowly my ship, the size of a soccer field, slid out of the slip. Thirty minutes later, it drifted a thousand meters above the marina. The screen displayed the keel camera image of the marina's pinwheel docking complex. Six of the twenty slips held vessels. Two were interplanetary ships, two were draggers, three were cargo vessels; in the last mooring sat a sleek and very modern stainless beauty, the emblem of the Catholic Church emblazoned on its flanks.

This morning, I had been on that same ship saying goodbye to my sister. The *Gypsy King* sadly shows its age when moored next to the latest in interplanetary travel. Sister Annie had completed her lunar meetings and negotiations; the *Steller Roma* would be leaving the next day for Mars. Their heading to the red planet would take them in the opposite direction of the *Gypsy King*'s flight path. It would be a fast one-month transit; Annie said she would stay two months and then return to Earth. The flight plan of our transit to the belt was filed with Interplanetary Space Command (ISC). We are currently under Space Command Luna control, a sub-command of ISC. The ISC is the quasi-governmental organization that maintains control over the comings and goings of vessels that transit between the planets, moons, and asteroids. After we are one million kilometers out, command shifts from SCL to ISC. Once we reach the asteroid belt, it is the Wild Wild West of space—every dragger and tourist for himself.

It would take ten days before the *Gypsy King* achieved full thrust and speed. Each day, its speed would increase by approximately ten percent. Since there was no drag, the ship would then maintain its intercept speed with minimal amounts of fuel. As we neared our destination, the process would reverse. The main fusion engine would be rotated and used to decelerate the *Gypsy* until it matched the orbiting speed of the asteroid we were chasing.

By the next morning, the *Gypsy King* was at twenty percent max-velocity and continuing to accelerate.

"Sir, I have an anomaly with the atmosphere readings," Hank said as he stood behind me. "It shows an elevated level of CO_2. The scrubbers are exceeding the estimated waste production numbers."

"You have taken into account Marcus, haven't you?" I asked, knowing full well the answer.

"Of course, the scrubbers and converters are showing the increase over a predetermined level with Master Marcus included," Hank added.

"Speculation?"

"Did Master Marcus bring a pet onboard?"

"Of course not, only his noid."

"Then, I'm working on it."

Twenty minutes later, I asked, "Update on the CO_2, Hank."

"Still statistically high; variations are higher in Level Three—Stores and Provisions."

"Please scan the level. Find out what's causing the anomaly."

"Yes, sir. Scanning."

"I have a heat source—temperature reading and mass is human; nothing shows on cameras."

"Goddamn it." I turned and glared at Marcus. "Garrett, you are with me. And grab our sidearms."

"Uncle, is everything all right?" Marcus said, crossing the command deck.

I stuck my finger in the air and then pointed it at my nephew. "If you have put a stowaway on my ship, I will space both of you."

Garrett, Hank, and I climbed down the stairway and entered Level Three. Seated in one of the viewing chairs in the forward lounge area sat Prophet Tassos. Across the room, a large servo-pack sat with its lid open. Stenciled on the side: *Hugo—1 Unit.*

"The peace of the Universal God be with you," the man said as he stood to meet us.

"Why the hell are you on my ship?" I demanded, waving a pistol in the face of the so-called prophet.

"Returning to the Creators."

* * *

Standing nose to nose with the man, my pistol at my side, Garrett held my arm, making sure it stayed there. I so wanted to whack the asshole against the side of the head and push him out an airlock. There was no way I would call him Prophet. To me, he was and would always be Tassos Orion, crew killer. His brown cassock lay over the servo-pack. He wore the simple clothing of a crewmember. Outside of his beard and the deep shadows around his intense blue eyes, he looked like any old dragger: worn out, pasty white, and creased with lines from a jillion hours pushing iron in space. Marcus followed us onto the deck, then sat next to Tassos.

"A thousand years ago, stowaways were tossed in the sea as shark food. I could justifiably space the two of you, citing the laws of space and provisions. This ship only carries so much; your little charade has jeopardized all of us."

"The additional cases I brought onboard carry significant amounts of food and supplies," Marcus said.

"I don't give a damn, kid. You two have violated every tenant of space law. And I don't care why, or that you are my nephew. However, I do care that I have a nimrod and a confirmed wacko onboard my ship. It puts this whole operation in danger. I don't like danger. Shit, this universe is dangerous enough without your crap."

"How fast are we going right now, Captain Strabo?" Orion said. "From the feel of my ship, I would guess we are at about ninety-five thousand kilometers per hour. We should reach two hundred and fifty thousand kilometers per hour in what, nine days?"

"It's not *your* ship Orion. I bought it fairly. And we've cut it to eight point seven days."

"I still like to think of her as mine."

"You lost her twenty-two years ago."

"You called him Orion. Why?" Marcus asked.

"Because his name is Tassos Orion, a worthless dragger, indicted murderer, and a religious crackpot."

"Wrong on all counts, Captain. I was rich beyond one man's lifetime when you found me and still am. I was indicted, but I killed no one. That's why the jury came in with a negligent verdict; I was not guilty of killing my crew. However, that didn't stop the ISC from stripping me of everything I had. The fine was huge. On the count of religious crackpot, one man's crackpot is another's saint."

"Never hide behind religion with me, Orion. That doesn't go far. More than a few zealots and saints have been spaced in the last two hundred years."

Orion ignored the remark. "However, I'm extremely pleased the *Gypsy* ended up with you. You have treated her well, even added improvements. I like this viewing area."

"I could make it your jail."

"A lot better than most I've been in. Besides, I will make an invaluable crewmember."

"You know the Prophet?" Marcus said, challenging me.

I looked at him. "Get one thing straight, Marcus, that man is not a prophet or even a fortune-teller. At one time, he was like me, a dragger. And damn good at it. Then six men died, lost forever; they were never found. While not convicted for their deaths, he was thrown out of the guild and has gone bonkers and bat-shit crazy. He's now parading around like some messiah . . ."

"Never use that term. The Messiah is real," Orion said. "That is blasphemy."

"I determine what's blasphemy onboard this ship, get it? And I determine who is onboard and who the crew is. Right now, there's too much to do until we reach our glide. I'd lose almost a month turning around and throwing you off the ship. Even if I spaced you in an e-pod, I'd have to stop. At this moment, our target is running away from us at twenty-five thousand kilometers an hour. I'd lose weeks, and add more than four million kilometers to the trip. So, lucky me, I'm stuck with you."

"If it gets bad, we could just eat him," Garrett added, his weapon still pointed generally at the stowaway.

"I'm way too tough," Orion said. "And besides, Captain, you are going to Sector Seventy-Three. There's much I can tell you."

"How do you know we are going to Sector Seventy-three?"

"The Lord provides," the Prophet said, looking at Marcus.

I was pissed, more pissed than I've been in maybe my entire forty-five years. The fine hand of my sister was behind this and most probably the Catholic Church as well. To get Orion to the moon and then on my ship required more than just sneaking around. It required papers, off-Earth permits, and pass-throughs. I just couldn't figure out why. The variables are all over the solar system. Maybe they hoped Tassos would end up as one more unfortunate spacer floating around in God's eternal vacuum. Or me, Buster Strabo, would be the righteous hand of the Almighty and shoot the son of a bitch or some other profound and final scenario that I hadn't thought of— yet. Maybe the Prophet was onboard to perform miracles, miraculously time-shift our way to the far reaches of the solar system—yeah, right! And why did this old dragger want to return to Sector Seventy-three? I knew every intimate detail of the *Gypsy King*'s logbook. Its servers still contained some of the entries of the old codger. They were the only ones that survived that final trip of Orion.

I punched up the log files and inserted a date. I was mildly shocked to see that it was the last entry with any reference to Sector Seventy-three. The log ended two days after this entry. It did not restart until my first entry almost three years later. It was also the last entry posted by Tassos Orion before he was recovered nine months later drifting in space. A younger Orion appeared on-screen; his eyes were just as intense.

June 10, 2432–Relative
We entered Sector Seventy-three at 23:04 hours last night. I have swept the sector; a strange reading has popped up, all from one target. The asteroid is exceptionally dense, is scanner reflective—however, it looks promising. We are fifty thousand kilometers from the object. We will approach and deploy one of the donkeys to assay the surface. All aboard are anxious, including me. We've looked at a dozen rocks; all were busts. I'm hopeful. I've never gone home without something.
Captain Tassos Orion, out.

Sector Seventy-three. What the hell was in Sector Seventy-three?

* * *

The transit to the asteroid belt was uphill—at least that's the feeling you get when you are chasing a rock in the same direction; another term is "lying in wait"—waiting for the rock to come to you. However, when heading back home with a million tons stuck on your lines, then it's like going downhill with a kiloton of expectations strapped to your back.

Fifty-eight days into the passage, we were about halfway to the sector. The days rolled one into the other; they always did in transit. Maintenance and service of the *Gypsy King* required extra vehicular actions (EVAs) with the donks. Grudgingly, the old captain fit right in. Orion, the experienced pro, remained calm and, when not handling one of my service orders, studied copies of ancient texts he'd brought. Marcus, when not training or studying, was bored. It was Garrett's job to keep his mind in the game; they worked on Garrett's slider. All I told Marcus and Orion was that we were alerted to a promising asteroid by a returning dragger. If it didn't pan out, we would drift back under speed to catch the next sector. From the data

that the *Chicago Glory* had sent, this Sector Seventy-three asteroid had promise. But there was something else, my drag-
ger-sense said so. And at the same time, Orion's knowledge of
the sector bothered me.

Clive had the watch, Garrett was sleeping in his cabin, and
I was having dinner with Orion and Marcus. Orion and I had
arrived at an amicable, though tentative, peace between the
two of us. Hank was serving.

I broke the silence. "Marcus, your mother mentioned that
you might be going into the Vatican after college—maybe join
the seminary, become a priest."

"I am not sure. There's a lot to think about," Marcus said.
"The Prophet has opened my eyes to many things."

"And yet, here you sit on an ancient dragger, heading into
deep space with the old soothsayer. That's not going to look
good on your application."

"Captain," Orion said. "Marcus is a bright and creative
member of my flock. He has skills that you are not aware of.
That is why I asked him to join me on this voyage."

Two months into the transit and he finally puts this on the
table. I leaned back, surprised. "You asked my nephew to go
with you? I thought my sister asked me to take him. And how
were you to get onboard without his help?"

"Marcus was always to be my aide; it was the only option
we had. And obviously, it worked. I'm here on the *Gypsy King*
heading to Sector Seventy-three. I have much to be thankful
for and to prepare for." The noid poured more wine in Orion's
glass.

"Thank you, Hank," he said.

"You are welcome, Captain," Hank answered.

"Hank, let's get one thing straight. I'm the captain, not
that guy."

"Captain Strabo, Captain Orion was my captain for almost
twenty years. I use it as a term of deference, not management
structure."

"Cute, defer away. Just remember who signs your paycheck."

"On that subject, sir, I will never forget."

I looked back at Orion. "Prepare for what?"

"Mysteries and revelations, Captain. There is much to discover in that sector. I've spent some time there."

"I know you were once in Sector Seventy-three, I have your log entry."

"My crew and I were there four times; the first two were during transits through the sector on the way home. That's when we found the anomaly. The third time it alluded us. Besides, as you know, there's not much in the logs to help you. Yes, the *Gypsy King* has made this trip before. I might even guess she would find her way if we all just . . . disappeared."

"Is that what happened to your crew?" I asked. "They just disappeared."

"Something like that."

The breach klaxon resounded through the levels, scratching any chance of continuing the conversation. Oxygen masks fell from emergency panels. I grabbed one and jammed it over my face. I tossed the second mask to Marcus. When I went to hand one to Orion, the man had his already on.

"What the hell is happening, Hank? Status!" I yelled.

"Main cabins and decks remain pressurized," the noid said. "Sensors say there are multiple punctures of the port hydrogen tank. They appear to be debris or micro-asteroid strikes. I've initiated three port-side bots to seal the punctures."

"You two stay here." I bolted to the stairs and pulled myself hand-over-hand up to the command level. Clive wore his mask and was studying one of the monitor screens. Garrett, still in his sleep gear, caught up and followed me. A minute later, Hank entered the level.

"Clive, status."

"We are losing hydrogen," Clive answered. "Not a lot, yet. The bots will be placing patches over the tank, but I need to get out there. It looks like only one of the interior tanks was punctured; other pressure deviations need to be clarified."

"Clive, I want you here. I'm going out on the *Horus*. Garrett, I want you as backup on the *Osiris*. Hank, get them heated up."

"Yes, sir. EVA in ten minutes."

Turning back to the stairs, I almost ran over Orion. He stood a few feet behind me. Marcus was just coming out of the stairway. "I told you two to stay where you were."

"Captain, I can be of assistance. I know my ship."

"Damnit. I'm not interested in a debate. If we lose hydro, we may not get back. Orion, you are with me. Garrett, take Marcus, you've worked with him on the manipulating arms. If we need them, four arms are better than two."

"Roger that, Captain."

We took the elevator to the equipment and EVA level. After donning our EVA suits, Orion and I climbed into *Horus*. Garrett and Marcus manned *Osiris*. Hank secured himself outside on *Horus*. He sat directly behind the command dome of the donkey. The equipment level was sealed and depressurized. We slowly lowered ourselves out into space through the open doors.

Maneuvering carefully, I took the lead along the flanks of the *Gypsy King*. Safety cables from the donkeys snapped automatically to the hull and then detached themselves as we moved along, always ensuring a physical connection to the ship. To me, they looked like thin snakes, biting then releasing themselves as we progressed.

"Where were the strikes, Hank?" I asked.

"Exactly eighteen meters from the nose of the port tank. The bots have already repaired the five largest holes on the outboard sides of Cell B. The debris completely pierced the tank. The interior bulkheads automatically sealed the remaining eight hydrogen cells. Sensors show leaks on the interior ship side of Cell B. The bots will move on to the smaller holes as soon as they can."

"Can the bots reach the other leaks?" I asked.

"They can reach three, but two punctures are in an area too narrow for the bots to enter. They will have to be sealed manually. Specifications note that I can't slide into that narrow space."

"Shit. Prepare the sealant patches; I'm going out."

"Captain, may I offer my services?" Orion said. "The ship can afford to lose me; it cannot afford to lose you."

"You remember how to do this?"

"Like riding a slider."

At the back of the *Horus*'s control room, an EVA pressure lock provided access to space. Inside were tools, repair equipment, and two EVA chairs that provided maneuverability and additional power for the operator and his tools. Attached to the chair was a three-meter-long manipulating arm to reach into tight spaces.

"Hank will go with you. If the tank is empty, you may not be able to find the holes."

"Roger that, Captain," Orion said.

I was impressed, even after more than twenty years, how deftly Orion entered the compartment, activated the chair, and requested depressurization. In minutes, he was powering himself over the top of the tank. Hank followed closely behind him. More security-snakes bit and released as they moved over the surface of the ship.

Below them, four robots moved precisely over the exterior of the tank, placing cold patches over the punctures.

"Clive, what are the readings?"

"Losses are dramatically lower. I'm still getting ongoing leakage, but the bots have done a good job."

"Orion is maneuvering himself over the far side of the tank."

"Captain," Orion said. "The bots have sealed the smaller holes here on the top of the tank; I can see two others on the inside. The largest is the size of my hand; the other is finger size. These are exit holes; the tank surface has peeled back. I need to cut them smooth, then stick on the patch."

"Roger that; can you reach them?"

"I need to leave the chair, all handwork."

"Hank?"

"I agree. I cannot fit in there, either."

"Dumb luck, I guess," Orion said.

"Hank, make sure there are retrieval cords attached to him."

I maneuvered *Horus* up and over the pair as they slid between the massive hydrogen tank and the side of the ship. There was not a meter of space between the tank and the hull.

"Watch the suit," I offered.

"I'm good," Orion said.

He waved, then slowly disappeared into the void. A light snapped on from his suit; the gap lit up.

Five minutes passed. All I heard over the com-link was heavy breathing.

"Captain," Garrett said. "I've completed the sealants on the far side; the bots are returning to their mounts. I'm directly over you."

I looked up and saw the orange undercarriage of the *Osiris*. It slowly moved away and down. In moments, Garrett and Marcus were visible through the windows.

"How's Orion?" Garrett asked.

"Hank?"

"Almost done," the noid answered.

"Finished, Captain, coming up," Orion said.

"Careful," I said. Then heard, "Holy God," then saw Orion jet out of the gap. His whole body was spinning uncontrollably.

"What the hell?"

"Captain Orion caught his suit on a fitting; his suit is damaged."

"Hank, it's a fucking hole. Get him—catch him, stop him."

From Hank's right side, a length of line shot out and tried to lasso the spinning prophet. It shot past, just missing him. Security snakes reached out and tried to grab some part of the suit. Always dangerous, their grips had the potential to tear additional holes in the suit. "Disable security cords," I said. They instantly pulled back; there was a double beep acknowledgment. Hank's maneuvering jets fired; he came within two meters of Orion; he reset his safety line and fired his jets. Hank caught Orion's right leg, and both began to spin in unison. Hanks refired his jets. The spinning slowed. Orion, regaining his senses, activated his jets. In space, actions and reactions are magnified a thousand-fold, no drag, no friction. Orion slammed back into Hank and knocked them both against the side of the *Gypsy King*.

"Stabilize, Hank," I yelled.

"Yes, sir. Stabilizing."

"Do you see the tear? Can you slap-patch it?"

"Yes, sir. I'm setting the patch now. There was some exposure to the vacuum."

"Get that man back inside."

"Coming, sir."

Hank quickly stabilized their tumbling and then, using his jets, headed back to the donk. He had Orion grasped in one of his extensions. I opened the hatch, and Hank and his human package dropped into the EVA lock. Ten seconds after pressurization, Hank and I dragged the unconscious man into the *Horus*'s control room.

"Is he okay, Uncle?" Marcus said over the intercom. "Is he alive?"

Tassos Orion moved his arm; his chest rose and then slowly fell.

"Yes, he's alive. I need to look at his arm where the fabric ripped. There may be some thermal damage. Hank, take us back to the equipment bay. Clive, you get all this?"

"Yes, Captain."

We slid into the bay; immediately behind me, the *Osiris* dropped into its dock. The level pressurized.

"The medi-bot is ready," Clive said. "Data says his suit automatically sealed the leak; the slap-patch helped. No additional hydro loss from the tanks, but we need to talk."

12

Clive was waiting in the airlock as the two donkeys docked. He ran to the *Horus* as soon as the level repressurized. With Hank's help, we lowered Orion to the deck. Clive and Marcus moved him to a cart and then up the elevator to the medical compartment on the third level. Garrett and I followed.

"Captain, we'll take it from here," Garrett said as he and Clive removed Orion's suit, placed him in the medi-bot, lowered the transparent shields, and activated the scanners.

"Is he going to be all right?" Marcus asked as his mentor was probed and lit up like the dance floor in a Corridor Three tingles bar.

"We'll know in an hour," Garrett said. "But right now, I'd say he is one lucky son of a bitch."

The medi-bot continued to scan, tweet, hum, and perform injections. The screen on the wall, opposite the medi-bot, showed bio-stats. All were close to normal. Looking at the almost naked body of Orion, I shook my head.

"Hell of a constitution, Captain" Clive said. "He should be spiking adrenalin. The screens read normal—like he was on a walk in a park."

"Let me know how he is in an hour; I'm going topside. Marcus, you are with me. Hank, get the donkeys serviced. I don't want to be caught short if this happens again."

"Yes, sir," Hank said and headed back to the equipment

level.

On the command level, I made myself a cup of coffee with a triple shot of caffeine. I made one for Marcus as well.

"Well, that was a lot of fun," I said, raising my cup to my nephew. "We haven't had that bad a strike in years. Shows you how quickly things change at a quarter of million kilometers an hour. You could be dead and talking to Saint Peter before you even know what drilled you. Orion came this close to dying out there. That's the way that space is, instant eternity. Marcus, we haven't talked about that man much. I've left it to you to come to me. That can't wait now. There's something more than just odd about him. When did you meet?"

Marcus looked out the glass of the command level; the stars filled every square inch of the di-glass. "It was three years ago. I was finishing classes at the Vatican Boys' School, and one of the kids suggested going to a lecture at a small college in the hills above Rome. Prophet Tassos was the speaker. I didn't know his other name, the one you call him, Tassos Orion. He spoke about God and free will and destiny, and that each of us must find our own souls and then lead them to our own eternity. All new stuff to us, radical thinking. He said we are all the children of the Creators. That's what's put him on the outs with the Church. He insists on calling us humans the children of the Creators. The Church believes in one God with three divinities, the Father, the Son, and the Holy Ghost. He says there are more, the Creators. Many who attended wanted to believe him; they also believe there is more than what is written in scripture. When he found out that you were my uncle and who my mother is, he took a special interest in my schooling. I did not know why then; I'm beginning to now."

"I'll bet. What does your mother say about all this?"

"I thought she would be furious; she wasn't. She encouraged me to ask questions, tape and transcribe what the Prophet says, find out what he believes. Then, a few months back, she told me that you were inbound from a drag and that we, including the Prophet, all were going to the moon to meet you. I thought it was all crazy, mother and the Prophet, crazy. When I asked the Prophet, all he said was: 'It has been foretold.' I had no idea what he meant."

"So, the man knew you were coming on this drag?"

"I guess so. Was all strange to me—even I didn't know. Prophetic; I guess so. When you asked, I was shocked. How did you know? How did the Prophet know?"

Clive walked onto the command level.

"How's he doing?" I asked.

"How old is that man?" Clive asked.

"According to his bios, he's sixty-seven."

"Well, Captain, he has the body of a twenty-five-year-old. His heart and lungs are pristine, no disease, and no scars. His beard and hair are white, but it's not due to age. And today's little mishap? There're no thermal burns from the vacuum and the cold, none. It's like he never left the ship."

"Interesting. I wondered about that when I saw him laid out in the medi-bot. What do you make of it?"

"Maybe the guy's found the fountain of youth or a wonder drug," Clive said. "I only know how to operate the medi-bot. I have no idea why that man is in that condition. From what you've told me, he's led a rough life—being a dragger for twenty years has to leave a mark. Shit. My own body's beat up from it. He's got nothing, maybe a few character wrinkles in his face, that's all. So, whatever he's been drinking, I want a bottle. Shit, I'll buy a whole case."

* * *

During the next few weeks, as we decelerated into the belt, I watched Orion closely. I tasked Hank with the job of being a spy, keeping a log about what Orion did when I wasn't around. For the first few days after the strikes, he stayed and took his meals in his cabin. Then, later in the kitchen, he was all warm and delightful. Telling old tales of drags, crewmen he remembered, and the quirks of the *Gypsy King*. He never said anything about the twenty-two years since he was found drifting in the *Gypsy King* and his arrest.

Hank reported that he downloaded and read scholarly books and religious tracks. Hank said his favorites tended to the teachings of Erasmus, the sixteenth-century spiritual writer. He also read books and essays by Erasmus's followers, especially the more modern mystic Benuvius, of the twenty-third century. I was comfortable with my knowledge of fundamental Roman Catholic theology. I did appreciate what he was reading—these were radical Christian theologies that took on the Church and its contemporary beliefs, but they were centuries ago. Look, I believe in the afterlife like the next Joe. Whether you die from old age at one hundred and forty or accidentally push the wrong button in the airlock, you are dead either way. But the whole intellectualizing by the Church, the earth's and Mars's old and new religions, and the omnipotence of God, any god, I leave to others. I'm a deep space guy. Every day—such as it is—shows the glory of the Great Somebody spread across the heavens. And out here, that's what they are: endless and forever heavens. And I also believe in the Golden Rule:

Omnia ergo quaecumque vultis ut faciant vobis homines, et vos facite illis.

Simply, do onto others as you wish they would do to you. If not, shoot the sons of bitches first; you may not get a second chance. It's always good to have a backup rule.

The stunner came the day after the strike when Clive said that the loss of hydrogen from the port tank reduced our safety margin by thirty percent. We had plenty of hydro for the trip, both going and returning. However, if this target in seventy-three was a bust and we had to chase another rock or two through the belt, it could become problematic. I never liked to have my safety margin fall below ten percent.

"If needed, we could mine some water from one of the dirty rocks," Garrett said. "I know it's not the best idea, but we've done it before. Distill out the hydrogen."

"And it took us two weeks, and we only gained a little hydro. Right now, monitor the usage. On the decel we'll watch the burn, minimize the flow to the reactor. Maybe start a few days earlier, take longer to slow down."

"I'll crunch the numbers," Clive said.

I tapped the screen where the hydrogen level held a static seventy-eight percent. It was habitual, as if tapping the flat screen might change the number.

"I used to do that," Orion said. "I've been watching you; you have many of the same habits I had as captain. Not sure whether it's because we are alike, or the *Gypsy King* changes a man to suit her needs. We believe we are self-made men; that we control our destiny; that everything we do is new and original. Then we start tapping screens, just like the last idiot."

"The philosophy of screen tapping, is that it, Orion?"

"Something like that. But deep in our DNA is a map, a map that we must follow. It is ordained. It's a map, unlike any other. Unique to us, like our fingerprints. To be truly human, you must understand your God-given map. You are the result of the Creators' plan."

"Kind of trite, don't you think? DNA, maps, predestination, old-school stuff."

"Maybe . . . but for humans and every other living thing that comes from Earth, there is a map. The difference between a rat and us is that we realize there is a map, we can envision the road, and we see how our map intertwines with others. From this intertwining comes civilizations, great feats of engineering, literature, music, religions, and to walk among the stars."

"Now, you are stretching it."

"Am I? A rat, he lives, he mates, he reproduces, but even he knows where his bread is buttered. That's why he hangs around humans. Where there're humans, he can always find a meal."

"Cynical predestination rat talk? Talk about old-school: *Ratus nobilius.*"

Orion smiled at my rodent joke. "To think better, very good. I make no bones about my philosophy; our future is out there in the stars, out there where from where we came. We humans must return to the Creators. I'm sure Marcus has told you this; that's why the Church and I have issues. Or at least with some of the people in the Church. Others are more . . . enlightened."

"My sister?"

"Yes, your sister, especially. She understands the message; she sent Marcus to me. He is beginning to understand."

"Understand what? That an old dragger finds religion, becomes a self-anointed prophet, then eventually leads his people to ruin and death? You are not the first and most probably not the last. Humans are predictable. If that's predestination, then you are right, it *is* in our DNA."

"Captain, there's much more to us than you may think. We humans are just one of many sentient species in the universe. I know that for a fact."

"And how do you know that? How can *you* be so sure?"

"Because the Creators told me," Orion said as he walked to the window of the com-level.

"What creators?" I asked, almost immediately realizing that the forthcoming answer was not something I cared to hear. "When we found you, you were as close to stark raving mad as anyone I've ever seen. It took three of us to secure you. And for the next few days, we locked down every escape hatch thinking you might want to space yourself. Finally, the doc knocked you out. After they took you off the *Gypsy* and hauled you to Earth, I never saw you again until lunch with my sister. So, Tassos Orion, what is your story? There is nothing in the logs about what happened here. Even Hank—who is one of

the few who actually likes you—can't fill in the blanks. Give
. . ."

"Captain," Orion began, "you've been good for the *Gypsy
King* and even better to Hank. Many would have separated the
two of them and sold them off; they are worth more together
than apart. You kept them together. I thank you for that. The
Gypsy and I go way back—hard to believe it's been more than
forty years; you know some of the history. I'm pleased you still
run her. She deserves the best."

I couldn't figure where all this stroking was going; I went
with the flow. "Thanks. She is a good ship, maybe the best."

Orion smiled. "We're getting maudlin. But the *Gypsy* will
do that. Buster, twenty-three years ago, this rock in Seventy-three begged me to come to it. That was the signal I heard;
it spoke directly to me."

"It spoke to you?" I asked.

"Yes, it spoke directly to me. It said: 'Welcome, Captain,
you are home now. Come to us.'"

I arched my eyebrow. "Really?"

"Well, not in a way that anyone could hear, and the words
just filled my head. What was more shocking was my crew
heard them as well."

"Your crew, they heard these words?"

"Yes, they were as real as anything said out loud. The voice
spoke to each of them."

Hank tapped on my cabin's doorframe. "Orders, Captain?"

"None for the moment. Captain Orion is telling me about
the day the *Gypsy* arrived in Sector Seventy-three. Maybe you
can add something?"

Hank took his usual place near the door; he reminded me
of a cigar store Indian I once saw in a picture. A tall, austere
figure, rigid and on guard; all he was missing was a handful of
cigars. To be honest, it was a little creepy. "So, you and your
crew began to hear voices?"

"Yes, in a manner of speaking. Lucas Dorman was number

one, Robert Thayer was tech; the other four had been with me and the *Gypsy* for four drags, almost unheard of for a seven-man crew. We were friends, and we all held some of the same religious beliefs."

I wasn't going to go down that rabbit hole; we never talked about religion or politics on the *Gypsy*. I guess every ship is different. "So, you all began to hear voices."

"Yes, Captain. They said the same thing over and over. 'Come to us.'"

I turned to Hank. "Did you hear these voices?"

"No, Captain. I did not. At that time, I did receive a series of strange radio waves that I couldn't decipher, extremely low frequency. But I cannot confirm what they said or meant."

"My crew and I debated about this at great length," Orion said. "We came to the same conclusion. We must go to the asteroid and check it out."

"Pretty ballsy if you ask me," I said. "And, Hank, what did you do?"

"I told Captain Orion about the risks. He said they were within safety parameters. I argued; he threatened to shut me down."

"Not a nice way to treat the one thing that could save your life," I said.

"We came to an understanding," Orion said. "Hank would stay with the donkeys when we arrived at the asteroid—we didn't know what it was then. We took both the *Horus* and the *Osiris*."

"How many of the crew did you leave on the *Gypsy*?"

"None. Everyone wanted to go."

"You abandoned your ship? You didn't even leave Hank onboard? You were all crazy as batshit."

"It was well within safety parameters."

"No, it wasn't, and you know it. It was stupid."

Ignoring my rudeness, Orion continued. "We locked down the donks next to the flank of the asteroid; only Hank could activate the controls. That's when we discovered the tunnel."

"There's a tunnel on the side of that thing?"

"Yes, Captain, a tunnel. It is the only entry into that rock that is the home of the Creators."

15

May the lights of the universe be praised and sanctified, you have come home. You have been missed, and yet it has been only a little time. Time that, you now know, has no beginning, only a middle. And the middle is never-ending. You have touched the face of souls; you are with them, and they are with you. Lights eternal.

But where are the others?—you ask. It is your first question. Your concern is for them. They are there with you, you sharply answer. You left them, they know you left them, they chose to leave you. You were Orion, the captain, when you left. You are now Tassos the Prophet. Your heart swells with the knowledge—your acolytes follow you; you will lead them.

Home. You are not alone; the others with you, do they know? Do they see into your soul? A million or is it a billion souls welcome you here, welcome you home.

Home. The image on the screen is black, blacker than the space around it. It is all shadow; shadows are cast by the light. You see it, but you see it in ways they don't. You see it because you have been there, walked with them through the lights, watched them rise with the light, and then you freed yourself.

Strabo asks a question while pointing at the vid: "What is that?"

"The wrong question," you answer.

"And the right question?" he asks.

"Why is it?"

* * *

As we decelerated to the coordinates of the asteroid that Oliveira on the *Chicago Glory* had given, Orion's question bothered me. Most of what he said bothered me. What did he mean about the Creators? On the face of it, it was the psychotic ramblings of a man who spent too much time in space. Someone who'd lost their crew and his ship. It would not be the first time a captain went bonkers over the sinking of his command. Out here, the vast expanse has gotten to more than one human. Sometimes the mind just can't deal with the limitless, with no up and no down. I kept the conversation with Orion away from the crew for a few days; I needed to think this all out. I needed answers to their questions.

We again inspected the damaged tank and the patches. Sensors recalibrated, arrays checked, and every thruster and jet on the donkeys tested. The small thrusters that would be mounted on the asteroid were run through their cycles. The new Martian thruster was double-checked. We even played out ten kilometers of the three primary cables. Everything was nominal.

"In a few hours, we will reach the coordinates for the rock that *Chicago Glory* sent," I said to the crew. "We will do a preliminary survey by circling the asteroid. Clive will handle all the probes and surveys. I want to know what this thing is before we leave the ship and do any surface assays. The *Chicago Glory*'s information is a place to start, but as Oliveira said, they didn't perform more than a passing flyby. The images are intriguing but still vague. They were more than a thousand kilometers from that thing."

I turned to Orion. "What else do you know about this asteroid? Everything in the logs, in the data on the computers, says that this is where you were when everything went to hell."

"You mean that man has been here before?" Garrett said.

"Yes, he has," I said.

"Yes, Mr. Borg," Orion said. "The *Gypsy King* and I have been here."

"Care to enlighten us?" Clive said. "We've come halfway across the solar system chasing this thing. We've waited, and you've said nothing. Why is that?"

"I was afraid that you would change your mind."

"It's a damn rock," Clive said.

"No, Mr. Jones, it is not a rock. It's not even an asteroid. It's far more than that."

"There's nothing but iron, nickel, and other metals in these things," Garrett said. "After twenty years, I've seen all the types. There's money to be made, nothing more."

"A man of faith sees far more than money. Isn't that so, Marcus?" Orion said.

"Yes, Prophet."

"What the hell do you mean by that?" Garrett said. "I'm here because of a payday. Faith can't be taken to the bank."

"Faith? What's this mumbo-jumbo they're squawking about, Captain?" Clive said.

"If I may, I'll explain," Orion said.

"You better," I said. "Or I will blow by this rock and wait for the next sector to come up. No skin off my back. We are here for the metal, not religion."

Orion glared at me. "Gentlemen, twenty-three years ago, the *Gypsy King*, my crew, and I were exploring Sector Seventy-three. We probed some interesting asteroids in the other regions of the sector, but they were either too large or the wrong types. We worked our way back toward the Mars side of the belt. Our sensors scanned the outer edge of the sector, near where we are now, and anomalies began to bounce back from something. It didn't appear on our screens. Curious, we came in closer to see what produced the readings. All we could see was a void created by its shadow, the sun being behind it. I slowed the ship to match the speed and orbit of the asteroid. We drifted in closer. Maybe ten kilometers separated us."

I couldn't help noticing that Orion left out the thing's calling to him and the crew.

From one of the speakers, an annoying beeping began. We all looked at the overhead screens; most showed external areas of the ship. However, the central vidscreen displayed a similar image to the one that Orion was describing. The sun backlit a black oblong shadow.

"What do the scanners show?" I asked Clive.

Clive had already shifted to his control panel. He punched in data as fast as his fingers could travel the keyboard.

"Everything is off the expected metrics. Density, I can't determine, radiation is minimal. I'm getting almost no returns of the probes. It's like a sponge; nothing bounces off. It's sucking up anything I send."

"It did the same thing when we approached," Orion said. "Captain, I suggest that we hold off twenty kilometers; we were too close back then. That's when it all changed."

"What changed?" I asked.

"The asteroid came alive."

"What the hell?" Garrett said.

"Garrett, back us out to twenty klicks—then hold."

"Roger that, Captain." Garrett started punching his keyboard.

"What do you mean, it came alive, Orion?"

"It projected another low-frequency wavelength burst. I wasn't sure if it was our signal bouncing back, or it originated from the target. We quickly learned it was not ours. My com specialist said it was noise, nothing cohesive, it was all over the place. But it was not background; it came from the asteroid."

"Is that when you heard the voices?" I asked.

"Voices," Garrett said. "He heard voices?"

"Captain, I'm getting a weak signal from the direction of the target," Clive said. "I can't make out any of it."

"Holding at twenty kilometers, Captain," Garrett said.

"Enlarge the image, Clive," I said.

The image, all black on black, increased until it filled the whole screen. The shadow was like a thick cigar, thick in the middle and tapering outward; it was clipped off at both ends.

"Clive, size?"

"Approximately five hundred meters long and one hundred and fifty meters thick in its middle. I'm still not getting any readings from the probes. It's about a hundred meters longer than the *Gypsy*, Captain."

"Too big?"

"It would be a lot to drag; it's easily three times the size of Castor. And yes, probably too big."

"Captain, that thing can't be dragged," Orion said. "It fought every attempt at repositioning."

"What do you mean, 'fought'?"

"Its orbit is stable, its mass immovable. We put one of our donkeys against it. After an hour of thrust, it hadn't budged. It fought all we did."

"That's impossible," Garrett said. "What was resisting the push?"

"Nothing that we could determine. It just wouldn't be moved."

"The laws of physics are not different out here," Garrett added. "Anything, with the right amount of force, can be moved."

"Not this."

"Prophet, is this the ship that you have been teaching us about?" Marcus asked.

"Yes, Marcus. This is *Kratos*, the home of the Creators."

said, "I want to know everything that you haven't told me. If that rock can't be moved, why didn't you tell me before we got this close?"

"You wouldn't understand," Orion answered. "None of you would."

"Bullshit—try me."

"Captain," Clive said. "I've run the data from the asteroid through the computers; they can't sort it out either. There is nothing to match it to. One analysis suggests that the thing is the size of the moon. Another says that it can't exist—that it is not there. I don't get it."

"And you won't," Orion said. "It is from beyond our solar system. It is not of our galaxy. We received the same signal; we probed the object for a week, even walked on its surface. Its gravity, due to its mass, is almost moon-like."

"Impossible, the gravity would be negligible," Clive said.

"Not with its density. It's a million times greater than it appears."

"You called it *Kratos*. Why?" I said, looking at the dark image on the screen.

"Kratos, from the Greek. He was the child of Pallas and Styx, a Titan and nymph. He's supposed to be the one who chained Prometheus to the rock after the Titan stole fire. Kratos is a god of power and rule. Besides, I liked the name."

"Asshole," Garrett said as he turned back to the ship's controls.

Orion looked at the crew and smiled. "After a week of probing, we found nothing."

"Why don't I believe you?" I said.

"We all believe what we want to believe, bless the Maker."

"As I said, asshole," Garrett added. "What do you want me to do, Captain?"

"Hold here. If there is a change in either the signal or anything from that rock, back us the hell out of here."

"Roger that, sir," Garrett acknowledged.

I wasn't sure what to do, as if doing something would change our situation. For the time being, we were safe—if what Orion said was true. I wouldn't risk the ship, and so far, other than the faint signal from the rock, nothing had changed.

I looked again at the magnified image on the screen. Nothing about it said "asteroid"; it was shaped wrong. It showed some damage from eons of meteoroid and debris strikes, but not as much as I, or any other experienced dragger, would expect. The damage was superficial; gashes on its side looked like glancing blows. The blunt ends had extensive nicks, but again almost inconsequential. Whatever this thing was, it had a density that would resist any strike or impact. I leaned into Garrett.

"Spooky."

"Roger that."

"Clive, the signal?"

"I would say we are being probed. Whatever it is, it's trying to find out what we are as much as we want to know what it is."

"It did the same thing twenty years ago," Orion said.

"And you went in close and investigated?" I asked.

"Of course, Captain, it looked good. The object's density was off the scale. We thought that it was a good find."

"And this signal?"

"There was no signal then."

"You said there was one," Clive said.

"It started when we were fifty meters off its surface. I dropped the two donkeys, and we scanned and mapped every square meter. At each end is a deep cavity, impossible to enter; some form of impenetrable force kept us out. Like a magnetic membrane or force field of some kind."

"I didn't find those reports in the data banks."

"I dumped them."

"That's enough to get you up before the Guild review board. To intentionally dump or overwrite data is a crime."

"So sue me. Force fields, signals, extremely hard surface, that's what we found."

"The Creators can do anything," Marcus added.

"How would you know? You weren't even born when the *Gypsy* visited this thing," I said, getting more annoyed with my godson.

"The Prophet told us."

"Not one more word about this fool, do you hear me? There's more than enough shit going on without—"

Klaxons began to blare throughout the ship.

"Garret?" I yelled.

"Something hit the ship."

"Hank?"

"External sensors report echoes of particle hits to the stern of the ship. Internal cameras and sensors say there are no breaches or penetrations. Something is hitting us; they are just not punching through the hull. It's like we're being pinged."

"Orion?"

"The same thing happened to us; they are intense radio waves. We believed they were intended to disable the ship, or at least that's what we thought. The wavelength is such that, over time, it might break down the physical structure of the *Gypsy King.* The sensors thought they were meteoroids, then the pinging stopped."

As if Orion ordered it, the klaxon quit.

"Like that, Captain," he said.

"Why do I think that you are still not telling me everything."

"You could not understand . . . everything."

"Captain, something strange now," Clive said. "I'm getting a signal on a low-band FM wave, 92.1 MHz."

"What is it saying?"

"It's static. Just a second, I'll try and clean it up."

"Orion?"

"No, Captain, we received no radio signal."

"Clive, what are you getting?"

"I think I almost have it cleaned up. One more second."

The intensity of the sound forced the men in the command level to cover their ears. Orion just stared at the screens.

"Jesus Christ, turn that down. What the hell was that?" I asked.

Clive punched in keys and then lowered the volume to almost nothing. He then slowly began to turn the volume up.

"What the hell is that?" Garret repeated, responding to the sound that was growing louder. Three distinct sounds repeated one after the other.

"Can you modulate it more?" I asked.

"Roger," Clive answered. Then he made a slight adjustment.

"Welcome . . ." blasted over the speakers.

"What? Welcome?" I said.

"We are . . . blessed . . . welcome. We are . . . blessed . . . welcome. We are . . . blessed . . . welcome," repeated over and over, filling the command level.

"Good Lord," Clive said. "It's being broadcast from the target. Who the hell is welcoming us?"

I spun around to Orion, who continued to stare at the image on the center vid screen.

"Who is it, Orion?"

Tassos Orion faced the screen, raised his arms, and opened

his hands. "I am coming, my children; I am coming."

* * *

"Who the hell is broadcasting, Orion?"

"My crew, Captain. I thank the Universal God that they are still alive. I told them I would be back, and I have returned. These men need our help. I request that we board that ship and retrieve them."

"What ship?" Garrett asked.

"That object that you believe is an asteroid, Mr. Garrett, is an alien spacecraft. My crew is onboard that craft. We need to access that craft and remove them. They have been marooned there far too long."

"Captain, this is all bullshit," Clive said. "How could anyone survive out here for twenty-two years? I don't trust that fool, and I certainly don't trust that signal. As I said, bullshit."

"Marcus, will you enlighten your uncle?" Orion said.

"What does he know?" I asked.

"Uncle, the Nostre Familia has six apostles on Earth," Marcus said. "They are in the monastery on the island of Lipari. They are the voice of the Prophet Tassos on Earth while he is here gathering the remaining apostles."

"Nostre Familia? Gathering what apostles?" Garrett asked.

"The six on that craft are the men who remained behind to learn," Orion said, his arms still raised. "They remained to become one with the Creator. They are my children, my apostles, my voice. It is they who we must rescue and bring home to the followers so that we can move outward to become one with the universe. This was foretold by the creators hundreds of millions of years ago when they arrived here."

"Hundreds of millions of years," Clive said. "Captain, that man is certifiable."

"The signal, Clive?"

"Still there, still repeating the same thing over and over.

No response to my return signal." He turned up the volume again.

"We are . . . blessed . . . welcome. We are . . . blessed . . . welcome," echoed through the control level.

"Uncle, you must help them," Marcus implored.

"I'm not going anywhere near that thing until I have a much better idea about what the hell is going on," I said. "Prophets, apostles, creators, million-year-old spaceships . . . not a chance until I know what that thing is. Garrett, back us up to a thousand kilometers."

"Roger that, Captain. A thousand klicks it is."

15

Standing in the window of my cabin, I looked at the invisible spot in the infinite blackness between the billions of stars. Each spec of light was a sun, or a solar system, or a galaxy. It was difficult to tell one from the other. It was also impossible to tell up from down, not that it mattered. That spot was *Kratos* or whatever that loony-tune prophet called that rock. I gave him credit for not demanding that we run back and find his crew. What's a few days after twenty-two years marooned? In my way of thinking, Orion left his crew on that thing, or in it, I guess. There was nowhere to live on the outside, no lunar camp, no bio-dome, nothing. Twenty-two years? I have twenty-two years of questions for the son of a bitch. How about just basic food and water? Six men, twenty-two years—fucking impossible. We would not find six Robinson Crusoes wandering about on this desert rock, six corpses maybe, or one very fat survivor.

"I brought you dinner," Hank said and placed a tray on my desk. "You need to eat."

I swirled the bourbon in my glass. I'd put in four cases of Kentucky bourbon in my locker; you don't even want to think about the price. Yes, a dragger's life has its ups and downs and personal expenses. Right now, I hoped four cases is enough.

"Hank, ship's status."

"Nominal and secure. Clive and Garrett are eating dinner.

Marcus is with Captain Orion in his quarters."

"Do me a favor, please don't call him that. Or at least make a note not to call him *captain* when I'm around."

"Yes, sir. Anything else?"

I looked at the concoction of steel and plasti-steel; we'd been tied to each other for more than twenty years—good times and bad times, which of course are human reactions. How Hank perceived them, I'm not sure. More than once, he'd saved my life and, in doing so, probably saved his own. Best guess is that Hank is as old as the ship, damn near immortal—if mortal applies to a box of wires, processors, and memory boards. "Yes, Hank. You were with Orion when the *Gypsy King* was here before, is that correct?"

"Yes, sir."

"Then why didn't you inform the grand jury about what you knew went on here?"

Hank paused for a moment. "Captain, I've wondered about that myself. I'm not programmed to speculate, but occasionally I analyze what happened at the inquest."

"And?"

"Simply stated, Captain, I was never asked. I respond to orders, input, and, when asked, to continue with the analysis. I will analyze until I'm told to stop, or the data runs out. In my memory, I contain the intellectual wealth of humanity for the past five thousand years; it takes up almost fifteen percent of my hard memory—history, literature, fiction, even a few how-to books. I do not have free will or the ability to empathize or even speculate. Humans have DNA; I have programs. I'm only as good as the programmer who created me and the data loaded. I am also aware of updates; as you know, I never update myself. You must authorize the update. That is the law."

"Some days, I think that's a blessing."

"I can't speculate on that, Captain."

"A joke?"

"I try, sir."

"So, you were never asked about what happened here? I wonder why?"

"That's speculation on your part."

"I get it. There has always been an anti-noid bias in the government. Will you answer a direct question?"

"Don't I always?" Hank said. "We may have our little disagreements, like with that circuit board, but I always respond to your requests with all the information I have available."

I refilled my glass to two fingers' depth; yeah, four cases would not be enough. The ship throbbed; I could feel its life through my shoes. After almost twenty years, the *Gypsy King* was, to me, as much a sentient being as a real human.

"How long were you with Captain Orion?" I asked. I generally knew the answer, but it had been a long time since I read the old logs.

"I was with Captain Tassos Orion for eighteen years. Before that, I was with Captain Gennelius for eight years until he died during the fusion reactor failure. Before that, I was with Captain Smythe-Rodgers for twenty-two years. She was my favorite, and she was a lot prettier than you, sir."

"Shit, an old onion looks better than me. However, no opinions, please. Just the facts."

"By my calculations, you were not even born when I joined Captain Smythe-Rodgers, just a fact."

"Please, nothing about my ancestry either. How many drags did you go on with Captain Orion?"

"During those eighteen years, we made seven drags. According to the logs, all were financially successful. Unfortunately, during the third drag from Sector Two Hundred and Twelve, we lost two crewmen due to the failure of the pressure seals on one of the donkeys. That was thirty-five years ago; it does seem like yesterday."

"Was it an accident?"

"Yes, the inquiry board reviewed everything when the *Gypsy King* returned to the smelter *Washington* circling the earth.

It was determined the reason was a deteriorated gasket and a failed backup. It was a minor seal around one of the elevators. When the elevator opened, the air explosively escaped. The men had no time to get to their rescue masks. Very sad."

"Was blame assessed?"

"Some. The court imposed a large fine on the captain; he paid it from the ship's share of the payload. If I remember, it was quite a sum—the asteroid was five percent gold. I also learned that the captain paid for the education of the men's children until they became of age."

"Not only lucky but a nice guy," I uttered under my breath.

"Sir?"

"Nothing. Other than that, no problems?"

"None. The remaining drags were successful; no one seriously injured. Quite a few crewmen retired wealthy. After the donkey failure, the captain started carrying a crew of six; at the start of the third drag, all were new."

"Three works well."

"Yes, sir. And with me and the other bots and noids, there is less reliance on human hands."

"Stop tooting your horn."

"Sir? I have a buzzer alarm, no horns to toot."

"Go on."

"Until the *Kratos*."

"The *Kratos*?"

"Yes, until we arrived here. We spent time, about four solar days, surveying and analyzing the object. We did not know what it was, even after the computer tried to figure it out. It came up with the conclusion that it was a moon, more than eight hundred kilometers in diameter. That would make it as large as Ceres."

"Which it is not," I said.

"Obviously. Size isn't everything; in space, it's mass that is critical," Hank said. "The effects that this object produced forced the captain to refigure everything about the object. I also could not determine the source of the voices. I knew they were from the object, but could not locate anywhere specific. That's when the captain decided to penetrate the outside shell. He had decided to use multiple lasers to burn into the object."

"You're kidding me."

"I do not kid, Captain," Hank said. "However, during the droid survey, an opening was discovered on the exterior, near its center or equator. The opening was approximately four meters in diameter. A droid was sent to the opening and slowly entered; at the twenty-meter mark of the tunnel, it stopped. The walls were wet looking, and seamless. To the right was a protrusion, a crystal-like globe set into the flat surface of the protrusion. The droid scanned it and collected images. We could not see what was happening in real-time; all transmissions failed once the droid entered the tunnel. It was after it returned to the *Gypsy King* when we could download and inspect the data. It told us nothing."

"Where are the records of this survey?"

Hank paused for a moment. "I cannot find them on the ship's computer. As Captain Orion said, they were wiped from the memory banks."

"That's impossible."

"That may be technically true, but they are gone. All I have is my internal records made during the analysis."

"And no one asked you for them?" I asked.

"Yes. I was not asked."

"Can you show them to me?"

"Of course. One moment while I connect to—"

"Stop. Do not put them on the ship's computer. Can you direct them to my com-pad?"

"Of course. One moment."

A few seconds later, dark images hinting of a tunnel appeared on my pad. A vague surface, rough and glistening, appeared. The light from the droid focused on the floor and the walls; they looked wet. I couldn't figure any of it out.

"Is this still in vacuum?"

"Yes, as far as I can tell, no sensor readings were made for atmosphere. It sensed gravity that increased as the probe went further into the tunnel," Hank said. "In a moment, the flat wall will appear."

I watched as the light began to reflect off a smooth surface; the droid hovered a meter away and slowly scanned up and down the face. It looked like a black window—there was some reflection of the light, but there was also the effect of the droid's light being absorbed. This went on for about fifteen seconds; then, the image rotated to the right. The protrusion that Hank had mentioned was approximately a meter above the floor. A globe of soft blue light sat on the protrusion; a quarter of it nestled into the surface. It looked like one of those ancient snow globes seen in museums. Only there was nothing inside this one, just a blue glow.

"Speculation?" I asked, knowing that Hank refused to speculate.

"Assumptions? I can only extrapolate that this is some type of apparatus to access a door or possibly a security device. But there is no confirming data. Scans showed no measurable energy emitted. The light was obvious, but there was no measurement of wavelength or power. It was there, yet everything reported by the droid's sensors was that nothing was emitting any frequency of light or radiation."

"That's impossible," I said.

"Yes, impossible. Yet, there it is. Of course, we found this out after the droid returned to the ship. We would have asked it to try other methods, but the captain decided to hold off for a while."

"Why was that?"

"You will have to ask Mr. Orion."

"Did anything else happen that day?"

"I don't have any of that information."

"Why not?"

"The captain asked me to deactivate myself about twenty minutes after he reviewed the images sent by the droid. I did as directed."

"He ordered you to shut down? Why?" I asked.

"You will have to ask Captain Orion. I have no idea what happened during the next twenty-four hours. When I automatically rebooted, the ship was empty, and the two donkeys were gone. I was confused, and I am designed not to be confused. I checked telemetry data for the donkeys. Tracking data revealed that both donkeys had returned to the object and were standing by near the tunnel. It also said that three men had entered one of the donkeys. The captain and three others crewed the second donkey. I sent messages and received no replies. My primary directive is the health and safety of the crew. My only logical response was to proceed to the object and find the crew. I put the *Gypsy* on autopilot with a standby directive. I then took one of the small sleds and traveled the twenty kilometers to the object. I then boarded both donkeys; they were empty. All EVA suits were gone, as well as some of the standard sensing arrays. My only logical conclusion was that the crew had entered the tunnel. I sent in another drone; all it showed was the same thing I had seen the previous day—the tunnel was vacant. So, I waited."

"How long?"

"Five hours."

"Why not longer?" I asked.

"Because I received a weak transmission that came directly out of the tunnel."

"And this transmission?"

"All it said was: 'Please help . . . please help.' It was Mr. Orion's voice. I quickly exited the donkey, and using the sled, I entered the tunnel. There I found Mr. Orion; he was incoherent and alone. I removed him from the tunnel and placed him in one of the donkeys. I gave him a sedative; he was extremely agitated. I spent the next three hours trying to find the rest of the crew. I had no success. In answer to my questions about the six crewmen, all he said was that they were with the Creators. I had no reference point to this information, so I had no idea what he was talking about."

"Did you check any of the crew sensors? Was there any signal from any of the crew?"

"None," Hank said. "I made an effort to investigate the tunnel while Mr. Orion slept. I came to the same tunnel wall. I could find no seams, doors, or anything that implied an opening. What I did discover, though, was that, at this face, the gravity was almost Earth normal, the wall gave off heat, and that there was an atmosphere—Earth-like atmosphere, the last fifteen feet. The door was about one hundred and twenty degrees warmer than space outside of the door. This temperature decreased and cooled as I exited the tunnel. I concluded that there was some heat beyond the wall. The ambient air temperature of this air was exactly minus forty-five degrees Celsius."

"Did you try to do anything with the globe?"

"Yes, I tried to rotate it. Nothing happened. The blue light didn't change. I even attempted to cut into the door. After twenty minutes on one spot, my torch barely left a scorch mark."

"So, Captain Orion just left them there? Why didn't you try and stop him?"

"When I returned to the mule, Mr. Orion again deactivated me. I was down for ten solar days, 240.37 hours, to be exact. When reactivated, we were millions of miles away, the crew was not onboard, and he would not leave his post. Eventually, he collapsed, and it was months before the recovery team met us. I managed his health as best I could, but he also fought me. He then bypassed all the safety measures and disabled me again. I was switched on after we returned to the moon. As I've said, I was never asked what happened."

"Unbelievable. Do you know why he turned you off?"

"No, but if I may speculate, Mr. Orion did not want me

asked about any of the information I had downloaded."

"Very curious."

"I agree."

"So now that we are back here, and you have had twenty years to cogitate over the problem, what do you think happened?"

"What happened? I have no idea, but I did calculate that the six crewmen who were left inside that object died. They are humans; they need food and water to survive. None of the onboard food stores were depleted, and no water was missing. They took nothing with them. The only objects missing from the *Gypsy Kings*'s inventory were the spacesuits designated for each of the crew. Other than that, they took nothing. Humans could, if atmospheres were maintained, live for up to two weeks before their biological systems would begin to fail. I can only conclude that they are dead."

"They are not dead," Orion said as he walked into my cabin.

"How the hell did you get into my cabin?" I demanded.

"When you don't change the ship's override codes, it's easy."

It was then that I saw the weapon in his hand—it was the last thing I remember.

16

You want me; you got me, you said when you opened the portal.

Hank was standing over me when I awoke. He was deactivated. I'd never, in my entire life, had the unpleasant occasion and sensation to be hit with fifty thousand volts of electricity. I don't recommend it. It hurts like hell! I pulled myself up to my chair and slammed my hand down on the internal com-link button.

"Garrett, Clive, you out there? Respond." I waited for ten seconds and repeated the order. This time I switched to full ship, not just the command level. Nothing. I tried again; I could hear the echo of my voice outside in the corridor. I placed my hand on the front panel of Hank's abdomen area; this was his central external com-link. I am the only authorized person to activate or deactivate him using this method. Ten seconds passed, and his eyes opened.

"Have a nice nap?" I asked. "How long ago did Orion enter my cabin?"

"One hour and twenty-two minutes ago," Hank answered. "When I saw the stunner, I tried to warn you, but he activated it before I could say anything. He then turned another device toward me. I don't remember what happened. Thank you for reactivating me."

"Are Garrett and Clive onboard? Are they alive?" I asked.

"Mr. Borg and Mr. Jones are on the command level," Hank said.

"I tried to reach them, no answer."

"Their life signs are shallow. However, they are alive."

I bolted out and took the stairs four at a time. On the command level, I found Garrett and Clive unconscious, still strapped in their respective command seats. I did a quick finger check for a pulse—both beat to the tune of the thumping of the devil himself.

"Hank, bring me the medical kit and two stim-pens."

Hank sat the kit on the bench next to Clive and extracted a six-inch-long blue stimulant pen. I set it softly against the side of his neck and activated the pen. I did the same to Garrett. Within minutes, they both slowly regained consciousness.

"Jesus, Lord almighty, my head hurts," Garrett said. "What the hell happened?"

"You tell me," I said. "Who was up here?"

"Your nephew was standing right there," Clive said. He pointed to a spot a few feet behind him. "The next thing I remember is you standing over me with a seriously bad fucking headache."

"Yeah," Garrett said. "I was talking with Marcus one second, then you. What's going on?"

"Punch in the command-level camera," I ordered.

For the next few minutes, we watched Marcus standing behind Clive and Garrett, then he removed a pen-like object, and tapped each of them on the neck. Both instantly fell asleep.

"Bastard," Clive said. "Why the hell . . ."

"I don't know, but we are going to find out. Hank, ship's status."

"The *Gypsy King* is nominal; all systems are functioning. However, *Horus* is not in its bay; the donkey is gone."

"Shit," Clive said and typed furiously into his keyboard. He also asked Hank, "Where is *Horus*?"

The panel above Clive lit up, and a long-range camera shot

picked up the brilliant yellow surface of *Horus*. Behind it, lit up by the sun, was the *Kratos*.

"Captain, the *Horus* is at that piece of rock," Clive said. "Telemetry says it's stable and holding about one hundred feet from the face of that thing."

"Internal sensors on the *Horus*," I said. "Do they show anyone onboard the mule?"

"No, Captain. They show no one is onboard."

"Can you pick up either Marcus or Orion?"

"No, sir," Hank said. "Their suits are missing, and there is no response from their monitors."

"Goddamn that man," I yelled. "Somehow, he's gone back into that thing."

* * *

For the next two hours, I assembled everything I would need when I found Orion and my nephew. The kit included stunners and tranqs, even a pistol. I hoped I wouldn't need them, but that son of a bitch had shown that he was not above using force to get what he wanted, whatever that was. I told Garrett to remain with the ship and away from any undue influence from *Kratos*. When he asked what that was, all I could offer was: "I have no fucking clue; use your judgment."

"Just keep the *Gypsy* out of harm's way," I said. "Back way off if anything happens and find a way to get back to us. I don't want to spend the next twenty years waiting for a ride home."

Clive was going with me, and so was Hank. I needed what little knowledge the noid had about that thing. We loaded the *Osiris*, rechecked all life support systems on the suits, and rechecked battery packs. We had enough stun power to knock the hell out a small army. I couldn't wait to put my sights on Orion.

"Garrett, when we get inside that thing, we will probably lose com-link. Clive will remain with the *Osiris*. Maybe I can set up a relay through Clive and the *Osiris*, but don't count on it. Give us twelve hours. If you don't hear from me, pass on everything we've found to Prasinus, attention the General Secretary; and to the *Washington* smelter, make that to the attention of Sarah Thomason. There's a link to a file that I've posted on my personal server account; attach that file as well. And above all, you two get the hell out of here."

"I don't like this," Garrett said.

"And I'm not thrilled about it either, but if that thing is dangerous—Luna Command needs to know. You ready, Clive?"

"Ready. No one stuns me and gets to walk away, nephew or not," Clive answered. I watched him rub the spot where Marcos had stuck him. I felt his pain.

Osiris dropped out of the bay and into the vacuum. Before we tried to engage the donk, I had Hank give it a thorough diagnostic and hull check. I wanted no surprises when we lit her up, and more especially when we were approaching *Kratos*. To be honest, I was shocked that Orion hadn't sabotaged the donkey. It would have been easy; he knew *Horus* and *Osiris*. He knew how to disable them. So, even as we crossed the twenty kilometers to *Horus*, we remained in our suits. Rapid decompression leaves a mark.

"Status update on *Horus*, Hank," I asked.

"Nominal, no change. It is pressurized and secure. And no change regarding Captain Orion and Marcus; still no signal."

"Drop that captain title, I've asked you," I said, annoyed at the noid. "You can call him a mutineer or a pirate, but not captain."

"Yes, sir," Hank said.

I wasn't sure what the sarcastic setting was for Hank, but it sounded a little too high.

"You have a plan, Captain?" Clive said as he slowed the *Osiris*. "We are about one hundred meters from the *Horus*."

"Right now, keep that ship between us and that rock. Might give us some protection."

"Protection? From what?" Clive asked as he stabilized the *Osiris*.

"I haven't a fucking clue," I said. "I just feel better with that donk between us and that tunnel or entry or whatever it is. The plan is simple: Hank and I are going into that tunnel. You will remain here and act as a relay, assuming I get a signal out that chunk of rock. You will also be here to help us escape if we need to get out fast. Can you take command of the *Horus*?"

Clive typed in a few commands on his keyboard and checked the screen over his head. "Yes, Captain. I have control. He didn't lock us out. This is all too strange; he didn't sabotage the *Osiris* and hadn't shut us out of the *Horus*. I do not like this."

"I don't like it either, so watch yourself. If anything goes sideways, back the hell up and wait. Like I said to Garrett— you still there, Borg?"

"Yes, sir, I'm monitoring," Garrett answered.

"I repeat, if after twelve hours you don't hear from Hank or me, get out of here. Clive, you will join up with Garrett, and boogie."

"Yes, sir," both of my crewmen said in unison.

"Hank, you ready for a little excitement?" I asked.

"Excitement is an emotion," Hank answered. "I do have some emotions, but they are at a low setting. I'll just make this an experience like no other.'"

Sometimes that machine drives me freaking crazy.

After leaving the airlock, Hank and I climbed aboard one of the service sleds attached to the hull of the *Osiris*. In a minute, we were slowly powering over the topside of *Horus*. Nothing looked out of sorts. It all seemed a little too normal. The gap between the donkey and the so-called alien craft had changed to about ten meters. The two service arms on the starboard side were in their stored positions. I studied the alien ship's surface; it looked like a billion years of asteroids and debris had chewed and peppered its surface. This thing was old, really old; old at the time of the dinosaurs, old.

"Hank, the tunnel?" I asked.

"Directly off the starboard stern corner, Captain. It is in the shadow of that portion of the hull deformed by an asteroid strike. That was why it was hard to see when we surveyed the object."

I slowly maneuvered the sled into an empty slot on the *Horus* and locked it in. Hank, leading the way with jets of air from the nozzles on his nav-belt, slowly towed yours truly to the circular black void on the side of the ship. This was a made object, with a door cut into its side. Welcome into my home, said the spider.

"Does it look any different, Hank?" I asked.

"No, Captain. It is exactly the way it was twenty-three years ago. The tunnel is approximately twenty meters deep. There was no discernable door at its end."

"Do you think that that orb you talked about might open the doorway?"

"Seems a reasonable conclusion."

"Then lead on," I said.

"Ah, I see. If there's trouble, the droid gets it first. But there is glory in being the first."

"Yeah, and I'll know when to duck," I gallantly said as the noid and I stopped at the edge of the roundish tunnel entry. It was about four meters high, and the same width at eye level; the floor was flat and smooth. My mag-boots sensed iron and locked to the floor. At least there was now an up and down.

"Do you scan anything ahead?" I asked Hank.

"No, just open space. Don't get too far behind, Captain."

"Wouldn't think of it," I answered and shuffled along behind Hank. When it's pitch black, and you forget to turn on your lamp, you feel a little dumb. I tapped the side of my helmet, and the wash of light filled the tunnel. Not that it showed anything. It matched precisely the same images that Hank had shown me a few days earlier. The farther we walked, the more

I could feel gravity, and the more the walls started to look wet and viscous—not a pleasant experience.

"Anything different?" I asked.

"No, it's the same as last time," Hank answered.

"Clive, are you getting any of this?" All I heard was static. I looked at the environmental sensor plate on my arm; it was beginning to show oxygen in the atmosphere. The fact that any atmosphere was showing was even more of a shock.

"Hank, I'm getting oxygen readings, how can that be?" I asked.

"I have no idea. Since the stuff doesn't interest me, I pay little attention."

"You're a big help." I looked farther down the tunnel; a blue light appeared on the right side about waist high. "Is that the orb you saw?"

"Yes, the same. Captain, I'm getting a rise in pressure readings and an almost normal atmosphere. However, it is minus forty-four degrees Celsius."

"The wall, how far?"

"Four meters; the temperature is now minus twenty, almost tolerable for humans."

"Eskimos and Swedes, maybe. Me, I like a nice—" Then the orb began to pulse.

"Did that thing pulse last time?" I said.

"No, not while I was here. I would suggest that you, being an organic life form, may have something to do with that."

"A guess?"

"An extrapolation."

Hank came to a stop. I scanned my light up and down the face of the wall ahead of me. Like Hank had said, it seemed to absorb most of my light and reflected very little. The blue orb continued to pulse like it was trying to grab my attention. Considering the space, it wasn't hard. I looked at my sleeve. "Environmental conditions, Hank?"

"Temperature is five degrees below zero; the atmosphere is

twenty percent oxygen, and the rest nitrogen, no carbon dioxide. The pressure is almost exactly like that on Earth."

"What's the volume in this area?"

"A total of about eighty cubic meters of atmosphere surround us, six meters behind us, you would die."

"Fascinating . . . it seems like someone has left a doormat for us. Do you think that the orb is a doorbell?"

"I haven't any data to support that idea," Hank blathered.

Not waiting, I reached out and touched the globe—nothing happened. I expected maybe a big bell chime or a magic doorway opening—nothing.

"You said the environment is Earth-like at this end of the tunnel?" I asked.

"Strangely so, yes."

"Might as well take a chance." I gripped the cuff of my right hand with my left and released the seal. The right glove came off. Usually, in space, all the air instantly and explosively blows out the sleeve of your arm, throwing you against the wall or spinning you around. Then, within a few agonizing seconds, the remaining air would be sucked from your lungs as well. Then unconsciousness. In a minute, you'd be freeze-dried. But here, in this way un-normal atmosphere, at near-zero degrees, all I felt was cold. I touched the orb with my fingers; a few seconds passed, then the globe turned from blue to yellow to a deep red. I stared at the globe, almost hypnotized.

"Captain, I do believe you were right; it is a doorbell," Hank said.

"What?" I said and turned to him. Behind him, the wall that only absorbed light a few minutes ago was becoming transparent.

17

Beyond the now open door was a vast chamber. Through my helmet, I couldn't see the ceiling or the walls. The chamber's floor matched the surface of the tunnel. Within this seemingly infinite space, I beheld the most incredible sight I'd ever seen, and I've seen a lot of bizarre things in my life. Here, millions of tiny lights flickered, flashed, and danced. Small constellations moved in concert with each other; others performed sweeping swirls that reminded me of videos of swarming earth birds. Others danced in pairs and small groups. Some were white, others pink, blue, and most probably, every color I could imagine. I was beyond dazzled; I stood mesmerized.

Hank followed me through the door and into the chamber.

"Tell me you see this. No, cancel that, what do you see?" I asked.

"I see millions of points of energy, like stars but smaller. I see organization and order; this is not chaos. However, Captain, I do not have a soul to see this the way you see it. I imagine that it is something else, a wonder."

"Hank, it is that."

I stood awestruck. My eyes couldn't move fast enough to follow most of the clusters; others just swayed while others waltzed and sashayed. A few times, a fist-sized clump of points zipped past my face, stopped, reversed, stopped again, and intensified, then quickly moved on. I felt like Hank and I were part of the furniture. We continued into the chamber, and the lights drifted out of our way, though at times I wasn't sure they would. I looked back at Hank and was surprised to see two points of light approach him and then just pass through him. It was like he wasn't there.

"Did you feel that?" I asked him.

"I felt an energy surge, Captain, that was all. It was interesting. A little like what you might call a tickling sensation."

We strolled slowly and farther into the chamber; beyond the lights was nothing. There was not a sense of depth or background. I clicked off my headlamp. The millions of colored lights made it feel like Christmas. Once every few seconds, a portion of the display—since I don't know what else to call it—would collectively brighten. Then that cluster of lights would fly around the room at head-turning speed. Then the whole show would go back to whatever you would call normal for a million hovering fireflies. It was impossible to gauge the size and volume of the chamber. I knew how big the outside was, but here, inside, it was impossible even to guess.

Then ahead, through the swirl of lights—most in this fellowship were blue and yellow—a shadow slowly formed, backlit by thousands of these sparks. The shadow walked toward us, and as these luminosities parted, I saw my nephew. He wasn't wearing a helmet or even his EVA suit.

"Isn't this amazing?" Marcus said, his arms up as he rotated on his heels one time. "The Prophet was correct."

I seized my nephew by his shoulders and looked into his face. The lights reflected off his eyes like stars. "Are you alright?"

"Yes, Uncle. I'm well. Isn't this a fantastic miracle?"

"Where is Orion? Where is that son of a bitch?"

"That's blasphemous, Uncle," Marcus said. "The Universal God would not be happy if he were to hear you slander his prophet."

"Prophet? You have got to be kidding me," I yelled. Instantly many of the sparks brightened at the sound of my voice rising. I couldn't have cared less. "Where is the bastard?"

"Behind you, Captain Strabo," a voice, almost ethereal, said. "My son, you must believe, for your eyes now know the truth."

Not five feet away stood Tassos Orion. Around him, a thick swarm of the lights, in all colors, flittered and crackled. Others would join the swarm and then quickly leave. Whether they were the same ones, I have no idea. But between the never-ending light show that rose high and swirled to the invisible ceiling and the small swarms that eddied around the four of us, I wasn't sure what truth to believe anymore.

Orion, as I did with Marcus, put his hands on my shoulders, and stared me right in the eyes. "Captain, all around you are the creators. They are millions of individuals and yet are one. They welcome you. Remove your helmet; you won't need that."

I paused, unsure, then cast my fate to the stars. I took off my helmet and passed it to Hank. "Don't lose this; I will need it later," I whispered. "And do not forget the time."

"Yes, sir," Hank said.

The air smelled like the spring day I experienced during my one trip to Earth—the memory of that day flooded my mind. I could see the roses, the sunshine, and taste the thick air of humanity's home. They say that smell is the most lasting sense; at this point, I'd have to agree. The emotions of that day with my sister and the extensive gardens behind the Vatican all came back. I looked back at Orion; he wore a strange smile. A million lights reflected off his eyes; it was as if the fireflies had found their way into his head.

"Heady stuff, Captain. It was the same for me the first time," he said.

I checked my sleeve. One hour had elapsed.

"What are they? You said the creators," I said.

"All things will be answered. First, I must show you something." He turned and walked away. "Please, Captain, follow us."

We passed through the swirling lights; I guessed we walked a hundred meters. There was nothing on the floor, no furniture, nothing. The ceiling high above was obscured by the busyness of the specs of energy. I reluctantly concluded that each pinprick was a dynamic sentient form of energy. Life possibly, but unlike any life I'd ever imagined. We stopped at a massive wall, its texture like the tunnel, rough yet curiously mottled and damp. Across its face, thousands of the sparks hovered, then each would touch the surface, brighten, then silently flit off.

Orion placed his hand against the wall. "Please touch this; it won't harm you."

It was warm and dry. Yet, I felt a tingling, an infinitesimal surge of electricity; the warmth flowed to my heart. "What is this?"

"Beyond this wall is the universe's greatest and strangest creation; we call them a black hole, a singularity. This one is about the size of a baseball, the size of my fist. There is one on the opposite side of this chamber. This one is positively charged, the other is negatively charged. The Pernix Lumen, as I call them, use these as their energy source, their food. Just as we carbon-based forms use our Earth's natural resources for sustenance, the Pernix comes to these walls and recharge. They go from one wall to the other; it keeps them balanced. Like whales that need to breathe in the ocean, they come and go without thinking about it."

I removed my hand and put it to my face. The fragrance was something pleasant, something I tried to remember. It was just out of my reach.

"What, or should I say who, are they?" I asked, looking back into the chamber. A massive swirling had begun high in the ceiling.

"Watch this, it is amazing," Orion said and pointed. "This

is for you."

Above, the lights began to eddy; a flower shape of lights began to form. Then, like an incandescent tornado, they spun upward and then out into a florid shape that turned back on itself. The colors were, all I can say, indescribable. This vortex twisted and turned, a murmuration of lights.

"You called them Pernix," I said.

"It's my term," Orion said. "What they call themselves is impossible to convey. Pernix Lumen means 'nimble light.' Kind of nails it, don't you think?"

"What are they?"

"We humans have to define everything, it's in our nature," Orion said. "We slap a name and a definition on everything, from the smallest bacteria to the greatest tree. We determine whether it has a use, fulfills a need, provides comfort or pain, is something to eat, or is it dangerous—it must fit into our world. Earth is a closed system, and underlying it all is the little-fish and big-fish rule. The small get eaten to allow the larger to survive. Harsh, but that's our nature. Yet beneath it, all is wholeness, the circle of life, the survival of the fittest, the realization that we are not immortal. Sustenance and life flow from this unending chain. From this awareness comes our religions, our philosophies, and of course, our baser natures. They are all a part of our wholeness. Captain Strabo, these are *our* creators. Marcus, tell your uncle what you have learned in the last hours."

I looked at Marcus. A firefly hovered before his eyes, then rose and disappeared through the skin of his forehead. He instantly smiled. "Uncle, the Pernix have been here, in this part of the asteroid belt, for hundreds of millions of years. They are pure energy and, as such, have no sense of time; a moment now is the same as a billion moments ago. We are here now. The Pernix have always been here. Hard to grasp, but that's how they see us and this universe. There is no before, or now, or after. At some point, hundreds of millions of years ago, in our terms of time, they discovered our Earth. There are thousands, maybe millions, of these Pernix ships spread throughout the universe. Beyond any sense of our time, they evolved into what you see about us. Billions of years ago, long before our system formed, they spread throughout their galaxy, then beyond to nearby galaxies, then outward to the whole of the accessible universe. This ship is both their vehicle and their source of continuing life and energy. Carbon- and silicon-based life could not possibly make these expeditions. To travel centuries, millennia, even eons, requires too much baggage—food and water mostly. These simple ships, with their captured black holes, provide an eternity of the energy they need. Even the Pernix have no idea about how long this power will last."

Stunned, I looked at my godson; his face glowed with warmth and calmness I'd never seen. "What happened when they discovered our planet?" I asked.

"Simply put, they colonized it. We are their children. That is why your hand was able to open the door. The amino acids on your skin told the Pernix that you were one of theirs. With that touch of your hand, the door opened."

"And that's why it wouldn't open to Hank's touch," I said.

"Yes, sorry, Hank. But you do not have the genetic and chemical configurations to activate the door."

"I guess I should be disappointed," Hank answered. A cluster of fireflies passed through his chest; he shivered.

"At some point in our past, Earth's past, the Pernix discovered that the evolutionary development of life on Earth had evolved far enough to create basic RNA, ribonucleic acid, the underlying basis for all life on Earth. The Pernix tell me that it varies from galaxy to galaxy, and planet to planet, but it is a relatively common chemical model. When they discover a chemical structure similar to RNA, they enable the evolution of that molecule by seeding it with a more complex form—in Earth's case it was the structure we call DNA, deoxyribonucleic acid. They tell us that these molecules, these nucleotides, are common throughout the universe. I'll take their word for it. What I do understand is that from that first infusion, an inoculation if you will, hundreds of millions of years ago, all life on Earth evolved from that adjustment. The Pernix have waited here until one of their children placed their hand on the doorbell."

I turned to Orion. "You? Twenty-four years ago?"

He smiled and bowed. "At your service. I am also called the chief bell-ringer."

"Cute," I said. The swirling had now progressed into an orgy of luminance, twisting, and folding in on itself. I had to shade my eyes. "And do you know what all this display means?"

"They are celebrating your arrival; it is a performance they are putting on just for you. They have waited a long time," Marcus said.

I looked at Orion; his head tilted back, and he watched the show. Six specs of light slowly danced in a halo around his head. Hank was standing a few feet away. A dozen more fireflies passed through him and out his back. To be honest, it was unnerving. What the hell were they doing to my noid?

"Orion?" I said.

"I will only be called Tassos, Captain. I have been asked by the Pernix Lumen to represent them to their children."

"Oh, really, that's opportune."

"One of human's best traits, cynicism. I understand."

"Where is your crew?" I asked, ignoring his remark. "When you were here last, you left six men. I see nothing that would sustain them for more than twenty years. You left them here to die?"

The six points of light stopped rotating around Orion's head. They formed a line about a half a meter in length and then advanced slowly toward me. At about two meters, they stopped. They then began to shimmer and expand until, within a few seconds, six humanoid shapes of light stood before me.

"Captain, these are my crewmen," Orion said. "I would introduce them, but they have told me they don't care, they have passed beyond the need of names. These are the new Pernix, and they are my friends. They are also the first disciples of Nostre Familia. And soon, my followers on Earth will join us, and they, too, will become Pernix Lumen."

*W*hoa, I said to myself—*hold those damn horses.* Talk about a Jesus complex. Orion or Tassos or Prophet Tassos had gone off the rails.

The light show continued. It now swept low toward the floor, and like twisting snakes of lights, enfolded in on itself, swirled about, then exploded into the most magnificent fireworks display I have ever seen. Millions of fireflies shot back and forth around the periphery. They were either enjoying the show or were generally nonplussed about the performance. Me? I was freaking scared to death about everything I'd just seen and heard. Right now, my universe had been kicked in the crotch, and I was about to double over from the pain.

"Are you all right, Captain?" Hank said as he moved to my side. I took the opportunity to check my sleeve; three hours had passed, nine hours left. I needed to find a bathroom, and I was damn sure there wasn't a restroom near the exit. Thank goodness for self-contained suits.

"Hank, I'm doing fine," I lied. I watched the ghostly silhouettes standing before me. They were kind of cool, if you got your head past the reality, at one time not so many years ago, they were living and breathing human beings. The forms slowly dissolved and became again singular specs of light that drifted back to encircle Orion's head. From this point on, I sure as hell would never call him Prophet Tassos, unless I needed to.

"Would you like to see the rest of this amazing ship?" Orion asked. "It is quite a marvel. We consider ourselves so brilliant, so advanced; the reality is we are just fleas to an elephant."

The analogy was silly; we were more like a grain of sand to the universe. I knew that, and he knew it, too. A tour? I re-checked my sleeve—you know what they say about a watched clock or pot or something.

I know space tech: H-tanks, pipes, electronics and servers, nozzles, and reactors—fusion or fission, your choice. After an hour, I was exhausted by what Orion showed me. I watched the river of specs as they flitted silently past, realizing that the little firefly in Marcus's pre-frontal cortex was doing the show-and-tell. What could I do? I also realized these bits of glowing space dust were a lot like their offspring, we humans. They had egos; I'd seen that during their aerial antics. Their display showed a sense of drama, and they wanted to impress me with their cleverness. I also discovered, through Marcus, that they were incredibly proud of their almost-billion-year-old ship.

And it was a fantastic piece of interstellar engineering. My guess, the two black holes are held in magnetic suspension in chambers at each end of the ship. When activated, one singularity draws in the bits of space around it and then, through some interconnecting worm-hole, discharges the material out the other singularity. All the laws of the universe locked up in two conundrums at each end of the ship.

"How fast?" I asked.

"As fast as it needs to be," Orion said.

"Foolish question, I guess," I said.

"No, not really. They have the ability, through these black holes, to bend space. Just enough to move quickly and almost instantaneously from one location to another. Certainly, within a solar system like ours, distances are almost irrelevant."

"And why did they stay here?" I asked. "They have a universe around them. They could come back and visit anytime."

"Because they had nowhere else they needed to be," Marcus added. "Again, time is relative. To the Pernix Lumen, they arrived yesterday."

"And they have an unlimited supply of energy to sustain them?" Hank asked.

"Yes, Hank. They do have that going for them," Orion said.

I looked at the noid—out of the mouths of babes come the most interesting questions. I realized then that Hank had more in common with these flickers than I might.

The Pernix technology *was* mind-boggling. The ability to move across or through space, unhindered by time, was man's greatest desire to travel the universe. We've built a few machines that accelerated nonstop until they disappeared from our solar system. A lot of good that does, unless you don't want to go back home. Home, now that's a human construct. And perhaps an Earth-born construct in our DNA as well: nests, dens, caves, rabbit warrens; even the dinosaurs had nests. These bits of light, I'm not sure. They flitted about inside this chamber like birds in a cage yet were also trapped here as well. I saw none at rest, no motel for the Pernix. Even a prisoner at some point will call their cell home.

Marcus and Orion—and I include the halo of six lights rotating over Orion's head—walked ahead. My godson pointed to things unseen beyond the lights; the Prophet waved his arms in circles. The crown of lights sometimes tilted, trying to keep up with his gestures.

"Hank, we are out of here in one hour," I said quietly to the noid. "I don't want to cut our time too close. I'm sure that Clive and Garrett are killing themselves not hearing from us. Any ideas on how to break away from this show-and-tell?"

"My bearings tell me that we are very close to where we started; we have come in a large circle. The entry is about fifty feet to your right."

I looked where Hank had directed, a blue spot, more significant than the hundreds of flitting specs, held stationary, the doorbell.

"Tassos," I said, not wishing to start an interstellar incident.

"Yes, my son."

I wanted to punch the condescending SOB so bad.

"Speaking for myself and my nephew, I'm hungry. Unlike these ethereal beings, I need a cheeseburger or something to exist. So, thank you for the tour. Hank and I will be going, and since my sister would be quite pissed at me if I didn't insist, Marcus is also going with me."

"I'm staying with Prophet Tassos," Marcus said.

"Marcus, you are still a member of my crew, and I'm your guardian. This is the responsibility your mother placed on me before we left the moon. You know that, and as long as you are on my ship, you will be obedient to my orders. I'm the captain, and there is only one captain." I looked at Orion. "The Prophet can do as he likes. He was never a crewman—his being a stowaway limits his standing and trustworthiness."

Orion looked at me with a smile. I balled up my fist.

"Marcus, my son, go with your uncle," he said. "He is right, he has the proper authority, and we must always show obeisance to those with authority. However, only to those we accept—remember that. I admire Captain Strabo; he was kind to me and has shown respect to the Pernix. They also appreciate that he understands what he has seen here. They have asked me to request that Hank remain here with them."

"What?" I said. "Hank, remain here?"

"They find him fascinating," Orion said. "They would like to know more about this . . . machine."

"Captain Orion, I do not accept their request," Hank said. "Tell them thank you, but no."

"That's not for you to decide, Hank," Orion said. "Your owner, Captain Strabo, is the only one to make that decision.

Captain?"

Hank started to move toward Orion; the halo of lights shifted and moved toward the noid.

"Stop it, you two," I said. "Tassos, Hank is critical to the *Gypsy King*—you know that more than anyone. He saved your life last time you were here; he's not some science experiment. So, no, I do not give permission. Hank, it's time to leave. And, Marcus, find your suit. We are leaving in ten minutes."

"I understand," the Prophet said. "He's an invaluable crewmember. Marcus, the Pernix will show you where your suit is. I will meet you tomorrow; there are things I need to finish here before I return."

Dumbstruck, I stood there, staring at the man. "You are returning to Earth with us?" I asked.

"Of course, Captain; did you think I would remain here?"

"Well, I thought after seeing your crew and all . . ."

". . . that I would remain here, and become a Pernix. No, my son, my world is here, at this time, in this solar system. Earth is my home, and the Universal God blesses me, and these eternal lights of the universe, to bring salvation to our world. Yes, Captain, I am returning home with you."

left *Horus* drifting a hundred meters off the flank of the Pernix ship. Orion could work out how to get to the machine when he decided to return to the *Gypsy*. I told him that if he didn't return in two days, I would have the donkey return without him. Fortunately, I'm not a betting man, or at least on sure things. I *knew* the SOB would return.

Clive was both thrilled and relieved when Marcus and I rode up the elevator to the command deck of the *Osiris*. I guessed that he thought he'd never see us again. Hank remained below securing the suits and then followed us to the main deck. The three of us and the noid filled the command deck. There wasn't much room for an afterthought. Hank took his customary perch in the stern quarter, near the sensor and tools display.

As Clive drove the *Osiris* back to the *Gypsy King*, two things became apparent. One, for the last six hours, I'd been a part of the most significant revelation in the history of humanity. And two, I still needed to make money. I'd spent millions crossing this part of the solar system looking for this rock, and we found it. Now, what the hell was I going to do with it? I was not going to drag that thing back to Earth; you can be damn sure of that. It would be like finding a cute little rat full of fleas infected with the Black Death and, for compassionate reasons, saving it and releasing it in some European port. Okay, that's an exaggeration—but not too far off. I can only imagine what the Earth-side politicians would do with something like this. And the jealousy between Mars, the moon, and Earth—don't even think about going there. This thing, this *Kratos*, filled with uncounted Pernix Lumen, was okay right where it was. And since there were only a few of us who knew about it, it's a good bet that if it had remained out here for the last half a billion years, it wasn't going anywhere tomorrow.

As a capitalist, I'm as greedy as the next dragger. I still must pay for the fuel and the hardware upgrades of the *Gypsy King*. I'm sure none of my creditors would accept a jar full of fireflies, even if they came from the far side of the known and unknown universe. Ahead, as we neared the *Gypsy King*, I could see the struts and cable spools hanging on her. They needed something to tow. If not, this dry drag would break me. And besides, I owed it to Clive and Garrett. They didn't sign up for galactic politics and genetic and religious mumbo-jumbo. As sure as Saturn's rings, there wasn't anything to monetize from that lump of alien tech floating twenty kilometers to my stern.

"What went on back there?" Clive asked.

"I'll tell both you and Garrett tonight. Right now, I need to process all the shit I saw. Hank, can you get a couple of those energy bars, I'm famished. And get some for Marcus as well."

"Uncle, I could have come back tomorrow with the Prophet," Marcus said. "I was fine. I had a few nutri-bars in my suit. I'd have been good."

"The only good thing, Marcus, is that you are here with me and not with that lunatic," I said.

"He's not a lunatic," Marcus said.

"In this solar system," I said, "there is no human crazier than that man. However, right now, I'm more concerned about how I'm going to deal with him during the next eight months. While I'd like nothing better than to leave him with his crew and those fireflies for all eternity, I'm just not that kind of captain who'd maroon one of my crew, even if a stowaway. He's certifiably nuts; I will deal with it."

I could see that Clive had questions—hell, I've got questions. Right now, what was more important was my ship and the crew.

"Clive, I've decided that we need to find a rock and make some money. Any objections?"

"To money? Never, Captain," Clive answered.

Garrett chimed in. "Include me in that vote."

"Roger that, Mr. Borg," I said.

"Nothing going to come busting out of the rock and bite us on the ass?" Clive asked.

"Lord, I hope not. Garrett, start figuring trajectories sun side and go through the logs to see if we've marked any asteroids worth our time. Pull up any that show rare earths or precious metals. We should be there in thirty minutes. I figure we'll boogie out of here in two days."

"Roger that, Captain. Borg out."

I said over my shoulder to Marcus, "There's a small shower in the toilet below. Why don't you get cleaned up—nothing exciting is going to happen." I had to smile when I looked at him. He was out like a light, no alien pun intended. He'd been awake for more than thirty-six hours, and, even in space, a man needs sleep more than he needs food. Me? I needed a drink.

The *Osiris* slowly drifted into its slot in the service level of the *Gypsy King.* I heard the foot clamps clank against the deck and lock down. Through the dome of the donk's control center, I saw Garrett looking down from the mezzanine of the repressurized bay. The empty bay for the *Horus* bothered me. That SOB had better return to my ship. I was trying to figure out how I could make him. I wasn't going to give him the satisfaction of becoming Robinson Crusoe in space.

The three of us and Hank exited the ship.

"Garrett, I want you to lock into the Horus. If I have to, I will pull that donk out its spot and drive it here. Can you do that?"

"Already plotted it; I have control."

"Love you," I said.

"I also started plots to a few asteroids that have been on our watch list in this and adjacent sectors the moment that you signed off. Captain, it's good to get back to work."

"After what I've seen, I couldn't agree more."

Whatever went on during the almost twenty-four hours that Orion and my nephew spent on that ship exhausted Marcus. He tried to stay awake while I began to brief Clive and Garrett about what happened on the *Kratos*. After ten minutes, he fell asleep again. I had Hank carry him to his berth and tuck him in.

Two hours and an empty bottle of my bourbon later, my crew sat in stunned silence. Hank showed videos that he'd taken while toured. The magnitude of what I'd seen and learned was also beginning to impress me as well. To discover that you are not alone in the universe—*that* knowledge will severely twist your mind around. I've seen more than enough crisscrossing this inbound quarter of the solar system to honestly believe that there is nothing out here but our measly planets. Space is big. So big, I can't even begin to imagine how large it is, and I've tried. Trillions of stars and planets, and that's just a truck driver's guess.

Nonetheless, to have a bunch of Christmas lights put on a show, and then tell you they are your creators, well that genuinely begs the question of what's out there. One thing that sets humans apart from the rest of the sentient earthly animal world is our stubbornness. It will take more than a light show to make me believe that Tinker Bell is my great-grandmother to the millionth power.

"You left Orion there, with those—things?" Garrett said.

"Not my choice or call," I said, pulling out another bottle and refilling our glasses. "He's a big boy, and he's been here before. What I'm trying to figure is why he wanted to come back. And now, why he wants to go back to Earth. All his mumbo-jumbo about going out into the universe with humanity—it spooks me. He wouldn't live long enough to get to Alpha Centauri, four and a half light-years from here. And, even with his blather about the Pernix and their disassociation of time and distance—shit, it's all magic and visions. Humans still need food, water, and toilets. The rules of physics don't just change; in fact, you can't change them. If he gets back, I will find out what's driving him." I looked at the panel over Garrett's head. "Any idea about targets?"

Garrett put up charts on the large overhead screen.

"There are no targets in this sector worth our time, there are a couple to the Jupiter edge, and most of those are ice. Besides, it would take a month just to get to them, and we would be going the wrong way to try and shorten our trip home. I propose falling sunward and catching up with Sector Seventy-one as it rotates to us—we will slide to it as we drop. There are some old surveys from twenty years ago that locate a couple of reasonably sized taters. A note on one of them says that it's possibly composed of titanium and iron. That suggests some rare earths. Other than that, we will have to do some prospecting. I don't have to remind you that we cut into our reserves with those punctures."

"Transit estimates?" I asked.

"From where we are now to the sun side of the sector, twenty-three days. If we wait to catch Sector Seventy-one, another ten days. So, that gives us a month of transit. We may get lucky and find another rock along the way. Assuming a two-week hook-up and thruster mount, we could be homebound in two months. Transit would be about one hundred and fifty days. We could boost that a bit; it would depend on the rock."

I knew Garrett was conservative; time in space just literally flies by. There is nothing to associate with its passage. Earthside humans have the sun's imprint on our souls; the twenty-four-hour clock is burned into our DNA. Only the clock on the ship's bulkhead told us what yesterday was and when tomorrow starts—a spacer gets used to it. But the circadian rhythms that rule our bodies kind of come unglued out here. Not a few have gone nuts trying to get their minds around time in space.

Twenty-two hours later, the klaxon squawked. It jolted me out of a sound sleep, the first I'd had in a week.

"It's the *Horus*, she's hailing us," Hank said.

"Permission to board the *Gypsy King*." It was Orion. I had wondered if his voice would have changed, become more electric—bad joke, I know—but still, I wondered.

"Are you alone, Mr. Orion?" I asked.

"Yes, Captain, I am alone. Who else could it be?" he answered.

"Some of your little sparkly friends?"

"Please, Captain. The Pernix must stay where they are. Yes, I am alone."

"Garrett will guide you in. After you are settled, I want to see you in my cabin."

"Yes, Captain."

I knew this was going to be a strange—no, bizarre would be the better word—conversation. I was quite pissed with the man; he knew about these fireflies from the very beginning but didn't say anything. Then he takes off with my nephew, and communes with Tinker Bell. Then there's his story, and it is his story, about millions of years, and DNA, and all sorts of other malarkey. The man is seriously deranged, and now he's back on my ship. Oh, joy.

An hour later, I looked up from my cabin's com console at the tap on the doorframe.

"Please come in, Captain," I said, extending a little bit of professional courtesy. I pointed to the mag chair in the corner.

Orion sat, looked at me with those blue eyes, and then stroked his beard. He looked like an aged professor of mathematics from Eastern Greater European University. I knew different.

"So, what do you think of my Pernix Lumen, Captain?" he asked.

"They'd make a nice ceiling feature in the Emerald City grand ballroom," I said. "And how do they feel belonging to you?"

"Don't be a fool," the man answered sharply. "And you are sacrilegious."

"I'm not. You and I both know the implications of your discovery. And once this gets out into the population, all hell may break loose. This revelation impacts every religion, philosophy, and political structure across the colonies, states, and nations. This shakes their very foundations—Orion, some will not like this. You know that. So why am I here—or, more correctly—why did you come along and make sure I came here with you?"

Orion stood and walked to the star-studded glass wall that filled the end of my cabin.

"I've known you a long time, Captain. We go back to almost the beginning," Orion said. He faced me. "I chose you because you are the only man I trust. This is more than you think it is; these Pernix *are* the Creators. Their ship is just one of millions; this they told me. For a billion years, yes, Captain, a billion years have passed since this ship began its voyage to be one of the catalysts, the initiators of sentient life across the stars. The others are doing the same across the universe. How many other planets have been fine-tuned with DNA, I don't know, and these Pernix don't know either."

"Others?" I asked. "Orion, you are repeating yourself. Do you mean that these fireflies have been doing this for eons?"

He smiled. "Naivety—we can only understand so much. You are quite right; the foundations of every social structure on Earth will be shaken. Our species has quite an ego; we are all so high and mighty. This revelation will change everything. We have evolved, believing we are the center of this universe. For thousands of years, we placed ourselves in the center of

God's moral and mechanical universe. Even the sun revolved around us humans. People were burned for not believing."

"There will be many who will want to stop you," I said. "The list of churches and religions is quite long and will probably even include the Atheist's Guild and every group that believes in evolution. The Pernix have kicked that bucket over."

"That is why I came back to Earth twenty years ago to prepare humanity for the future. My writings and my disciples are laying the groundwork for this revelation. Our greatest philosophers knew there was something greater out here. From Buddha to Aristotle, they would talk of the greater soul of humanity. It was as if the Pernix had left a message in our DNA that this day would come."

"You left your crew to die."

"You met my crew; they did not die; they joined with the Pernix. The Pernix themselves are sentient beings gathered from a hundred other cultures, cultures that were old and mature when our solar system was forming. They became what they are because it was simply the easiest form of life to allow them to live forever."

"That's not life," I said. And as soon as I said it, I knew that I was wrong. Good God, now I was falling for his gibberish.

"The Pernix are proof that life comes in many forms. Our religions claim that there is an afterlife, a heaven, a paradise, a nirvana. It's as old as our cultures and societies. We rationalize it, twist it, even pervert it. The Pernix are the souls and the memories of the past. They are forever and yet are here in the present; they are also in the past and in the future at the same instant."

"You are totally insane."

20

I stared at the man. It was as if a tsunami had smacked me up-side the head and then drowned me. When humans are faced with danger or something so foreign to our nature, our first reaction is to throw up a defense or just throw up. Something so intense and vivid that, whatever our beliefs, our historic cultural theses must be defended. Humans are damn good at this; the death of Socrates and the Inquisition come to mind. The nuclear bombings of France, England, Italy, and the Alps showed this. During the past three thousand years, humans were quite prepared to kill a million innocent people to defend a belief, or a cause, or an institution—no matter how tenuous or ephemeral.

Orion put his hands together. "Captain, whether I'm in-sane or not is irrelevant. It is always the messenger that takes the blow."

"I hate martyrs. They accomplish little, and the cost is too much—seventy-two virgins notwithstanding."

"I do not intend to become a martyr. I intend to become a teacher, a leader. There's a big difference."

"You think?" I said. "Captain, we will have a lot of time on our hands over the next few months before we reach Earth—unless, of course, your Pernix have a way to move us instantly across space and time?"

"That I do not know. And yes, we will have time to discuss this further. I'm going to get something to eat—as you reminded me, this body still needs food. Then I'll be in my cabin. I assume that you will try and pick up a rock on the way home?"

"Yes, the first sensible thing you've said today," I said. "Regardless of your higher plain and the infinite universe thing, I still need to pay the bills. My crew needs a paycheck, and the earth and Mars still need raw materials. Garrett is laying in a course that will hopefully get us near a couple of rocks that we can check out. If they look good, we'll hook one up and drag it to Earth."

"Excellent. It will be good to get back into the business. Captain Strabo, you may not believe this, but I miss this. I was good at it, and so are you. We will talk more about this later."

* * *

A month later, I filled my tumbler with two fingers of bourbon, one of my finest. It had been hidden for such a celebration as now. I passed the bottle to Garrett, Clive, Orion, and Marcus.

Behind us, hanging two kilometers back, was one of the best asteroids we'd harvested during the last ten years. It was a solid mix of titanium, iron, and rare earths. There were veins of gold, silver, and platinum. We even found a few cavities of diamonds and other precious crystals. Our communications with the Great American Metals smelter, *Washington*, gave us a good price. As we increased speed, we would lay back the rock even farther. Garrett estimated the travel time at three months. A month to accelerate, a month to travel at speed, and a month-long deceleration, or something close to that. I left the figures to Hank, Clive, and Garrett. We hadn't plowed into anything solid, yet. And besides, if we hit anything zipping along at over two hundred thousand kilometers an hour, we'd never know it. We'd be just space debris—forever.

Orion and I had come to an understanding: I wouldn't talk about the fireflies, and he wouldn't bring up all the shit he was bringing to Earth. I was more worried about Marcus. To him, this was more than an adventure. He'd been brainwashed, that was obvious. And seeing that speck of light slide in and out of his head gave me the willies. From what Tassos said, I surmised that the fireflies would not or could not leave their ship. They needed the unlimited power that the black holes gave them. I believed that Orion was telling the truth, as far as he knew.

My attempts at conversation went well with Marcus. We talked about his mother, his schooling, and his relationship with the Church and the Vatican. When it drifted into the subject of the Pernix, he got defensive and turned the conversation away. That bothered me—a lot.

Hank took the watch after our celebration; Clive and Garrett went to their cabins. Orion, as he always did, wandered away to his.

"You did a good job out there, Marcus," I said. "Not many could have done that work, especially a rookie. There may be a job out here if you want it. It's good money, and with the new city on Mars, they will need a lot of what we provide."

"My home is on Earth with the Prophet," he answered. It was his usual answer. "There's more to our lives than money." The glass of bourbon in his hand was having an effect. I smiled.

"I get it. I was once excited about my future. And when I had the opportunity, I took it."

"And here you are, dragging rocks through space. I have bigger dreams; the Prophet showed me this future. You saw it with the Pernix; they showed me the future. Our world is ending. The Prophet says our future is in the stars."

"And you believe him?" I watched as he sipped his bourbon.

"Of course I believe him, and the Pernix do not lie; they

cannot lie. The Prophet will lead us. We will follow him."

"It's that simple? And what makes you think that the Pernix don't or can't lie?"

"Faith. I have faith in them. And not everything is complicated. There will soon be a time when all is revealed. The truth will show both believers and unbelievers; they will then have to make a choice. That is when we will have the stars as our own."

"That's a big belief—the universe."

"Isn't this what we have been taught—that we are just part of a universal whole? Isn't this the word, the word as it has been told to us for thousands of years?"

"There have been a lot of words thrown about over the millennia. And millions died because of words. How do *you* know that these are the truth? That these are the truest words?"

"Belief, Uncle. That's what the Prophet has told us, and that's what we believe."

The circular logic of his faith was not unlike a thousand other religions. If I hadn't seen those fireflies myself, I would argue with the boy. But when it comes to faith and beliefs, often logic is the first casualty.

"Are you prepared to follow that man to ends of the universe?"

"Uncle, there is no end to the universe. Our journey will be never-ending."

"We humans know that there is an end. We have a beginning, a middle, and we will die. That is our lot in this life."

"Not according to the Prophet. With him, there is life never-ending."

"You said this never-ending line, twice. How can you be so sure?"

"Prophet Tassos has told us. It is the basic tenant of our faith."

"He's not the first to use this tenant; over the centuries there have been others."

"Yes, and they were correct, as far as their knowledge went. However, our belief is true. The Pernix Lumen are the proof. You have seen them; you must now believe."

"And why is that?" I asked—the liquor was doing its work.

"In a moment, they showed me the past and the future. We are all a singularity in the vast universe. Each of us is our own universe; we are each a point of singular thought and action . . ."

"That's enough, Marcus," Orion said from behind me. "I think the captain is having difficulty understanding our beliefs; he's baiting you. And is doing it at your expense."

"Yes, Prophet, I understand," Marcus said.

"No, go on," I said. This was becoming fun—the exuberance of youth and self-discovery aided by the weirdness of Captain Tassos Orion.

"Captain, we will continue this conversation some other time," Orion said. "Marcus is a novice in the order. He has much to learn. And I think you used liquor to ply the boy. That's not a good thing or a fair one either."

"We all employ defenses," I offered. "He is my charge and responsibility. I am concerned."

"Please, don't be concerned," Orion said. "He is part of a great undertaking, a revolution, and he has seen the Pernix. He is like a son to me; I care for him. He is humanity's future."

"And that future is what? And remember that he is my nephew and godson; there are responsibilities."

"The universe is his future," he said as he helped the boy to his feet.

They walked to the elevator and disappeared to their cabins. Beyond the glass of the control room was the vastness of the uncountable stars.

"And that was circular logic," Hank said as he turned toward me.

"Yes, my friend, it certainly was that."

21

It would all be downhill from here. I wasn't sure what the kid was babbling about—it was a mishmash of a thousand philosophies, beliefs, and creeds all rolled into one simple faith. My questions all fell into one simple one: To what end; where was Orion going with this? Me? I was heading to Earth with a paycheck tied to my ass.

I looked up from my station; Hank stood near his usual place near the entry.

"Problem?" I asked.

"No," Hank answered. "Captain, everything is nominal."

"Did Clive give that rock a name?"

"He did. He wants to call it *Ferrum*; it's the Latin word for—"

"Iron. I get it. It works. *Ferrum* it is."

"It does assay out high in the metal. Clive thought about calling it *spodium*."

"*Spodium?*"

"Latin for zinc."

"Doesn't have a ring to it, let's stick with *Ferrum*."

"Roger that. I'll let Clive and Garrett know."

"That's not the reason for the visit, is it?"

"No, Captain. I apologize, but I heard what you and Captain Orion were talking about."

"Everyone heard. Circular logic."

"Yes, I was with Captain Orion for twenty years. While not as pleasant, or pretty as Captain Lucia Maria Smythe-Rodgers, he was organized and treated his crew well. I respect him."

"Coming from you, that is a compliment," I said.

"Thank you," Hank continued. "He was always fair with his crew, and they seemed generally happy."

"What happened?"

"As I told you before, I don't know. The crew went into that thing and did not come out. I was sure they died. I was never asked during the hearing. So now, twenty-three years later, we see the crew. They are now sparks of energy; they have become Pernix Lumen, as Captain Orion calls them."

"I asked you not to call him captain."

"I'm sorry, as Mr. Orion calls them. I have no idea what they are. I do not have enough information."

"When you saved Orion, you said he called for help."

"Yes. Do you wish to see the images again?"

"No, that's not necessary. He called for help. If these Pernix are benign, why would he need your help?"

"I can't answer that. After we got back to the ship, he shut me down. What happened during that period, I have no memory."

"Could he have gone back?"

"Yes, it's possible, even logical that he would. However, I do not know if he did. When he reactivated me, he was in stress. His actions were illogical; I tried to get the ship back on course for Mars; it was the closest port. Then he shut me down again. It wasn't until the rescue that I was activated. I assume that's why I was not asked any questions; the assumption by the rescuers is that I knew nothing. You were there; you remember that."

"Yes, it was strange. Others were in charge. I followed orders."

"Like me."

"Yes, like you," I said, remembering that day. "Can you

speculate on what you think might have happened while you were deactivated?"

I watched Hank. If a noid could process data, I guessed that's what he would have looked like. A million logic tracks must have been zipping through his processors.

"The best conclusion is that Mr. Orion went back to the object. After his return, he wiped all the data from the computer, even the data for the donkeys. It is the absence of data that leaves me to speculate that he went back."

"To what purpose?"

"Even I can't speculate about that, Captain."

I took Marcus's glass; there were a couple of good swallows left. I finished his bourbon.

"Can you tell me about what Orion has been doing on Earth since his return?" I asked.

"After he was found negligent and fined, for almost ten years he traveled extensively throughout Europe. I have nothing specific about his journey. From news reports, he went to Lipari Island near Sicily, and people began to visit him on the island. In a published story five years after his arrival, he announced that these followers—his term, Captain—are to be called the Nostre Familia. At a news conference, he stood with six of these disciples and called them the Twelve. There were jokes about his math since there were only six. When he was pressed, he said that the other six would soon return to Nostre Familia."

"I assume that the six we saw inside the *Kratos* would be these others?"

"A speculation, Captain?"

"A deduction."

"A fair one. There are also reports of Mr. Orion—he was now calling himself Prophet Tassos—meeting with cardinals and bishops of the Catholic Church as well as visiting many of the newer monasteries built in Europe and Africa since the end of the war. There are lengthy articles about the growth of his monastery on Lipari Island and the increase in numbers of his Nostre Familia."

"How many?"

"The authorities report that he has over ten thousand members and affiliations with hundreds of churches and leaders."

"Interesting. Now, how could the leader of such a cult pick up and leave? That's strange."

"A cult? I understand your conclusion; they certainly act like one. However, his political and religious associations tend to support something more substantial."

"One man's cult is another's truth and belief. I get that."

"I wouldn't know. Human philosophy is often more irrational than I care to speculate about."

"Amen to that, brother."

* * *

Marcus spent his days working with Garrett on the magsled. Garrett hoped to enter the machine in the races at the Emerald City arena. These low-slung, almost slab-like, vehicles use magrepelers to push the machine a few inches off the iron plating of the track. Then with a high-temperature converter, they blast jets of steam out the rear giving thrust. It is all a strange mixture of space tech with directional nozzles, frictionless flying, and human balls. Once past inertia, these steam thrusters can push the sled-like vehicles to over two hundred kilometers an hour. On the face of it, it is crazy. No drag, no brakes, and only jets of steam to control direction. The moon's lower gravity made crashing only slightly more tolerable.

"Garrett is going to let me drive it when we get to the moon," Marcus said.

I lifted an eyebrow at Garrett. "I'll make sure that your mother is also a part of the decision," I said. "These things have been known to get wonky, spin out, crash. There's a reason there are airbags around the track and onboard the sled."

"I'm not worried, Garrett's one of the best," Marcus said.

"Is that what he's been telling you?" I asked, raising my other eyebrow.

"I've been driving these sleds for twenty years; you know that, Captain. He couldn't have a better teacher."

"Marcus, ask Mr. Borg to show you the scar where they inserted the titanium rod in his tibia. That might make you reconsider."

"Spoilsport," Garrett said.

"You have a titanium rod in your leg? How did they do that? Did it hurt?" Marcus asked as I went up the elevator to the command deck.

Clive was in his chair. Hank was standing behind him.

"Status?" I asked.

"Nominal," Hank said. "Systems all green; we have adequate hydrogen to complete the trip."

"Since we started the deceleration," Clive said, "I've been using the thrusters on the *Ferrum* to slow us—that way we don't use too much of our reserve. As Hank said, all nominal."

I scanned the central screen that displayed almost every aspect of the ship and the tow. My greatest concern is cable tension, especially on deceleration. The last thing you want is to have that chunk of rock to go sideways on you. Its mass is significantly more than the *Gypsy King*, and all the rules of physics still apply. So, caution is the better part of every move we make.

We'd passed through Mars's orbit a month ago. Right now, the planet was on the far side of the sun, something like four hundred and fifty million kilometers away. Earth was moving away from us; we would intercept in approximately two weeks. All we had to do was slow our speed while racing to catch a planet that was spiraling away from us. The whole operation, from beginning to end, is like a pile of clock gears, each spinning at separate speeds, all connected to the same hub, with us flying out in a loop that would fling us back to where we came from. I leave all the calculations to Garrett and Hank; that's why I'm the captain. Some say I look damn good in my uniform.

22

If one more drunk calls me a truck driver, I will kick his ass to Uranus. I can take a lot, I'm patient, and I know a few people who tolerate my company. But a drunk, in a suit, at a bar, connected to the hotel built into the *Washington* smelter holding stationary thirty-five-thousand kilometers above the old city of Washington, D.C., having the huevos to call me a truck driver? That was all it took; I did kick his ass to Uranus. That's also why they had me cooling off in what they officially called a holding cell in the security office. Sadly, they had not improved its appearance or food. Clive and Garrett were sitting on stools in the hallway, watching me. They were smiling—revenge smiles — probably copies of the ones I've used on them.

"Come on, guys, get me out of here. We have business to take care of." I rubbed my jaw where the drunk's one lucky punch managed to make it through my stellar defense.

"It's such a nice picture," Clive said. "I wish I had my camera."

"Here, use mine," a voice I knew but did not wish to hear or at least hear, here.

"You should see the other guy," I said to the CEO of Greater American Metals. This smelter, and through the magic of corporate ownership this jail cell, was owned by her company. One could extrapolate that she then owned my ass. I guess that's not so bad.

"Can you help spin the wheels of justice and get me out of here?" I pleaded.

"Begging's beneath you," Sarah Thomason said. "I hear from you once during the last six months, and then, when you get home, the first call is from Garrett here, about you needing bail."

"I hadn't paid them yet," I said. "By the way, anything you can do to help that bitunit transfer—I'd be much obliged."

She raised her PD, and I heard a click.

"Really?"

"Should I send the pic to you, boys? Might come in handy someday," Sarah said.

"No, it's firmly planted here in my memory—kind of like a solar flare of justice," Garrett said.

"Cute. Please, can you get me out of here?" I sounded pathetic, even to myself. And my head hurt to holy heaven.

"Just push open the door," Sarah said. "It's been unlocked for an hour. You are on your own recognizance; there will be a fine to be deducted from the payment. I don't know what I'm going to do with you."

I rubbed my head, thinking of a hundred things, many not for public discussion. "No reason to bring that up. I hurt too much."

An hour later, I was treating my head with a bag of ice and bourbon in Sarah's apartment.

"During the first walkover, they confirmed it's a nice rock," Sarah said. "The analysts sent me the preliminaries, and they are good, very good. They also found a brilliant, flawless diamond that might weigh in at three thousand carets; it's the size of a rugby ball. I'll leave that to the gem guys. I'm more interested in the rare earths—good job."

"Your wishes are my commands," I said.

"Clive and Garrett hinted at some trouble, but you and the crew look good. Your nephew left the *Gypsy* with that Prophet Tassos. How the hell did he get onboard?"

"If you would mercifully renew my medicine, I'll tell you every shocking detail. Most of it, I still don't believe."

She did, and I did.

"That will turn the mitered heads of a lot of high priests and bishops on their pointy noggins," Sarah said.

"That's just the half of it," I answered; the medicine was working. "Orion is pushing for a revolution or at least a rebellion. I saw it in his eyes. When he talked, it was more like the righteous true believer looking to change everything. That will force some to stand against him and his people."

"The story is, he has ten thousand followers?"

"Yes, and if he gets to Earth, that number will increase. The man is charismatic, and I think that he's enlisted my sister into his plans. Marcus, I'm not sure. But he has seen the lights, so to speak, and it changed him. All I can see is trouble, big-time trouble."

Sarah's PD pinged, and she scrolled down through the screen. "You asked about Orion and his travels—here's what I've found. He left *Washington* twelve hours after you docked. His itinerary had him going to the moon first, Prasinus. He's booked at the rectory. He has a two-day layover, then is scheduled on the Vatican transport to Earth—that's next Monday, six days from now."

"He thumbed a ride on the Vatican's transport? He does have pull. Marcus?"

"His schedule jives with Orion's—it looks like they are traveling together. They have reservations on the Eurounion's slide on Sicily, Friday—a week from now."

"He said his followers are on Lipari Island. It's somewhere near Sicily."

"About thirty kilometers north of Sicily, the *Siciliano* daisy is the Eurounion's fourth. I've used it a couple of times; it's the closest to Rome. Makes sense, I guess."

I mulled over what she said. "I figure he's going to assemble his followers and then move on Rome. No clue why."

"You said revolution. Is this a possibility?" Sarah asked.

"Revolution, rebellion, an insurrection—I don't know. He blathered on and on about the universe and the stars, being one with the Creators. Stuff a prophet would spout. To what end? And those lightning bugs are two hundred million miles away—where is he going with all this? If my sister is involved, that means that some of the clergy of the Church are involved. That means he has access to money. Why did he stow away on my ship? He could have taken any of the Vatican's ships. And he didn't seem to be in a hurry; now he's bouncing between the moon and Earth. He could have taken the *Washington* shuttle to the daisy, slid down from there. I don't get it."

My PD buzzed. It was Borg.

"Is the *Gypsy King* ready?"

"Yes, Captain. The hydro tanks are filled; nice system here, only took six hours. And Clive has laid in a course to Marina 3. We still on schedule?"

"Yes, I'll meet you at twenty-three hundred," I said. "Orion and Marcus took off for the moon and the EC just after we arrived. I want to talk to that man."

"I'm racing on Saturday; they found a slot for me," Garrett added. "Will you need Clive or me for anything?"

"No, don't think so. I'll try and make your race. See you tonight." I clicked off.

"I thought you were staying a few days?" Sarah said. I heard the disappointment.

"I need to get the *Gypsy* to Marina 3; their fees are a lot less than here. And I also need to talk to my sister and find out what she knows about all this firefly stuff."

"I can make some allowances for the fees. You could stay here."

"Bribery? What will your board say?"

"After the last rock you dropped—they will agree to anything I ask."

* * *

My crew and I took the shuttle down to the Emerald City; Garrett's sled in the cargo bay. It would be transferred to the racetrack after we cleared customs. Garrett would stay with his machine, something about last-minute adjustments due to air pressure. He also wanted to walk the track to get a firsthand view of the conditions. Clive said something about a girl; I put my hands up and told him to be careful.

It took all my willpower, such as it is, to walk away from Sarah. Everything about the *Washington* smelter is first class, from the commissary to the kitchens and bars, to its CEO. Complications, there are always complications. If I had my druthers, I'd get a great condo on the moon, and have someone else do the dragging. However, Sarah was one of the few and only things that dragged my sorry ass back to Earth.

What did concern me was that Annie was still in Prasinus. She said she was going to Mars, but she hadn't left. During the drag, we talked a few times. Marcus called his mother often. She said that she did go back to Earth for three months, then returned to the moon. It must have been damn important—the slide down the daisy, any daisy, was tough on the body. It's the speed under gravity thing; you didn't want to put your body through it too many times. When I pressed her about why she went, she said it had to do with the new colony on Mars. I can always tell when she is telling a fib; her left eyebrow twitches.

My first job after finding Annie was to find Marcus; I hoped they were together. Tassos Orion—that's a man who should not be going back to Earth, not now, maybe never. I found Annie at the Convent for the Revealment. I sat in the pew behind her as she prayed. A dozen other people in religious vestments, civilian clothes, and suits sat in the chapel. She was the only nun in a habit. Angelic voices filled the sanctuary.

The order had not spared the bucks on the interior of the chapel. Polished stone arched upward to colored windows that allowed the sunlight to pierce the space in crisp bands of light. The altar used for Mass was an expensive slab of Carrera marble transported up from Italy; a small village in the Apennines could have eaten for a month on what it cost to ship that here. Golden fixtures, sconces, and iconography hung on the walls. The Stations of the Cross were pieces of art from sometime in the eighteenth century. The pews were slabs of polished black basalt excavated from a mountain range to the south of Prasinus. It was quite a place.

A choir rehearsed; their chants, Gregorian I think, filled the nave with voices only heard in some of the most famous chapels and churches on Earth. I waited patiently for Annie to finish her prayers.

She stood, turned, and saw me. I was shocked by her smile. I was expecting more of a "What the hell are you doing here?" look.

"Aren't they divine?" she said as she pointed to the choir. "They are from a village in South Africa. My order invited them to sing at the celebration next month. They are here for six weeks before they slide home."

She said celebration like I knew what she was talking about; my expression must have given me away.

"The Pope's consiglieri is coming in two weeks; he is the Vatican's emissary," Annie said. "He is involved in the planning and funding for the colony on Mars. There is a festival planned to celebrate Pope Julius's one-hundred-and-twentieth birthday. These voices will fill the cathedral—it will be wonderful."

My tin ear agreed, they did sound beautiful.

We walked out of the chapel and into the wide corridor that extended past city hall and the piazza fronting the cathedral. We didn't talk. She knew why I was there. It had been that way since we were kids. After our folks died, I raised her—that is, if you could raise someone with an IQ of 183. Often it was an intellectual standoff. For the past thirty years, I was the one standing off in the corner, amazed by what she accomplished. When I bought the *Gypsy King*, she was the first onboard. I swear she secretly sprinkled holy water on the floorplates. She wanted to rename the ship the *Gypsy Queen*; I told her no. It's an old aphorism that you never, ever rename a ship—bad luck and all. She was disappointed. That's also why I'm sure there's a statue of some saint hidden behind some panel somewhere and the holy water thing. If you hadn't guessed it, I'm what you call an agnostic. Organized religion and I—we go down separate streets. But we are in the same town. And after what I saw three months ago, it either reaffirms my agnosticism or blows it the hell out of the water. And yes, the singing was beautiful.

"Do you know where Marcus is?" I asked.

"He is at the rectory with the Prophet," she answered.

"Stop calling him that. It gives me the willies when you say it. The man is a certifiable crackpot, and Marcus's reverence for the man is not healthy. I did what you asked. Why did you make sure that Orion also got onboard?"

She turned away, trying to deflect my accusation.

"Damn it, Annie, I know you were behind the permits and the passes that got that man on the moon. He is big-time persona non grata, yet there he was, and on my ship. If you wanted that man at the alien ship, you should have sent him on the Pope's bus, and left me out of it."

"That would have been impossible. What are you talking about?"

"Nonetheless, Pope Julius could have waved his fingers and, voilà, a miracle: Orion has a ticket—and left me out of it. Now, your son is up to his brain cells in this. Did he tell you that? Did he tell you that those fireflies just buzzed in and out his head like there was nothing there?"

The shock on her face stunned me. Marcus and Orion had not told her what happened. I'd assumed that she knew everything.

"What are you talking about?" Annie asked. "Fireflies?"

"Well, Sister, it seems that your Prophet Tassos has been communing with aliens more than a billion years old. He calls them the creators; these specks of energy are our ancestors. There are millions of them, and they want us to join them."

She turned white, almost matching her habit. She grasped the wooden cross on her breast and squeezed it; her knuckles turned even whiter. She looked past the plaza and toward the cathedral; her eyes slowly rose to the glass that wrapped the city of Prasinus.

"I need a drink," she finally said.

"I know a place."

23

We talked for more than an hour; her questions about the Pernix Lumen were probing, perceptive, and for the most part, negative. She knew more about what was going on than what she admitted. It was the details that freaked her out. I knew that, and she knew that I knew. Families are like that . . .

"And the Pope knew this?" I asked.

"His Eminence knows what he knows," Sister Annie answered as she gazed up to the high glass canopy that stretched overhead. "I don't know the full extent of what he knows or has been told."

"An evasive answer."

"Like the Pope, I only know what I know."

"Annie, please. That's a child's answer."

"God will lead us."

"I hate repeating myself; I know you are not naïve. Your son is wrapped up in this; I've seen these lights, these beings. On the surface they seem benign; beneath is something else, I know it. Orion has tapped into this—I'm not sure who is using whom. If what he says is true, these Pernix have waited millions of years to see what they have created. Unlike us—their little science experiment—they will be here long after we are gone."

"Buster, I'm not sure what his Eminence will do with this knowledge. I fear for the Church."

"Did Orion come to you and the Church to assist him, to find out more about these beings? Or did he come to threaten you?"

"The Church has been threatened many, many times over the millennia," Annie said seriously. "The hordes from the east, Islam, Luther, the Reformation, agnosticism, even atheism, and two hundred years ago the rise of the Africans. Each had their charismatic leader, a belief in themselves, and their version of the promise of heaven. Humans are always looking for something. These zealots, like the Nostre Familia, offer something beyond the Church. We fight back. Each time we reformed and changed. Sometimes it succeeded; other times, it failed. We are still here."

"So, this is one of those moments?" I asked.

"His Eminence believes it is, and potentially the most serious."

"Why does he believe that?"

"Because man has not caused this—it came from the outside, the universe."

"Some might say from God himself."

"Or herself," she said, chiding me.

"Please, that's an argument with no answer. These fireflies are powerful; I've seen that."

"Truth is powerful as well."

"Your truths will have problems with this power," I said.

"There is an old saying, 'Keep your friends close, and your enemies closer.'"

"Another says, 'The enemy of my enemy is my friend.'"

"Those are little morality plays; it's all nonsense, you know that," Annie said. "The Church, for a thousand years, has known that it's all about power."

"And money."

"Who was it that saved our world two hundred years ago? Who was there to rebuild our world after it nearly annihilated itself? Who was there to turn this world back to truth and morality, reconstruct the governments, and bring stability? It was the Catholic Church, not religion, but the Church. And it was done from right here, in this building." She pointed out the door of the tavern to the cathedral.

"To its own ends, that's been shown," I added. "The Church's power and its reach are evident and awe-inspiring. There has never been a time when its wealth and power reaches as far as it does. Your mission to Mars is proof of that. Earth is turning into the heaven that was foretold. The planet is recovering from thousands of years of avarice and pillage, all due to humanity's need to expand, to invent, to grow."

"And with the Church's benign leadership."

"And bank accounts," I added. "Those EU armies, under the leadership of Archbishop Metz, that landed in Africa and annihilated the Islamic armies, that was hardly benign."

"We did not play a part in that."

"Of course not. Bankers never get their hands dirty."

She turned and glared at me. "Those are unfounded rumors."

"Most rumors come with a modicum of truth. It's the interpretation of the execution that matters to history. Metz's generals proved that on all accounts."

"That was more than two hundred years ago. What do you want us to do? Stand back and wait, to be patient, to see the future forced on us? Allow the darkness to grow?"

"Where is Marcus? You said he was here with Orion; I don't believe it," I said, changing the conversation. Ours was an argument that would have no end, at least right now.

"He has gone to Lipari Island with Prophet Tassos to be with that man's followers and disciples."

"And you let him go?"

"I was in transit. I learned about his travels after he arrived in Sicily. They are being watched."

"Marcus or Orion?"

"All of them."

"The Church has always had its spies," I said.

"One of the reasons we have survived for twenty-five centuries. It's that enemies' closer maxim."

"I suppose that I'm one of those spies—can't say that the pay is all that good. Are you my watcher?"

"Your reward is in heaven."

"Hard to cash the checks from that bank."

"Don't blaspheme. Buster, bring Marcus back to me."

* * *

To say I was pissed is an understatement. I left Annie in front of the cathedral and returned to my hotel room. It was what she didn't say that upset me more than what she admitted to. I couldn't figure out why she lied to me. I was a truck driver; I knew that now. I'd been tricked into taking Orion back to that ship, to the Pernix Lumen. To be the Church's eyes and ears to all that he did, and I reported it dutifully to Annie. And I'd done that. I felt like a two-bitunit whore in the east corridor.

For the next few hours, I walked the hallway outside my room, thinking about what was going on. That thing drifting in Sector Seventy-three—filled with an innumerable number of sentient beings slowly revolving around the sun—scared the hell out of me. Orion said they had been there for half a billion years, waiting—waiting for this confrontation? The never-ending squabbles that man engaged in: the philosophies, the armies, the murders, the assassinations, the many nations that rose and fell. This moment felt different, as a student of history. I knew this was different; I knew it in my gut. Had these twinklers been playing in our human sandbox for the last two hundred and fifty thousand years?

I called Garrett and Clive, set up a dinner for us later that night. I wasn't sure what they could do to help, but they had been there. Garrett said that he was racing in the morning. I told him I would be there. Then I called Sarah.

"Where are you?" I asked and waited.

"I'm still on *Washington*," she finally answered. Sometimes the time delay was infuriating.

"I'm going to Earth to find Marcus," I said.

"You haven't been on Earth in years; the gravity will kill you."

"I have to get him away from that fanatic. There is no way I'm going to let that fool destroy my godson."

"That's noble, but within days you could drop dead from a heart attack."

"I can take it. He's on that island that Orion is using as his base. He's cooking something up, and I'm going to save Marcus from his lunatic. I'm coming to *Washington* on tomorrow night's shuttle, then transfer to the *Siciliano* daisy. From then on, I'll make it up as I go."

"That's not what I'd call a plan," she said.

"That's the best I can do."

"There's a Great America ship docking at Marina 3 tomorrow; I'll make arrangements for you to use it. That will cut two days out of your trip. I'll meet you here. I've got something that will make your life on Earth easier—and I'm going with you."

"I can't ask that."

"I'm not asking. I like that kid, and I don't like Orion. It's that simple. We'll go Earth-side and rescue the kid. Do you need any help? I have a dozen well-trained men who would be extremely—"

"No, just us. Showing up with some of your people would send up a flare. I'm guessing that Orion has his people all over Sicily. We'll be spotted the moment we land. You and I will go in as tourists, that will be our cover."

"So, you do have a plan," she said.

"As good a plan as I've ever had."

24

Dinner that night was the first time that my crew and I had
had a chance to get together since we'd dropped the rock
and split from the *Gypsy King*. I told them that I'd transferred
the bitunits to their accounts; Clive said he already had seen
the number. He was pleased. Garrett smiled and said thanks.

"How's Marcus?" Garrett said. "I like that kid. He's grown
into quite a man, even if he follows that crackpot. But a year in
space will do that; you either become a man or become dead."

I told them everything I'd learned; they were shocked.
Clive said he was going with me. I told them both no. They
were disappointed.

"Earth will be worse on you guys than me. This must be
low key. If I have to, I'll snatch Marcus. After I get him out of
there, the authorities will deal with Orion. What they do with
this prophet, I don't care."

"I think we made a mistake with that fool," Clive said.
"We should have left him with his Pernix Lumen. Let him
become one of their little lights, buzzing around for eternity.
It's an image I can live with."

"Who was to know?" I answered.

"Cap, we make a living making snap decisions—this was
one of them," Garrett added as he finished his wine. "That
man is trouble."

"Hindsight is always twenty-twenty."

I waved to the bot to bring me the bill.

"I'm racing in the morning. Second flight."

"I'll be there; someone needs to be there when they cart your carcass to the hospital."

"I never crash," Garrett said. "And the sled's good, damn good. You'll see."

We shook hands, and I watched the two men, who I'd grown to call brothers, walk away, arms wrapped on each other's shoulders. I hadn't mentioned—in case I did not return from Earth—that I'd left them the *Gypsy King*. I knew she would be good hands. They loved the life of dragging, and at their ages, they had a good number of drags left between them. My time in deep space was over—family is thicker than water.

* * *

It's been five years since I saw my last sled race at the Colosseum, a ponderous name for the soccer-sized track and dome located on the west side of Emerald City. It was the venue for big events, speeches, and athletic events. Wrapping the main parade ground and soccer field was the mag track. It banked sharply at each end. On the moon, sliders race for ten laps, the usual duration due to the sled's water supply. The races are a series of flights, five sleds to a flight, then a final race of the flight winners. For thousands of years, after chariots became race cars, dirt tracks became asphalt, horses became horsepower, the big winners were always the gamblers. The largest sportsbook on the moon runs the Colosseum; anything humans do is worth a bet.

Here they race over an iron track; the field generators built into the sled keep it a few inches off the deck. The onboard thermal electric cooker produces high-pressurized steam, which is directed through nozzles. The nozzles control the direction and speed of the sled. Sure, we could use wheeled sleds, but why be conventional. On the moon, with its lower gravity, these heavy sleds fly across the deck. There's no friction to manage the direction, just the jets. The sleds, using power supplied by a long arm that drags the ceiling above the track, are slow to start and almost impossible to stop. The driver sits atop the six-meter-long sled, the vertical power arm directly behind him, while a thin strip of titanium drags the deck, completing the circuit—the jets fire in a dozen different directions.

The first flight went well, three finished. The other two, on the third lap, collided and slid up and off the course, losing power instantly, before crashing back into the airbags. Both drivers limped away.

Garrett walked over to me. "Thanks for coming, Captain. Need all the moral support I can get."

"Morality has nothing to do with this," I said. "I want you to kick their asses. The *Devil's Own* is a good sled, none better. Where's Clive?"

"He's in the pit area, making a few minor adjustments."

I looked toward the area filled with sleds, techs, and drivers. I waved at Clive; he waved back.

"Make them eat steam, Garrett."

"Will do, Captain."

The support teams pushed their sleds onto the track; their power arms deployed; the whining of the generators filled the air. A tether held each slider in its place as it ramped up the force of its accelerator nozzle; it's like the gates in horse racing. Here, as the lights count down, the driver pumps as much push through the rear nozzle until the track releases the tether. Freed, it instantly goes screaming down the track.

Garrett grabbed the lead through the first bank; the crowd felt the sudden increase in humidity as steam billowed out the rear of the sleds. Above, massive video screens displayed the race; onboard sled cameras supplemented the overhead views. Two laps into the race, Garrett kept the lead. Rounding the far end of the track and heading into the straightaway, the sled directly behind him attempted to pass. When the attacker's forward starboard orifice failed to balance out the pressure from the port, he began to spin and, in a split second, spun up and out of the track, clipping the top rail. The rebound off the retaining rail forced it into two of the trailing sleds. Did I mention that the sleds moved with no friction due to the mag-lev? The racetrack instantly cut the power to the two rogue sleds. Losing their repellant fields, all three dropped to the steel deck in a display of sparks and the unholy shrieking of metal on metal. Garrett flew by, his fist in the air.

Six laps later, Garrett slowed to a stop in front of the viewing stand. Only two sleds finished his flight; second place was three seconds behind.

I wandered out into the pits, avoiding the fistfight between the slider who'd been knocked out of the race by the crash and the slider whose sled failed the turn. Such is the life of a sled driver. Win, lose, or draw, you still might get punched in the face.

"Great race, Garrett," I said to my number one. "You're in the final?"

"I qualified and made a few bucks in my heat. Seven to one, not bad," Garrett said. "Unfortunately, the thermal couple and the cooker cracked during the last lap. I'm done for today. It was good to see the modifications I made worked. Even the small secondary nozzles at the port and starboard quarters performed well. They were Marcus's idea."

Clive wiped a tool on a rag and looked past me. "Marcus, any word?"

"No, he's dropped to Earth with Orion. Sarah is chasing down permits and passes."

"Captain, don't lose that woman," Clive said. "She's good for you."

"Ah, Clive Jones, lead mechanic and matchmaker?"

"Garrett and I are here to watch your back. Be safe. If you need anything, call us."

"I will. I'm shipping out tonight to *Washington*; then we'll see what happens."

* * *

What I hadn't counted on as I checked in after shuttling up to the *American Zephyr* was Hank waiting for me in the lounge.

"Why are you here?" I said to the noid. "Who's taking care of the *Gypsy*?"

"Captain, I received a com from Ms. Thomason. She asked me to join you on this ship. I came over an hour ago. She explained that you need my assistance, for what she did not say. She also said you would explain it all to me. Captain, I assume that you need help."

"A supposition?"

"An informed decision. Besides, I like her. You two should get married—you always come back to her after all our coming and going. I see it. So, am I here to be your best android?"

"First Clive and then you. Your humor escapes me."

"I was not trying to be humorous. What big adventure are we embarking on? Dragging chunks of rock has become boring after almost two hundred years."

"Noids can't get bored."

"Captain, I've been bored for half a century."

"Damn, you are impossible."

"I do my best."

During our thirty-six-hour fall to Earth, I explained to Hank everything that I learned and speculated on the rest. His knowledge was helpful. His data bank included information about Lipari Island and its thousands of years of history. We discussed tactics and scenarios. What he didn't know he found on the ship's database or Earth-based libraries. If required, he communicated with sources at the Vatican and other archives. By the time we docked at *Washington*, the noid and I had formulated a scheme. But schemes are subject to the vagaries of the usual things that impact a plan, mostly the actions and reactions of the enemy. Orion wasn't a lump of stellar rock to be pushed around; this was a man backed by a billion years of something, something I didn't understand.

Sarah met us in a private vestibule off the main corridor of the smelter's primary circulation system. Hundreds of people filled the passageway; many were heading to ships like the *American Zephyr*. There were departure signs for the other smelters in Earth orbit, some for the moon, and even one for Mars. Sarah's company was the largest in the known universe.

"Records show that Orion and Marcus met four days ago, with two other people at the space docks at the *Siciliano* daisy," Sarah said. "They were a man and a woman. They slid to Earth the same day they arrived, then disappeared. I found no additional contacts on Sicily."

"My guess, they had excellent off-the-record connections and the ability to cover their tracks," I offered. "They went to Lipari; I'd bet on that."

"And how are you, Hank? It has been a long time," Sarah said.

"I am pleased to see you again, Ms. Thomason," Hank said. "Thank you for inviting me on this adventure."

"Adventure? What did you tell him?" Sarah said with a smile as she placed her hand on mine.

"He knows everything. He was there twenty-three years ago and saved Orion. He has skin in the game."

"I have no skin," Hank answered.

"He's also a little too literal at times."

"That's one of the reasons I asked him to meet you," Sarah said. "Emotions will run deep; his eyes and ears will be helpful. I've something to show you."

We walked through the public rooms of a wing that extended out into space from the side of the primary docking facility. The sign on the door read COMPANY OFFICES. An armed guard stood to one side. When Sarah approached, the guard went to attention and saluted. The door slid open.

The interior reminded me of the Great American offices on the moon. Through glass walls, I saw personnel dutifully at work. It had been years since I'd walked these corridors, but nothing had changed. Sarah waved us into her office.

"I need a drink," she said. "Would you pour me a bourbon and one for yourself?"

I did as ordered—pure Kentucky nirvana. Hank took a spot near the door and watched.

"We've been working on those," she said and pointed to a pair of black metal legs standing to one side of her desk. "They will make your time on Earth more manageable."

I looked at the contraptions and immediately knew what they were. "I'm not wearing those. They are too heavy, and besides, I'll be fine on my own two legs."

"These are better," Sarah said as she picked up one of the braces. "They weigh almost nothing, spun carbon, servomotors at the joints, and they are linked directly to your brain through pads pasted behind your ears. There is an additional back unit that plugs into the top of the legs—that will relieve the stress on your spine. Tests have been excellent. And an advantage over Hank—he will have a tough time keeping up with you."

"Great, half-man, half-robot," I said, still not sure about the need for all this hardware.

"Buster, you know what will happen when we hit Earth's gravity. These will make it easier."

"Do they come with ray guns and ticklers for defense?"

"Cute, no. Good idea, but no. They are to support your weight and ease the stress."

"Thanks, I think. Are you going to wear them?"

"And mess with these legs? Not a chance. Besides, I go to Earth often; I'm conditioned."

We took another of Great American's shuttles to the docks that encircled the blossoming head of the spiral shaft of the

Siciliano daisy. It was easy to follow the four-hundred-kilometer stem as it curved Earthward to the triangular-shaped island that floated in the Mediterranean Sea visible off the toe of the boot of Italy. Dozens of shuttles were moored to the daisy's docks. Others were leaving, and some waited for an open berth. Two bulk carriers from the smelters were docked. They would transfer their cargos into pods that would use the stem's elevators to spiral down to the base.

These daisies saved Earth from itself. All pollution was gone; all the hard rock mining on Earth had ended. Electricity, now generated in space, was the source of unlimited and pollution-free power; the stems were their conduits. During the last hundred years, food production increased exponentially; a quarter of the food grown on Earth was now sent up the stems to space and distributed throughout the interplanetary colonies. In time, these colonies would expand their facilities, but Kentucky bourbon needed to be distilled on Earth, and so did corn, and soybeans, and what man craved most, meat. Did I mention that man was a creature of habit and a slave to his genes and stomach?

I slapped the braces on before we left the smelter. Hank thought it was funny that I was joining his clan. I raised an eyebrow over that supposition.

"You may have to join my guild, Captain," Hank said. "Right now, you are a few servomotors short of a full robot. If we replaced your brain with a more efficient data processor, I think I can get you a union card."

Sarah snickered. "You wouldn't replace everything, would you? Some parts are more than adequate."

"That's enough from the two of you; these will do just fine. Nothing more."

"It's a shame, that's all I can say," Hank said as he picked up our bags.

The slide, as it's called, can totally wreck you if you are not prepared. The ride up from Earth is like a long elevator ride. There are pressure changes, some disorientation, and a welcomed gravity-free arrival. Down-slide was something else. You are injected with something that eases the stress on your heart and circulation system, and you lie back in a lounge chair and watch the countdown clock at the end of the pod. At zero, your stomach instantly arrives somewhere near your throat and continues to stay there for the entire drop. The pod spirals downward among the fibrous shafts that twist upward from the stem's base secured more than a thousand meters deep into the hard rock of Earth. To go up, the pod must overcome the pull of Earth's gravity. The slide Earthward uses gravity and friction. One mistake and that controlled free fall will fuse you and the pod into that massive foundation. At ten thousand meters, the pod slows to two hundred kilometers an hour, and you begin to try and swallow your stomach. Some get a kick out it. The whole thing just sucks; even my braces didn't help.

We recovered in a nice hotel; the price included in the ticket. Hank didn't bat an eyebrow if he had them. After an hour of Earth gravity, I thanked Sarah for the braces. Another reason I like her . . . a lot.

25

You touch the back of your hand. Is it real? Are you Tassos Orion? Are you truly the man you believe you are? For twenty-three years, you have played the part. Or has the part played you? With each year, your world grew, and more of the followers joined you, they believe in you. Now you must believe in yourself—hard to do when you aren't exactly sure who you are. Do you believe in yourself? Are there doubts?

Space is infinite. That's like saying the sun is hot—you know that. It's so vast that it would take a thought an eternity to cross from one edge to the other. And a thought, your thought, can travel the breadth of the universe in zero time.

You try and understand; you try to think of the millions of years that came before and the millions that will follow. You are a bump in the road of time, barely a blip in the readout of the passage of time.

Your followers are here; they wait for your words, words of hope, of redemption, of love, and of eternity. You will promise eternity; you can deliver eternity. Humans want to live forever, you want to live forever, and it is faith—faith in you, Tassos—that they want.

It is a trick, a ploy to stop you. You know something will happen, something the Pernix will allow. Do you need permission? And if so, from whom?

* * *

I've breathed canned and recycled air for the past twenty years;

the atmosphere of Sicily literally took my breath away—literally. When we walked outside into the sunlight, I fainted. Thanks to the braces, I remained standing. Hank caught me as I began to fall on my face.

"Have I died and gone to heaven?" I asked, looking up into Sarah's eyes.

"I told you, be careful," she said as she helped me up.

The next few days were going to be a challenge in more ways than trying to find Marcus. The last time I was on Earth, it was dealing with the blowback and debris of what Captain Tassos Orion left in his interplanetary wake. The grand jury questioned me, or specifically the attorney for the ISC, about what I saw and did during the recovery of Orion and the *Gypsy King*. We believed it was a recovery, not a rescue. The beacon that signaled the trouble with the *Gypsy King* continued to flash for the two months it took us to trek the hundred million miles to the ship. We used a high-speed government liner; she was about half the size of the *Gypsy*. During transit, we were sure all we would find was a holed ship, completely decompressed, and a freeze-dried crew. What we found was stranger than that: one man, semi-catatonic, emaciated, and a switched-off android. Four of us stayed onboard the *Gypsy* to get her to the moon.

The ISC ship took Orion onboard and began the recuperation process for the man. We followed. It was six months later that I found myself on Earth at the ISC headquarters, answering questions about Orion's actions I knew nothing about. You know how much they pay a juror on a court case? They pay a witness even less. However, I did see Annie. She had completed her novitiate at the Revealment convent outside Rome—she was full of her calling then—she radiated God and the Church. I was pleased for her. I went back to the moon, signed on for a crew headed to Sector Two-thirty-eight, and made good coin. Over the next two years, I packed a few more short but profitable trips under my belt. By then, I'd completely forgotten Tassos Orion, but I never forgot the *Gypsy King*. It was after my last trip, after dropping our rock at *Washington,* when I made my decision. I stood at the window of the command level of my ship and watched as the *Gypsy King* drifted outside the glass. Right then, I took the biggest chance of my life; I wanted that ship. Six months later, with help from my new girlfriend, Sarah Thomason, I stood on the command deck of the *Gypsy King* as its captain. Hank was sitting in the control seat, and Garrett Borg was at the communications board. Clive would join us two drags later. Life was perfect in my little portion of the universe then. Right now, standing on the rocky ground of Sicily, I hurt in places I didn't think existed.

"Marcus will have to wait until you get your Earth legs under you," Sarah said. "There's a small hotel overlooking the Mediterranean Sea an hour from here. I've booked us rooms. Two days from now, we'll find that son of a bitch and get your godson back."

I wanted to argue, but all I could do was nod my head— even that hurt. The doctor knows best.

Two days later, and with a bright red sunburn on my shoulders to show how sensitive I'd become to sunlight, Sarah and Hank led the way to a sleek heli-cruiser. **GREAT AMERICAN METALS** was painted on the door. Having Sarah and her deep pockets as a partner has its advantages. Hank took the controls, and we lifted off for the short hop to Lipari Island.

"My sources tell me that when Prophet Tassos landed on the island a week ago, the celebrations went on for days," Sarah said. "Reports also say that Marcus was with him. That's where we will start."

"How many of his followers are there?" I asked.

"They believe more than five thousand gathered to meet him. He made a great show. His followers were ecstatic. He gave a long and rambling speech about the universe, their place in the future of humankind, and the great revelation to come. I have a copy of the speech if you want to read it."

"Later," I said. "Right now, we need to find Marcus."

"We will need these." She pointed to a bundle of brown robes. "The faithful wear these; they will help us blend in and move about more easily. I have also tasked two of our com-drones to monitor us and our progress. Hank can follow on his screens and relay info to us as needed."

"Com-drones? I thought they were old tech, unnecessary."

"Fairly benign and are lost in the electronic clutter. Safer than satellites, at least for now."

"Hank, after you drop us, can you find a place to stash this ship and wait?" I asked.

"Captain, there is a level spot on a small, uninhabited island just off the coast. I'll wait there. I can be wherever you need me in less than fifteen minutes."

"Excellent," I said. "We will both be wearing com-links; keep track of us. When we call, I'll tell you where to pick us up. If there's a problem, find us. It's your decision."

"Roger that."

It was night. We flew low and silently over the ancient castle and the grounds that surrounded the old church. Infrared sensors showed a few people were about; I assume most had turned in for the night. In a clearing, north of the town's center, Hank lowered the cruiser to a rocky shelf, and we quickly disembarked. Just as Sarah and I cleared the ship, I felt another wave of vertigo wash over me. Sarah grabbed my shoulder and steadied me.

"I knew it was too soon," she said.

"I'm all right. Give me a minute." I breathed in a lung-full of the salty air—damn, it tasted good. As we walked away from the ship, Hank silently took the ship skyward. In seconds, only Sarah and I stood on the narrow plateau above the village. The lights from the city filled the darkness below; we followed the narrow trail toward them. After a few hundred meters, the tents of the Prophet's followers began to appear. Small camp-fires burned, and the rich smell of wood smoke tickled my nose. I had a flash of such a catechism scene from two and a half thousand years ago where followers of Jesus would camp and wait for their prophet. The voices from around the fires were soft and muted; there were no drunken yells or even raucous laughter. The campground was comforting, warm, and inviting.

A woman stood when she saw us. "Come and join us, brothers; I've made some lamb stew," she said. "There's plenty; I don't want to waste it. Come."

The smells were intoxicating.

"Certainly, sister," Sarah said and took my arm.

"Are you sure?" I whispered.

"We need information, and besides, I'm hungry."

We walked arm in arm to the campfire. Around the flickering light, a group of men and women sat on the ground; their eyes turned to us. They smiled.

"Here, brothers, there's room," one of the men said, sliding over. "Amanda, do you have extra bowls?"

We sat. Stoneware bowls and spoons were handed to us; a ladle poured stew into each.

"Where are you from?" a woman with a sweet voice asked.

"We have just arrived," I said. "We came over on the ferry from Sicily; we couldn't miss this."

"Isn't it wonderful?" another woman said. "I came from Great America. We are from almost everywhere. It's a blessing to see the Prophet again. We are all full of hope now for the future; he has shown us the light. I am sorry you missed his message."

"And so are we," Sarah said. "I am Sarah; this is Buster. We are from the moon. We briefly saw the Prophet before he left for the—"

"You saw him before he went to the Pernix to gather the six?" a man asked.

"Yes," I said.

"That was a wonder I would have loved to have seen. But

he is with us now."

"What did the Prophet say?" Sarah asked.

"He started by thanking us for welcoming him home," the man began to say.

"John, it was more than that," the woman sitting next to him interrupted. "He began by welcoming us to the new universe, the one where we will lead the way for the earth's people to the stars and to the future. He talked of love and respect and all the wonders that lay before us. Then the six appeared and circled his head; their lights shown in all our eyes."

"The six, they are here?" I asked incredulously.

"Yes, Buster," John said. He raised his hands above his head, opened them, and the six illuminations rose and encircled his head. A joyous wonder, I'll tell you that.

I placed my hand on Sarah's leg. She was shaking.

"He brought the six here . . . to the island?" I asked again.

"As he prophesized before he left. He said he would return with the first six of his disciples, and they would be joined to all of us. When the time is right, of course."

"I wish it is soon," a woman across the campfire said. "My heart is bursting."

"Mine, too," said another.

"Would you care for more stew, Sarah?" Amanda asked.

"Yes, please," she answered. "It is delicious."

"My mother's recipe," Amada said. "I'm from hills above Ephesus; John and I came as soon as we heard that the Prophet was returning. Our children are with my mother."

"You left your children?"

"We will gather them up when things have settled down. The Prophet will tell us when it is safe. He asked that we leave our children with our families."

The group sat silently; the smoke rose in a twisting column to the dark sky. Above, a million stars blanketed the sky.

"Did the Prophet bring a young man with him?" I asked. "I saw him on the moon with a boy, a teenager, I think?"

"Marcus?" another woman suggested. "Yes, Marcus was with him. I saw the two of them in Rome before the Prophet went to gather the six. A fine young man. He was introduced as the Prophet's son, not his real son, but he called him his son. He told us that when we believe like Marcus, the universe will be ours."

I squeezed Sarah's leg; the shaking had stopped.

"You are from space? You saw the Prophet and Marcus on the moon?" John asked. "I've never been in space—what is it like?"

"Very different than here on Earth," Sarah said. "It is a wonder."

"Amen to that," John answered.

"Did the Prophet tell us what he expects from us?" I asked.

The followers all looked at each other like they shared a secret. One reached out, and those nearest to him placed their hands on his.

"We all leave on boats the day after tomorrow and go to Rome," Amanda said. "There, we will join thousands of other followers and demand that the Pope take the Prophet into his bosom and have the Church join us in our travel to the universe."

26

Sarah and I thanked our new friends for the delightful stew and the information. We stood and said we had to set up our camp. They offered us beds and breakfast in the morning; we declined, thanked them, and walked farther down the hill.

"I have never met a softer and more likable group of people in my life," Sarah said.

"I agree, true believers," I said. "I can't understand if they truly believe or does Orion have this much power over them."

"All movements begin this way," Sarah answered.

"A wondrous following or a dangerous cult. I'm concerned. We must find Marcus."

The farther we walked, the denser the complex of tents and campfires. In some camps, we heard songs, soft voices full of expectation. I tapped the com-link in my ear.

"Hank?"

"Yes, Captain."

"Where do you think Orion and Marcus might be?"

"Captain, the main complex is ahead of you about two hundred meters. There is a building south of the church. From the infrared signatures, this is where the greatest concentration of people is. I suggest this is the best place to start."

"Walk us in," Sarah said.

We followed Hank's directions. We passed through a gate with two guards; they did not stop us. They gave us a welcome and called us brothers. We climbed stairs and then crossed the main piazza in front of the church. A few tents were set up and more campfires; luckily, there were few of the followers. Lights burned in the windows of the building. We passed through a tall pair of open doors and stood in the vestibule. More stairs climbed upward. The hallway was empty; then twenty men and women quickly appeared and encircled us. They were dressed in the same type of robes that we wore. I saw no weapons. One of the men stepped forward.

"It is good to see you, Captain. Welcome to Nostre Familia," Tassos Orion said.

Stunned, I stared at the man. "How did you know?" I asked.

"Like you and Ms. Thomason, I, too, have spies. Well done. Seize them."

I was surprised at how gently we were held. I thought about trying to bust myself free and escape, but it would be foolish. There were too many. Sarah looked at me; I was expecting fear or at least shock, but there was none. She shrugged. I looked at our captors; Marcus was not among them.

As a group, we moved across the vestibule to an open door. No one said anything. We followed the leader down a series of stairs and landings until we were pushed into a dark room.

"Keep them here until I decide what to do with them," Orion said. "Bring them light and food and water. We are not jailers." The men holding our arms released us. My ingenious plan had met the enemy.

"I assume that you are here for Marcus," Orion said, standing in the door to our cell.

"Is the boy safe?" I asked.

"Yes, he could not be safer. He is well and will see you in the morning." The door slammed behind him; the lock clicked.

Sarah took in a deep breath. "Good plan."

"All plans are good until they aren't. What's next?" I said.

"We look for a fake panel or another miraculous way out

of here. There's always a secret exit."

"Now, that's a plan."

A minute later, the door's lock clicked, and two women entered; one carried a light and set it on a ledge. The other placed a basket filled with bread and cheese and containers of what turned out to be water. They quickly left. The door clicked behind them.

"We're probably the first prisoners here since . . . hell, only God knows how long," I said.

"Another paragraph in my memoir," Sarah said with a snort. "Imprisoned by zealots in a medieval dungeon. 'Her body was found dried and withered, only a dead lantern and an empty basket to mark her final days.' I like the sound of that, mysterious."

"What happened to me?"

"I ate you."

"Cute."

We sat in the dim light and talked about our past; the discussion eventually led to escape. Then my ear began to squawk.

"Captain, are you still there?" Hank's voice interrupted our scheming. I'd completely forgotten the noid, what an idiot.

"Of course we are still here. We're stuck in a jail cell."

"I believe if it's underground, it is properly called a dungeon."

"Thanks for the clarification," I answered, wondering which of us was the more useful idiot.

"Your infrared signatures disappeared. I assume that you are in the bowels of the castle."

"Good word," I said. "Bowels is where we are, dipshit."

"Dipshit? I do not know this word."

"I'll define it for you later. We are safe for now. Are you secure?"

"Yes, I am picking up nothing that can be perceived as a threat. Do you need to be rescued?"

"No," Sarah said. "We are well, have food, and are in the

heart of the enemy's camp. Things couldn't be better."

In the light, I saw her face. Her comment about being eaten put a smile on my face. She raised her hand and pointed a finger at me. I shrugged.

"Hank," Sarah said. "Just keep monitoring. In the morning, we will probably be taken out and paraded around as spies. Watch for any attempt to compromise you. If they knew we were here, then they probably know about you. They may attack or try to disable you. At the first sign of anything, lift off and stay safe. We will need you tomorrow."

"Yes, ma'am. Captain, you promised an adventure—is this now an adventure?"

"Yes, Hank, this is now an adventure. Anything that includes a dungeon in the bowels of a castle is officially an adventure," I said. "I'm not sure how long they will allow us to keep in contact."

"Excellent. If I lose you, what should I do?"

"Wait, stay where you are," Sarah said. "At some point, there will be a time to act. Until then, wait until we contact you."

"Yes, ma'am. Out."

"Wait? This is your plan?" I asked as I took a long drink from one of the containers.

"That could be poison," Sarah said.

"If it is, then you couldn't eat me. This is self-protection."

"You are an idiot."

I couldn't argue.

A few hours later, a cold light appeared in the window high above the dirt floor of our dungeon. Words carved into the stone walls appeared almost magically. Some were in French and others in Italian, love notes from past residents. None of them gave us comfort, especially the one that Sarah translated from French. "My last day in this hole, they come soon to kill me."

"Reassuring words," I said, as it grew brighter. I didn't die from the water, and the bread and cheese were quite delicious. An hour later, the door clicked and opened. Marcus, the cowl of his robe resting on his shoulders, walked into the room with a woman.

"Good morning, Uncle, and you, too, Ms. Thomason. You should not have followed me. You can see I am well," he said. "The Prophet has provided."

I hugged the boy.

"Ms. Thomason," Marcus said. "You are the last person I expected to see. Don't you have a company to run?"

"We came to rescue you," she said.

"I would suggest that you failed," Marcus said. "There are some who want to leave you here; it is being seriously debated. The Prophet, of course, has the last word."

"Of course," I said. I looked at the woman. She was about Marcus's age, pretty. A long strand of blond hair hung along her cheek where it had escaped the cowl over her head.

"Uncle, this is Mary. We are betrothed. At the proper time, the Prophet will bind us together. He has selected Mary to be my wife."

Stunned, I said, "Does your mother know?"

"There will be a time to tell her, but not right now. We have much to do before we can plan for the future. How is Mother?"

"She is concerned," I said. "She was the one who asked me to find you and bring you home."

"I am well, and content—this is my home."

"Do you understand what is happening?" Sarah said.

"I understand all that happens."

"So, you are going to Rome to convince the Pope to join you," I said.

"Good luck with that," Sarah added.

A surprised look came on the boy's face. "You know this? How?"

"Not all your followers are as secretive as your Prophet.

It's a fool's choice."

"You know him, Uncle. You saved his life. The Prophet is here to lead us."

"As your uncle said, a fool's choice," Sarah added. "There is nothing about this that seems to be what it is."

"I know all," Marcus said.

Marcus's forehead began to glow, and a small, brilliant spec of light appeared. It floated motionless above his thick head of hair and then rose to the ceiling. Mary looked up and closed her eyes. The Pernix then made a slow traverse of the dungeon; its light filled the room. I heard Sarah gasp.

"How did that thing get here?" I demanded.

"Uncle, it has been with me since *Kratos*. As I said, I know all. The creators have always been with us. These are here to help, to lead us."

"To do what?"

"To be one with the universe," Mary said.

The Pernix came back to Marcus and hovered just above him, then slowly descended until it disappeared inside his head.

"We are leaving tomorrow," Marcus said. "You will be detained here until we leave, then you are free to go. Goodbye, Uncle, give my love to my mother. Ms. Thomason, it was a pleasure to see you again. Take care of my uncle; he looks confused."

Marcus and Mary left the cell; I heard the door lock after them.

"Good God, was that a Pernix?" Sarah said.

"Yes, and in their ship there were millions of them. Right now, I'm not sure who is controlling whom. There's something not right about any of this."

"We have got to get out, tell someone," Sarah said.

"For now, we are stuck. There will be time," I said.

"Time? We seem to be running out of that commodity. Hank, did you hear all of that?"

"Yes, Ms. Thomason. Most worrisome."

"No shit. Can you tell me what's happening out there?"

"Surveillance feeds from your satellites show a large convoy of ships headed to the island. Some have already arrived, and the followers are loading onto the boats. I assume they are headed away from the island."

"What is the closest port to Rome?" Sarah asked.

"That would be Ostia, on the Tiber River," Hank said.

"How long will it take for them to reach the port?" I asked.

"About twenty-four hours—the weather is excellent. A slight swell from the south, little wind."

"You are now a weatherman?"

"I am here at your service."

"Then tonight, come and get us. I want us to be in Rome to meet them."

27

We landed in the car park area of the Villa Borghese about two and a half kilometers from the Vatican. We kept our robes, and I had Hank wear one as well. He was not pleased.

"I look outlandish in this; it impairs my mobility," Hank complained as he slung the rucksack filled with a tent, food, and blankets over his shoulder.

"Pull the hood over that whining head of yours, and walk slowly," I said. "It is a disguise; can you get that through your tin head?"

"No need to be insulting. Of course, I know this is a disguise. I suppose that this will help us find Marcus."

"That's the plan," I said.

"If I hear one more word about plans, I'll hit you in the forehead and see if one of those fireflies has made its home in *your* cranium," Sarah said.

"Cute—I'm bug-free, I assure you."

"I'm not so sure," she answered.

"Really, I am."

"When this is over, I'm going to have your noggin scanned just to be sure."

We walked through the Piazza del Popolo and then along the boulevard that paralleled the Tiber River. Two centuries earlier, Rome had been declared an international city of great historical importance. Per the designation, nothing has been allowed to change since the massive reconstruction of the ancient city after the war. Sarah said that it looked like it did five hundred years ago. I couldn't argue; I wasn't there. The few vehicles moving about were modern, but the architecture and the cafés that lined the river were now as they had been for more than a thousand years. After all the glitz, glass, and steel of the outer colonies, it was remarkably comforting. The stone bridges, the cobblestones paving the sidewalks and streets, even the great trees that lined the river gave a quiet yet essential reminder of the past, a human past. Beyond, above the river, stood the dome of St. Peter's. Sarah was correct; the braces did help; I was beginning to be energized by the city. Walking was easier.

Hank narrated the ten-bit tour as we strolled along the river. He talked about the buildings, the history, and the period before the city was almost eradicated from history. It was the Church, and its money, that rebuilt the city from the ruins. No relics remained from those dark years, no memorials to man's stupidity. I also saw dozens and then hundreds of the Prophet's followers as they walked along the same streets that had carried the Romans, invading barbarian armies, Napoleon six hundred years earlier, and the most heinous, the Nazis in the mid-twentieth century. There was seldom an era when Rome wasn't fighting back the advance of time, armies, and politicians. The followers walked in silence toward the physical and spiritual center of the Catholic Church, St. Peter's Basilica, and the Vatican. An institution that was now the heart of an interplanetary empire that extended well beyond the dreams of a carpenter's son two and a half millennia before.

"I've never been here," Sarah said. "It is wonderful."

"It is that," I said. "It's what's going on behind the walls of that complex that interests me. Intrigues, collusions, plots, all in the name of God."

"Don't be so cynical," Sarah said. "People live here. It isn't just the home of a religion; it is the home of millions of people. Most probably don't know what's going on, or even care."

"And I'm cynical? I say lucky for them. Me? I'm hungry; a bowl of spaghetti and glass of Chianti would be a nice change from our enlightened jailer's bread and water."

We sat in a comfortable sidewalk café; OSTERIA BENE was painted on the awning. We waited for service. When no one arrived, I went inside.

"Can we get some service?" I asked the older man behind the counter.

Over his thick glasses and even thicker mustache, he looked me over, then said, "We don't serve your kind here."

Stunned, I looked at him. "Our bitunits aren't good here? And what do you mean 'your kind'?"

"I don't serve heretics and unbelievers," he said sharply. "I understand they are serving you people in the park up the river. There's not a restaurant in this town that will even give you a glass of water. So, just go—I don't want trouble."

"Trouble, from us? We mean no trouble."

"Then go. But I need to ask, why is there a noid with you? You people don't believe in them. Why is it with you?"

"He is my valet," I said.

The man wrinkled his brow and looked out to my companions. "Valet? Never heard of such a thing. Just go. If the local police see you here in my restaurant, they will tear the place apart tonight. Please leave. I don't need the trouble that you people bring."

"The trouble seems to be with your locals, not us."

"Please, signor, just go. I beg you."

The man's hands were shaking. I looked at Sarah, a questioning look on her face.

"Thank you, signor. I'm sorry, we mean no trouble."

I walked to the front and told Sarah and Hank we needed to leave.

"I heard the conversation, strange," Sarah said.

She stood, and Hank moved away from the table. The three of us continued along the river. Hank broke the silence.

"Valet? I'm not your valet," he murmured.

"Today, my friend, we are a lot of things that we are normally not. And the rest of the day will be a lot stranger, that I'm sure of."

"Amen to that," Sarah said.

* * *

After crossing the Tiber River, we found the park that the restaurant owner mentioned. A thousand followers filled the grounds. Along one side, tables full of bread, cheeses, and meats were neatly aligned. The followers, all dressed in brown robes, took what they needed. We joined them. No one asked for money. Again, the voices were cheerful, almost gay. Music filled the air. I'd never been to a picnic, a real honest to goodness picnic—a first for everything, I guess. I still wanted a glass of wine. I was beginning to suspect they were teetotalers, which ran contrary to my cocktail sessions with Orion and Marcus on the *Gypsy*. The differences between dogma and practice, you got to love it.

Sarah engaged a pair of young women who were sitting on the ground. As she talked with them, Hank and I stood under the shade of a massive tree. Don't ask what kind, I know moon rocks and asteroids, not Earth-side botany. It was a big green leafy thing; the bark was rough, it smelled lovely. When the followers saw Hank, they turned away. I was interested in why but did not pursue an answer. Hank stood motionless and watched them; other than to occasionally mention the word "valet," he was silent.

"You know I didn't mean it," I said.

"I understand, I'm just confused."

"You and me both, buddy," I said.

"I believe they do not like me."

"There seems to be an aversion. Yes, I agree."

"I wonder why?"

Sarah walked back to us.

"And?" I asked as I handed her a plate with sausages and cheeses.

"There is to be a gathering of the followers in St. Peter's Square," Sarah said. "They have been asked to gather there tomorrow night. They said there was a promise that the Prophet would also join them. One asked me if I knew why they were asked to be here. I told her that I did not know. They were disappointed. No one knows why. I asked them how they knew to come to Rome. They said they received a com-link request on their PDs. All it read was that for those who could come, they were to join the Prophet during these holy days here in Rome, nothing more."

"A lot of faith going on here; it's also strange that I see no children," I said.

"I've noticed that. It was the same on Lipari."

"Hank, Sarah mentioned holy days. Are we in the middle of a specific Catholic religious period?"

"This week is the celebration of the Revealment," Hank said. "It is a week of quiet reflection over the discovery of the tomb of one of Jesus's original disciples. However, some religious archeologists and scholars disagree with the find and the interpretation. That was two hundred and fifty-three years ago in a village in what was, at the time, southern Turkey. There were rumors of miracles and healings soon after the discovery. Your sister's religious order was founded on that discovery, or Revealment, as it was called. As a minor point, it is called the Revealment, not revelation. Divine Revelation is an important and fundamental part of the Catholic liturgy. The Prophet has mentioned this several times in his speeches and sermons. He has said, 'All will be shown at the time of the coming Revealment.'"

"Thanks, I think," I said. After lunch—excellent by the way—we continued to the reconstructed Castel Sant'Angelo. The grounds surrounding the edifice, originally built two thousand years ago to house the cremated remains of pagan Roman emperors, were filled with the followers. Campfires had been lit, and the smells of food filled the groves of pine and cypress trees. Songs carried through the fragrant air; soft voices came from the small encampments. We found a clearing near the west wall of the castle where Hank set up our tent. As the sun set, the dome of St. Peter's dominated the skyline. It was a different perspective of the sun than I was used to for the last thirty years. Here the orb was glorious; in space, it was just the brightest spot in the black of the universe. This view was much better—it *is* all about context.

The followers surrounding us shunned us. When I caught them looking, they turned their eyes away. I remembered the bistro owner's remark about Hank.

"Hank, old buddy, why don't you pull that hood over your head and try not to be so conspicuous. You are pouring cold water over our clandestine activities."

"Are you embarrassed about having me around?" Hank mumbled. "First you call me a valet, now an embarrassment—what's next? Denial that I even exist?"

"Is he always this touchy?" Sarah asked.

"Needy is the word I'd use," I said. "Just do as I've asked, please. Sarah and I are going exploring."

"Yes, Captain. Please keep your com-link open in case you need help."

"From these people, I don't think so," I said.

"Humor me, okay?"

Sarah and I strolled through the confusion of tents and campfires. An entrepreneurial fellow was driving a small auto-carrier through the crowd selling firewood and bread; it looked like his business was good. Again, I was amazed at how quiet it was, though a constant soft murmur filled the air. In an area shaped like a small half bowl, a woman sat. A cluster of followers sat around her. We found a spot and listened.

"... it was then that the Prophet came to us," the woman

said. "It was in the dry hills above the old city of Avila, in the country once called Spain. We were a group of pilgrims headed to the shrine to Santa Teresa. The night before we entered the city, we camped, not unlike this, on a small knoll that overlooked the city. As we prepared our dinner, the Prophet came into our camp. We did not know who he was; traveling with him were two men. Later I learned they were the disciples Hubert and Conal."

At the mention of the names, the crowd whispered among themselves.

"Yes, Hubert and Conal, may they be with us always," the woman offered. "We offered them food and beds; the Prophet spent the evening with us. He talked of the universe, the creators, and our need to be among those that came before us. It was also a sermon of love and expectations. Our place among the stars as foretold by the Pernix Lumen."

At the mention of those damn bits of light, I heard a murmur that was as close to a prayer as any I'd heard. The followers whispered, "Let there be lights to lead us."

"Blessed are the followers of those lights," the woman answered. "I am disciple Teresa Espana; this is the name the Prophet gave me when he asked me to join his other disciples. There were four of us then, disciples Hubert, Conal, Van Tran, and myself. Within a year, disciples Jules and Ruth joined us."

"Let there be lights to lead us," came softly from the crowd again.

"For six years, before the Prophet returned to the Pernix"—more murmurs—"we traveled across earth talking to the people. It was Prophet Tassos's words about the universal nature of humans that convinced many to join with us. We knew in our hearts that we were part of a great hope and future for humans; it was in our DNA. His words and ideas sang to us."

"Were you there when they martyred Disciple Hubert?" a voice asked.

Disciple Teresa took in a deep breath. "Yes, my sister, I was there. My heart was broken that day. We were in Mexico City; the day was warm, and the sky a blue as the Prophet's eyes. We were crossing the large plaza in the center of the city. There, a man ran up to us and aimed a pistol at the Prophet. Disciple Hubert jumped in front of the weapon just as the man fired. The bullet killed Disciple Hubert instantly. The followers seized the man, his name is Alfonso Juarez, but you all know that. They wanted to do justice on the killer right there; the Prophet said no. He told the followers to release the man; he escaped into the crowd."

"Is it true he was later found dead?" the voice asked.

"Yes, it is true. The man was sick, deranged—someone murdered him."

"And the killer was never found?"

"Yes, that is what I've been told," Teresa said.

"He deserved it," another voice said.

"No one deserves death," Teresa admonished, looking at the man. "We are not entitled to make that choice; it is the universe's choice. Juarez was sick, but what happened was not justice. For the followers and the believers in the lights, it is not our place to seek vengeance. We only seek the truth and the light."

"Why is the Church so afraid of us?" another voice asked. "Why do they persecute us? Some have said that the Cardinal of Mexico paid Juarez."

"Rumors, nothing more than that. Brothers and sisters, those that challenge authority are often persecuted. It is those in power, their fear that makes them act that way. But we have each other, and we have the lights."

"Let there be lights to lead us" again filled the small amphitheater.

"Tomorrow will be glorious; the other disciples and I are talking with you tonight to prepare you. I only know what the Prophet has told us, and I assure you it will be a wonder. However, if you are not full in your heart and have misgivings, you must leave. This the Prophet has said. Now I must go and meet with others; I won't be getting much sleep tonight."

Teresa Espana stood. She was tall and thin; her robe matched everyone else's; the only difference was a deep red cord wrapped around her slim waist. Four men walked behind her; their robes were also like the others. They wore white cords around their waists. My guess, they were part of the Prophet's militia. I'd seen the various colored cords in the crowd, but it never registered until now. The followers wore brown cords, some yellow. Even among the followers, there was a hierarchy and a police force.

We rejoined Hank at our encampment. The night had chilled; we bought wood from the vendor and started our fire. Hank's presence still deterred anyone from joining us.

"I am finding it hard to understand these folks," Sarah said. "They are peaceful, yet there's something about them that makes me nervous. It's as if they have a secret that they keep to themselves. Yet, I don't see fear."

"I agree," I said while looking at Hank. He stood just beyond the light from our fire. If I didn't know better, I thought he was leaning against the stone wall of the castle. "What do you think?" I asked the noid.

"Captain, I'm getting chatter over old FM wavelengths. I can't make out any of it. First, they are in Italian; that's not the problem; it's that they make no sense. I can translate the Italian parts, but the phrases are confused or something else."

"Code?" I asked.

"Possibly," Hank answered. "With no point of reference, I don't know what they mean."

"How long have you been monitoring them?"

"Only the last hour; it started just before you returned."

"Interesting," Sarah said.

"How so?" I asked.

"Do you think the Roman authorities are going to stand back and allow all this to happen?" Sarah said. "After the comments from the restaurant owner, I assume they are monitoring everything. How many of the followers are here?"

I thought for a moment. "Guessing more than ten thousand, probably more. We only see a small portion of the crowd." A buzzing began high overhead.

"What the hell is that? Hank, what do you see?" I said, pointing to the sky.

The noid walked away from the wall and looked upward. He slowly scanned the night sky, which was clear.

"Drones. I count at least six passing overhead."

"That's to be expected," Sarah said. "Goes with the Church's paranoia."

For the last hundred years, the city of Rome and the surrounding countryside were controlled by the Church. From the time of its reconstruction after the nuclear attacks two hundred and fifty years earlier, it had taken over the management, both politically and physically, of the old city. None dared to stand in its path. Benign, to be sure, it nonetheless is the government of this part of Italy. Its influence extends to the moon and Mars. Its banks are among the strongest financial institutions on Earth and the solar system. While coins were an old form of exchange, most citizens used PDs to conduct their business. However, here in Rome, the coins carry the images of Popes. Someone was watching what was going on, someone with a vested interest in what Prophet Tassos and his followers were up to. Why I thought of my sister at this moment surprised me.

"Wouldn't take much to gin up the paranoia of the Romans," I said. "Hank, what the type of surveillance?"

"The drones are small, recon types. I see no weapons. All are compact, nimble, XT33 designs. Their cameras are excellent. Unfortunately, their transmissions are hard to crack—I've tried. Data collectors, I would suggest."

"Let me see what I can do," Sarah said as she scrolled down the screen of her PD. I watched as she furiously typed on the screen. "Give me a half hour. My people are looking into it. It's always good to have friends in high places."

"Like up there?" I said and pointed.

"Where else?"

To my utter shock and delight, Hank removed a bottle of bourbon from his knapsack. He poured two glasses and then returned the bottle to the bag. Damn, I'm really in love with that bag of circuits. Don't tell him.

"Better?" Sarah asked.

"Much," I said. "This is the life. Nice evening dinner, surrounded by a couple of thousands of our closest zealots and true believers. What's not to like? I could use a cigar."

"Sorry, Captain, no cigar."

"Really?"

"Really."

"That was a joke."

"Captain, if I'd known that . . ."

Sarah held up a finger just as I was about to ask her a question. "Hold that thought. I've got something coming in on my earpiece." I watched as she nodded. She said "got it" three times, and "Jesus" twice. When she got to "You have got to be kidding me," I could tell she wasn't.

"The Legions of Rome, under the command of Cardinal Ludwig von Fisher, have advanced to the outskirts of the old city, near the Porta San Paolo and the Aurelian Wall. Heavy weapons, crawlers, and bots. My observers guess more than twenty thousand legionnaires. They've essentially encircled the city. I would put all this in the Not So Good column."

"I don't get it—what's their end game? These few thousand followers have little impact on the Church and its operations. Maybe it's an overreaction on the Pope's part? A show of force?"

"Maybe, but right now, it appears they want to contain these people, like sheep in a pen. Buster, this is not good."

I pulled out my PD and said, "Call Annie."

In the light from the fire, I saw Sarah's eyebrow rise, then she nodded.

It rang five times before my sister answered. "Where are you? Have you found Marcus?" Her face, wrapped in the black and white wimple of her order, appeared on the viewscreen.

"You damn well know where I am. I'm in the middle of Rome, surrounded by thousands of your legionnaires. And no, I don't have Marcus."

"What are you talking about?"

"Please, Annie, no games. Right now, and you know it, there are thousands of Orion's followers camped outside the walls of the Vatican waiting for some miracle or phenomenon tomorrow. They've been called here by their Prophet, probably to confront your boss. We are surrounded by the Pope's defense force, and they are beginning to squeeze these people toward the Vatican. There is no way you can't know about this. Where are you?"

There was a pause, a long pregnant pause.

"You are here, aren't you?" I said. "You know exactly what's going on. Annie, this is crazy, people are going to die."

"It's all under control. The legion is there to preserve order, protect the city in case there is a riot, or—"

"Bullshit. These people are calm and as docile as lambs," I said. "They have come at the request of Orion, their Prophet Tassos. I haven't heard a foul or vile word from any of them. And you certainly aren't going to gain their confidence by pressuring them."

"The legionnaires are there to protect—"

"Just stop it. I know exactly why they are here. What I want to know is, *why are you here?*"

"The Pope summoned me," Annie finally said. "He believes that I have knowledge that would help diffuse this problem."

"There is no problem; you are forcing it to become one," I answered. "And what knowledge is this?"

"It's Marcus."

"What about Marcus?"

"He has been made one of Prophet Tassos's six disciples. He has taken the place of Hubert, the assassinated disciple. After you returned to the moon, Tassos took Marcus to Earth."

"I know that. I am here in Rome. I saw Marcus on their island."

"The island? It was there that Tassos announced to his followers that Marcus was now one of the six. He told the people gathered that Marcus has a special place among the six. Marcus had seen the Pernix Lumen; he was now one with them."

"At the time, we were stuck in a dungeon under the castle. House arrest or something like it. I saw Marcus then. Do you know he's betrothed?"

"Betrothed? We? Who is with you?"

"Sarah is with me, so is Hank."

I could tell from the expression on her face she was not pleased.

"Why is she there with you?"

"She was looking for an adventure," I said, watching the smile on Sarah's face. "And, by the way, the girl can't be older than, maybe, eighteen. Blonde, cute—did you know?"

"No, I didn't. When is this wedding supposed to happen?"

"I haven't a clue. Your son has other things on his mind, like little lights that buzz in and out."

"The Pernix? He's got one of those in his head, like Orion?" Annie said.

"You know about that?—of course you do. Spies and more spies."

"Buster, I strongly suggest that you, Sarah, and that noid leave Rome. I will let the commanders know that you are coming out. You will be safe."

"Safe? I thought they were here to protect the city and these followers. It sounds a lot more intimidating than that."

"They have been ordered not to take any aggressive actions against the followers. But you know how this could go."

"Yeah, I get it. Someone pops a balloon, and a hundred automatic weapons return fire. Yes, accidents will happen."

Annie turned her head; someone was talking to her. "I've got to go. Buster, just get out. Will you do that for me?" Not waiting for an answer, she broke the connection.

I turned to Sarah; she was listening to her com-link. Again, she held up a finger.

"I'm out," she said and looked at me. "Not good; in fact, much worse. The legion is actively pushing into Rome from all sides. There have been a few incidents; some have been hurt—stun-guns and ticklers, no bullets—yet. I'm bringing two high-altitude drones in from Greater America; they will be here in three hours. They will take positions at twenty thousand meters. Their camera's resolution will make our observations as good as almost being here."

I looked at the followers asleep in their tents around us. I saw no tech, or com-units, or glowing from PDs. They were blissfully unaware of what was surrounding them.

"Do we tell them?" I asked Sarah. "Do we let them know that they are about to be attacked?"

"We don't know that," she answered. "It could be as Annie said—they are here to protect the city."

"You don't believe that any more than I do. Hank, anything new?"

"More coded voices are adding to the cacophony. My impression is that there is confusion."

"That's when problems start," I said. "Confusion breeds chaos, chaos begets fear, and fear kills. Not good. Orion is here somewhere; I need to stop this. Right now. He's the only one who can prevent a massacre."

24

We spent the next day going from camp to camp looking for Orion and Marcus. There was no apparent change to the followers and their demeanor. We did hear some singing and people were meeting in small groups. Hank, when noticed, was still shunned. Sarah asked about the Prophet, if anyone had seen him. The response was always, "He was here just an hour ago. He asked for our blessing. Us—he asked for our blessing. May the lights be with us. He then moved on, that way."

"Was he alone?"

"Marcus and Teresa were with him; someone said Van Tran was at the next camp. May the lights be with us always."

We found the followers were from everywhere. Central Pan Africa, India, Australia, Southeast Asia, Eurounion, the Levant, and Greater America. A mixture of the world's cultures and races. Without exception, smiles and blessings greeted us. I've seen baskets of kittens that were greater threats than these people. But no children—that was a puzzlement. When I asked, we were told that they were safe; they would "be with us soon in the universe."

The word we heard from our fellow pilgrims was that we should walk toward St. Peter's Square in the late afternoon. How this information, or any information for that matter, was passed on to the people camped around the Vatican, I had no clue. I saw no PDs or other communication devices. Sarah and her drones kept me up to date on what was happening around the city. For the moment, the army had stopped pressing in toward the Vatican. How long that would last was anyone's guess. By midmorning, the followers had become aware that the legion had encircled the city. They showed no fear; I thought this was all too strange. Me? I was scared shitless.

When the warm day became late afternoon, I suggested it was time to go. I told Hank to stay with our camp; he objected, saying that he should go with us for protection. I understood his concern but insisted that he remain. If a noid could be disappointed, Hank showed his. Others in the surrounding camps were also preparing to leave; they all left their tents and personal items.

"Everything points to a confrontation between the followers and the legion," Hank said. "My primary job is protecting you and Ms. Thomason."

"Thanks, but right now, just monitor the situation. If we need you, I will let you know."

"Hank," Sarah said. "I'm sending you the frequencies and com-links for my drones and satellites. You can monitor them, keep us aware of what's happening. If it becomes hot, you will know. If you can't contact us, come and get us. Does that work for you?"

"I understand. I will monitor."

Sarah and I left Hank and began walking toward the Vatican; thousands flowed along the streets. The late afternoon sun stood behind the massive dome of the Vatican; a few clouds drifted across the darkening blue sky. The shadow cast by the dome extended down Via della Conciliazione, aptly named the Road to Conciliation—how much conciliation? We would find out. Time was running out. Thousands of the followers filled the street; all were silent. Then, with almost a whisper, they began to sing a hymn, a song I'd never heard.

Let the lights of the universe illuminate our way,

Let the lights in our souls rise to the sky,
Let the peace in our universal hearts lead us not astray,
Let the lights of the universe shine within our stars.

They repeated the words over and over as they headed toward the basilica. I was taught about the church's postwar herculean task of rebuilding it exactly as it had stood for a millennium. Between the hymns, the crowd, and the architecture, even my hard dragger's heart began to understand this building's visceral importance to the faithful. When Sarah took my hand, I felt a shock. I looked around; hundreds were walking to the basilica, also hand in hand. *How could these followers be a threat to the Church?*

Let the lights of the universe illuminate our way . . .

"My drones are in place," Sarah whispered. "They report that the legion is again pushing forward; many on the outer edges are being crushed by their advance. This is not good."

"Hank?" I asked.

"Yes, Captain. I heard."

"Stay awake, stay sharp."

"But, Captain, I never sleep . . ."

"It's a figure of speech. Don't lose contact. Where are you?"

"I am still at the castle. The grounds are empty—thousands have passed through and followed you and Ms. Thomason. Now there are only empty tents. The drones report that the legion is only blocks away; their main advance is across the river to the east. They are also taking positions in the hills to the west, behind the Vatican. Video shows heavy weapons are located in prominent positions. I should be there with you."

"Hank, begin to move toward us."

"Yes, Captain."

"Thank you for your concern, Hank," Sarah said.

"You are welcome, Ms. Thomason."

"Sometimes he acts like a mother hen," I said.

"A mother hen?" Hank said.

"Another figure of speech."

"If you say so."

We reached St. Peter's Square. Dominating the expanse of cobblestone was the red granite Egyptian obelisk that was five times the age of the Vatican. Like a sundial, its shadow pointed east out and over the followers, then down the boulevard to the river. We stood in almost perfect alignment with the cross at the top of the cupola and the cross on the tip of the obelisk. We pushed our way into the crowd and then past the pillar. Ahead, across the oval piazza, rose the stone steps that lead to the entry to the basilica. A hundred perfectly aligned Swiss Guards, in their colorful uniforms, stood shoulder to shoulder along the top step. A single opening between them allowed access to the building's massive front doors. Two men, side by side, climbed the steps. Directly behind them, five more figures, also wearing the brown robes of the followers, solemnly followed. I knew the first two were Orion and Marcus; the others must be his disciples. No one else approached the steps. At the top of the broad stairway stood a purple canopy, additional Swiss Guards, flanked by the cloth structure that billowed in the soft afternoon breeze. Halfway up the stairs, Orion and Marcus stopped. The disciples turned to the crowd and stood shoulder to shoulder one step below them.

"We have come to address our Holy Father," Orion said. His voice boomed across the square and down the Via della Conciliazione. From under the robes of the followers, ten thousand PDs rose to the sky; every device amplified the voice of their prophet.

"Pope Julius the Eleventh, we, your brothers and sisters, have come to speak with you. Please, Holy Father, come out and meet your children."

Sarah and I moved closer; we now stood at the bottom of the steps. The guards were stoic. An eerie silence filled the square. I looked out over the thousands of upturned faces, their arms skyward holding their PDs.

"Holy Father, your flock awaits you," echoed the voices of the followers from the surrounding buildings.

Minutes passed, then high over the entry, the doors of the central balcony opened. A banner unraveled from the railing—it was that of the Pope. A small, withered man in a simple white cassock and white cap slowly walked to the rail. Behind him stood a dozen other men dressed in priestly robes of gold and red. To the right, against the frame of the doorway, stood my sister.

"Who addresses the Holy Father? Who comes to demand an audience?" a strong voice asked over speakers placed around the square.

I recognized the voice. Pope Julius had led the Catholic Church for more than sixty years, the longest tenure of any Pope in the two and a half millennia of the Church's existence. The crowd was stunned. My guess: they didn't think that he would face the multitude.

"Holy Father, I am Prophet Tassos, and these are the believers of the Universal God. We have come to petition—"

The earsplitting and violent crack of thunder knocked me to the pavement; it was a sound louder than anything I'd ever heard. Sarah lay next to me; blood oozed from her left ear. Using my braces, I stood and looked across the square. It was a sea of brown. Thousands sprawled across the pavers; many tried to regain their feet. I looked for the obelisk; it lay broken and shattered across the cobblestones. Bodies lay beneath its rubble. Many of the Swiss Guards were trying to stand. Only Tassos, Marcus, and the five disciples remained standing, seemingly unaffected by what had happened. And me? I had no idea what had just happened.

My earpiece buzzed. "What?" I yelled, my eardrums barely functioning.

"Captain, something approaches," Hank said.

From high above the square, another crack of thunder shattered the numbed silence, a silence that was just beginning to be punctuated by the shrieks and wailing of the injured and afraid. Then I saw the *Kratos* fill the twilight sky. It glowed red from its passage through the earth's atmosphere. The screaming increased until everyone under its shadow had fled the center of the piazza. The slug of molten iron hovered motionless over St. Peter's Square. It extended down the length the square, the road, to almost the Tiber River. It was as wide as the central oval of the square itself. A wave of claustrophobia passed over me. Impossibly, the alien ship hung, stationary, maybe two hundred meters above us—I believed I could reach out and touch it. Sarah grabbed my arm.

"Is that what I think it is?" she asked.

"Yes, that's the Pernix Lumen," I said and pulled her tight.

"Hank, why didn't you warn us?"

"Warn you of what?"

"That the Pernix were about to crash Orion's little party."

"I did not see the alien ship," Hank said. "And neither did any of Ms. Thomason's drones and satellites. Is that what made the sonic boom?"

"Yes. There are hundreds of injured; some are dead."

"Would it be appropriate for me—"

"Get your tin ass over here," I yelled—my hearing rang like church bells. "Many need help."

I looked for Orion; he was still looking up at the balcony that once held the Pope. The people on the balcony were helping the old man to his feet. Annie was in the middle of the group. The Pope stood, Annie at his side.

"What is meant by this invasion, Prophet?" a voice boomed. "Is this how you betray the Church and all that she has given you?"

Stunned—it was my sister's voice.

"The universe is not mine to control; we are just part of its light," Orion said. "We are here to welcome the Creators."

"Blasphemy," she yelled.

"Is it our blasphemy, or your lack of belief? Behold the

Creators."

He pointed to the *Kratos*. From the black opening of the tunnel poured thousands, then millions, of the Pernix Lumen. Resembling a shower of white sparks, they poured ceaselessly into the night. A dense rope of illuminations wrapped themselves around its battered hull, like a snake strangling its prey. I felt the heat of the ship's metal hull quickly ebb. It was as if these specks were absorbing the heat, the energy, accumulated by its entry.

"These are the Creators," Tassos exclaimed again. The followers, those that had regained their feet, held up their PDs. His voice carried across the assembled.

The fireflies now coalesced and billowed upward into fascinating and bizarre shapes. It was like what I saw in the belt, only here, they danced in shapes and forms unlike anything I remembered. Upward they curled, then folded in on themselves, then rose high over the Vatican and spiraled downward around the great dome. Then they split and flew down the flanks of their ship, joining together on the far end, and then they climbed upward again to the stars. It was mesmerizing. Across the square, I saw the followers slowly refilling the plaza. Their faces illuminated by the millions of lights. Then, directly over the collapsed obelisk, the lights collapsed into a ball of light so bright it was blinding. It slowly ascended until it was like a new sun had risen. Its cold light washed across the multitude; there was no warmth in this sun.

"Pope Julius, these are the Creators; these are the Pernix Lumen," Orion said as he turned to the man standing on the balcony. His voice projected from the people. It was as if he was everywhere speaking to everyone. "Each of these lights is a being, a sentient entity from our past and our future. They were here when we were first formed from primal DNA and clay, and they will be here when we become part of the energy of the universe."

"These men and women before you are my followers and

disciples, all filled with the energy of the Pernix. And these are my disciples who have been with the Pernix for the past two decades."

The Prophet put his hands together, clasping them tightly. Then he raised his hands and his arms to the sky. When he opened them, six flickering bits of light rose and then, encircling his head, formed a crown over the Prophet's head. Marcus stood to one side, watching. Then, from the sphere of Pernix illumination, a cluster spun free and zipped across the square. They stopped above the five human disciples standing on the steps. Above each man and woman, the fistful of lights began to spin, like a spider ensnaring the humans. A gasp ran through the crowd as the mortal disciples began to turn from matter to energy. In moments, all that remained were illuminated shapes of the humans they once were. Some in the crowd screamed. I'd seen these same forms when the six were Orion's crown in the *Kratos*. Somehow Orion had managed to keep these things on my ship without any of us knowing. It seriously pissed me off. These illumined disciples then collapsed in on themselves, until they, too, were like the first six. They rose and joined the rotating crown over Orion's head, eleven lights. At this point, even I was beginning to believe that Tassos was a prophet.

"Captain?"

"Yes, Hank. What's up?"

"Incoming."

From every direction, hundreds of missiles and projectiles impacted the hull of the *Kratos*. Fire and shrapnel exploded across the ship's surface and over the followers below. Nothing could damage the dense metal of the vessel. I remembered the scars of asteroids that had barely left their mark. To think that some shell or missile would have an impact on this ancient technology only proved how ignorant we actually are. Hundreds were being hurt and probably killed by the exploding shells and debris. Why would the Church do this?

I ran up the steps to Orion. "Why are you doing this to your people? Tell the legion to stop; this all must stop. Please, for the love of God, stop killing your followers. Marcus, make him stop."

The Prophet raised his hands. The sun, made of the Pernix, exploded outward and formed a dome over the square and the followers. No shell or missile penetrated the shield. The shelling of the *Kratos* stopped. I looked back, astounded by what this man had done.

"It is the Church that attacked us," Marcus said. "We had nothing to do with this."

"Bullshit," I said. Even though I was his godfather, I wanted to punch the son of a bitch in the mouth. Teenagers will do that to you. "Ask him, Marcus. If there is ever a time that you needed to hear the truth, this is it."

Marcus looked at his mentor; his eyes implored the truth. "What is he saying? Is he correct?"

Orion ignored the boy and turned back to the Pope. I couldn't see Annie on the balcony. "See what you have done; these people meant you no harm. Have you no mercy?" he demanded.

The words echoed across the illuminated square and up into the sky. The Pernix returned and became the ball of light again, its surface roiled like the sun itself.

Orion looked at me. "Captain, take the boy. There is nothing for him here. I know that he was working for his mother and the Church. Take him away. There is still much to do here. He is in danger."

"I won't leave you," Marcus said to Orion. "I have seen my errors. I understand. I am with you and the followers, please."

"Go, Marcus. Your mother needs you."

He pointed to the doors of the Vatican. Sister Annie was running across the porch of the church toward us. Orion looked at me. "Captain, Marcus needs you in his life. Please take him."

I grabbed the boy and pulled him down the steps to Sarah. Annie rushed to our side and wrapped her arms around her son. I turned back to the Prophet. The eleven lights that orbited his head began to spin faster. As had the lights earlier over the disciples, these sparks began to enclose and enshroud Orion until he became as bright as the orb spinning above. Then they all ascended, a brilliant ring of light. It intensified until it was too bright to look at. The ball of Pernix Lumen also began to spin, until it grew even more brilliant. Then, in an electric display of lightning bolts, they exploded outward across the square. Each light found a follower and began the same transformation that Orion and the disciples had experienced. Even the bodies beneath the broken obelisk and those injured and scattered under the ship were transformed. I watched dumbfounded—why didn't they come for me, or Sarah, or Marcus, or the guards? Then, in a fete of thunderous sound and clicking electricity, the Pernix and their new converts spiraled up into the sky, forming an illumination a thousand feet high. Then they began to pulse and glow in a hundred colors. Slowly they began to rotate, then spin; within seconds, they disappeared into the ship. I looked back at Marcus; from his forehead, a single firefly of intense green light emerged and followed the other Pernix back into the *Kratos*. Within moments the ship began to rise and ascend to the star-filled night. In the space of a single breath, they were gone.

It was eerily silent across St. Peter's Square. Pieces of paper drifted about like lost souls in the dim light of the streetlights. Haphazard piles of debris and robes, like brown carpeting, spread across the ancient paving stones—one robe for each of the followers. Had I witnessed a tragedy of unimaginable horror or the unbelievable transformation of true believers to the welcoming arms of the universe? Whichever it was, I was unforgiving. This was somehow wrong, inhuman, an abhorrent aberration. A just God would not have allowed this.

"Captain, are you alright?" a familiar voice asked. Hank was climbing the steps.

"Yes, Hank, we are okay." I looked at Sarah and Annie. Marcus was turned away and had buried his head in the bosom of his mother. Annie mouthed the words, "Thank you." For what, I wasn't sure. Ten thousand humans had just been converted into specs of energy by those insidious fireflies. Was this what *they* wanted? Did they have an option? Hell, were they even given a choice? There was no way to know now. Faith can be a bitch if you get my drift.

"The *Kratos* escaped the atmosphere at an unimaginable speed," Hank said. "Physics should have ripped the ship to pieces. It left Earth and the orbit of the moon seconds after leaving here. It disappeared from any of Ms. Thomason's sensors twelve seconds after leaving Earth. By then, it was almost at light speed. According to my data banks, what they did was impossible."

"Hank, what happened here was even more impossible," Sarah said.

"What happened here? Where are the followers?" the noid asked, scanning the square.

"They are one with the Creators," I said.

"Captain, I dislike your archaic phrases. Please, what happened?"

"Hank, I haven't a clue. Right now, I need to talk with Annie and Marcus."

My sister and godson were climbing the steps toward the open doors of the basilica. Sarah followed behind them. I quickly stumbled up the steps trying to catch up. Hank followed. The Swiss Guards, looking stunned and confused, stood to either side, watching as if we were miracles that survived a murderous assault of lightning. In the doorway, a cluster of cardinals, bishops, and priests stood. In the middle of the group, sitting in a hover-chair, was Pope Julius IX. He extended his hand toward Marcus.

Marcus stopped and lowered himself to one knee and kissed the Pope's ring; my sister placed her hand on his shoulder.

"I am sorry, your Holiness, I lost faith. I wanted to go with them," Marcus said.

"We understand. My son, you did well. Please join us," Pope Julius said.

* * *

There's a game that starts with dozen people sitting in a circle. You begin by telling a simple three-sentence story to the person next to you. They then tell the story to the next person and so on until it gets back to you. By that time, it's changed so much you don't even recognize it. Each person believes what they hear and repeat, but at some point, the story changes from the original truth to the interpreted truth of the last storyteller. Such is what I faced now. Which person was telling the whole or real story? Let me tell you the version, or at least one of the versions, I want to believe. However, *want* is a strange verb, implies a preconception, a need, maybe even a bias. But then again, raised in a religious school on the moon, one will tend to have biases and hurt knuckles. We want to believe in the past, and the great stories told over and over. Stories passed down or translated from one generation to the next are examples, and time steals a little of the truth at each telling. Such is the Bible and the other books of lore.

I got off the earth as fast as I could. Sarah, Hank, and I returned to the *Washington* smelter, and within a few hours, we were safely secured in her suite. So, let me begin. I can't say that what I'm telling you is the truth, but you will get my drift. After all, I was there, and you know how reliable eyewitnesses are.

Plain and simple, Marcus had been sent by the church into Orion's religious camp to spy. Stupid, I know, for an organization to use an inexperienced eighteen-year-old kid, but he says he volunteered. And it was probably his naiveté that saved him. Knowing my sister, it's a good bet that she was behind this. Orion was smart, damn smart, so I'm certain he had a good idea about what was going on. And the Pernix Lumen most probably had some form of communication going on between them and Orion, so that spark flickering in Marcus's head was their modus of a spy system. I'm guessing they read his every thought. Maybe that's why they left him on Earth when they took the followers. What went on that night had all the trappings of extreme religious dogma, a miracle, something that will forever be codified in some new gospel or sacred text and dogma yet to be written. Sarah tells me that within days new groups of Pernix followers formed around the world. Orion made sure the world saw their assumption into the Pernix Lumen's ship and their zipping out into the universe. A PR firm's dream episode of *Stars in Our Lives* . . . coming to a church near you. They are popping up everywhere, even on the moon, where I hope to be in a week.

Contrary to what you might believe, gravity sucks. It is a relief to be back on the artificial gravity of *Washington*. My back doesn't hurt, my insoles don't hurt, and best of all, my eyelids don't hurt. It's the simple things in life. That contraption that Sarah put together for me probably did save me from a heart attack. The muscles in my legs still hurt, but that's enough about me. I'm sure you're dying to find out what happened right after the Pernix left, so here goes my version.

As we approached Pope Julius, I wasn't sure what would occur. Would the Swiss Guard arrest us for complicity in the mass disappearance of ten thousand people? Would Annie bust my chops over her son? Would the world, as we know it, end? Would the Pernix return as avenging angels and punish their children for being self-centered assholes? Would a firestorm of retribution fulfill the Book of Revelations?

None of that happened. I was disappointed.

We passed through the nave of the Vatican. The Pope led in his hover-chair. He drifted silently along with his entourage, past the tomb of St. Peter and the Baldacchino. A guard opened a door, and we continued into the labyrinth of halls and rooms deep inside the Vatican—most I assume had been built after the reconstruction. Annie held her son's hand; Marcus just looked ahead. His head high, good for him. Sarah and I, and to my surprise Hank, followed. Usually, noids are forbidden in most religious sanctuaries. At the end of a long and ornate hallway adorned with artwork and statuary, we arrived at a massive oak-paneled door. A Swiss Guard twisted the bronze handles and opened it; the Pope floated in. The other great work of art by Michelangelo in the Vatican, the detailed reconstruction of the artwork in the Sistine Chapel, arched above us.

"We would like to speak with these people alone," Pope Julius said. He pointed to the five of us.

A bishop, I didn't know his name, was the leader of the entourage. He started to say something.

"Bishop Tatu, we will be safe; there is no need to worry. We need to talk with Sister Annie and her brother. We have many questions. So, please excuse us."

I watched the group reluctantly leave the chapel; they chattered amongst themselves. If there were listening devices planted in this room, that's probably where they were headed.

"We are alone," Pope Julius said. "They will find that all the surveillance to this room is mysteriously silent. We will be finished before they find out how to reactivate the microphones and cameras." He turned to Marcus. "My son, you did exceptionally well, beyond what Sister Annie and we thought that you could achieve."

Marcus genuflected on his right knee. "Thank you, Holy Father; I am just your servant." The Pope extended his hand, and Marcus again kissed his ring.

"And you, too, Sister Annie, for allowing us to employ your son in this dangerous task. The Church, for two thousand years, has been attacked by outside forces many times. We have survived all, and despite some very bad times, we have triumphed and thrived. However, this alien force is the greatest challenge to the Church and the people we serve. We did not understand their power until they appeared. It is formidable." He turned to me.

"Captain Strabo, we wish to thank you as well. You played your part, and as such, the Church owes you a debt."

"Holy Father, I had no idea," I confessed, and I genuflected.

"The Lord works in mysterious ways."

Yeah, I get that. However, I was learning the machinations of humans are far more mysterious.

"Do you know where they went?" the Pope asked.

I had the same unasked question.

Marcus turned to me. "Holy Father and Uncle, they have returned to the universe from where they came. Everything that Prophet Tassos said about them is true. He was their voice; they spoke to the followers through him. However, they are now in the vastness of space. They came here to our solar system to seed our planet; they waited until we were mature enough to understand. Then they took a sample of our species, added them to their collective, and returned to join the others."

"We are a science experiment?" I asked dumbfounded.

"You are always the cynic," Annie said.

"My son," Pope Julius said. "It was important to the Church that it be purified. We couldn't allow this to grow. It would challenge everything that it has been founded on."

"Purified? Cleansed?" I blurted. "Good God, can you hear yourselves? The greatest event in the history of the human species, and you see this as a threat? A threat to what?"

"Someday, you will understand," Marcus said.

"How did Orion stop the shelling?" I asked.

"It was through the Pernix; they placed a force field over the church," Marcus said. "After the first shells were fired, they somehow electronically jammed the weapons. They overpowered all the electrical systems of Rome, nothing worked. Only after the *Kratos* left did they regain their function."

I filed that away; from the look on the Pope's face, it may have been as Marcus said or not.

* * *

Sitting in Sarah's suite hadn't changed any of my notions about what had happened. I swirled my bourbon and continued to stare out the windows onto the blue ball fixed thousands of kilometers below us.

"How many other planets and species do you think there

are out there in this universe?" Sarah asked.

"There's an infinite number of galaxies and planets," I said. "Our little system here in the Milky Way showed up ten or fifteen billion years *after* all that out there exploded from nothing. More than enough time for other planets to evolve and reach for the stars before our piece of heaven coalesced into what we call the sun and Earth and Mars. So, who the hell knows what's out there?"

"Makes me feel insignificant," Sarah said.

"Don't let it," I said. "I don't know if Orion will be back; in fact, I hope he doesn't return. His followers here continue to grow in strength. The Church will do its best to marginalize them, and will, as it has for two dozen centuries, do everything it can to survive. And they will also grow. Such is our species. Someday, maybe the Pernix or something like them will return. If they do, we will be long gone."

"Does your drink need refreshing?" Hank asked.

I raised my glass and watched as Hank poured. It is nice to have a valet.

EPILOGUE

lied. I am back at the only job I know how to do, dragging. I thought I could settle down, get a nice place on Prasinus, marry the love of my life, retire. That lasted all of three months. I did buy an apartment in the new wing under development; it will be ready when Garrett, Clive, Hank, and I return in two years. One last hurrah. So, there's that.

We cast off a week ago, H tanks topped off, cables all bright and shiny, bots loaded, and I finally did get a settlement from the insurance company about the failed thruster—only took three years. My insurance premium went up twenty percent. No big deal, I'm rolling in it. I also have a rich contract from Sarah for a rock to be delivered to the Mars smelter. I'm charging the church an arm and a leg for the metal; I also finagled a good advance, a first. And it would be Sarah who would charge them. I got an excellent pre-flight deal with Great American Metals as well. My contract is just to deliver the goods.

Sarah and I talked a lot about the future but came to no conclusions. She did spend a few days on Prasinus before I took off. It's nice to have a warm shoulder to lean on; I'll miss that shoulder during the next few years. I didn't ask her to wait; she didn't say she would. Then again, she didn't say she wouldn't. Human relationships are just messy.

I received a note from Marcus; he thanked me for allowing

him to work for me. His piece of the rock we hauled to *Washington* would pay for his schooling at Notre Dame. He did not mention Orion or the followers. I was grateful for that. I've been trying to get that man out my head since we cast off.

Sarah also kept me informed about what was going on in Rome. Pope Julius IX is ill; the rumor is that he has just a few months left. I bear the old man no ill will, but he pissed me off. Then again, he is just the latest Pope to lead the Church; the next few years will be difficult. There are rumors that the followers are being marginalized, called a sect, a faction; the word *cult* appeared in the news. That's what you do: first, you separate, then isolate, then you begin the blame game. Another rumor is that Mars is being built as a new home for the followers; I'll believe that when it happens. Humans and their games—what's not to like?

Sister Annie's position and influence in the church, even in the three months since the Assimilation as the followers called the incident, has grown. She left a communication saying she was going back to the moon before heading to Mars to take over the construction of *Domus Dei Martis.* I wished her well. Families are complicated; everyone knows that. Ours is just a little more so.

I climbed the stairs from my cabin. Garrett and Clive were in their respective command chairs. I took my seat and looked out into the vastness of the universe. It was mesmerizing; it always is as we head out.

"Coffee, Captain?" Hank said as he sat a cup next to my chair.

"Thank you, Hank," I said, putting my fingers around the warm mug.

"You have not informed us of our destination," Hank said.

"Anywhere except Sector Seventy-three," I said.

"Roger that," the crew answered.

The End

A Note from the Author
The Alex Polonia Thrillers

There are two other Alex Polonia thrillers, Venice Black and Saigon Red.

Gregory C. Randall was born on a hot and muggy day in Traverse City, Michigan. He grew up in Chicago. Greg has never forgotten his roots. Mr. Randall makes his home in California.

Mr. Randall is the author of fiction and nonfiction works available through the usual outlets.

For more information about the other books that Mr. Randall has written and planned sequels, please visit and connect with Greg online:

www.gregorycrandall.info

See his blogs:
http://www.writing4death.blogspot.com
http://www.cogitourbanus.blogspot.com

Other books by Mr. Randall:
Fiction
The Cherry Pickers

The Sharon O'Mara Chronicles
Land Swap For Death
Containers For Death
Toulouse For Death
12th Man For Death
Diamonds For Death
Limerick For Death

The Alex Polonia Thrillers
Venice Black
Saigon Red

The Tony Alfano Thrillers
Chicago Swing
Chicago Jazz
Chicago Fix

Nonfiction
America's Original GI Town, Park Forest, Illinois

Additional copies can be purchased through these sites as well
as through the usual online bookstores.

www.ingramcontent.com/pod-product-compliance
Lightning Source LLC
Chambersburg PA
CBHW032052260626
47157CB00020B/2838